# WAHIDA CLARK PRESENTS

## VENOM IN MY VEINZ

### By

### Rumont TeKay

Wahida Clark Presents Publishing
60 Evergreen Place
Suite 904A
East Orange, New Jersey 07018
973-678-9982
www.wclarkpublishing.com

Library of Congress Cataloging-In-Publication
Rumont Tekay
Venom in My Veinz by Rumont Tekay
ISBN 13-digit 978-19366497-2-3 (paper)
ISBN 10-digit  1936649721 (paper)
LCCN: 2014914596
1.    Chicago - 2. Drug Trafficking - 3. African
       American – Fiction - 4. Urban Fiction 5. Street
       gangs-  6. Gangster Disciples

Cover design and layout by Nuance Art, LLC
Book design by Nuance Art, LLC
Edited by Linda Wilson
Proofreader Rosalind Hamilton

Printed in USA

# VENOM IN MY VEINZ

## Acknowledgements

*GiaVonna, no matter what, I will always Love & Protect you till the end of time.*

# RUMONT TEKAY

Chicago is not just a city. . . It's a Nation!

# RUMONT TEKAY

## PROLOGUE

B romise slowly awoke from his unconscious state, a bloody mess. He felt like he had been hit by a truck and it was difficult to breathe. He reached for his rib cage and realized his wrists and ankles were all shackled, bonding him to the frigid concrete beneath him.

*Where am I?* Bromise looked around to see what he could with impaired vision, but the pitch darkness made it impossible. "AHHH!" he yelled. "Let me the fuck out of here!" He became hysterical, pulling at the chains with all of his might. But there was no use. He stopped struggling and fell on his back, screeching in pain. Defeated, he pushed his back against the damp cold wall with the bottom of his soles, and reflected on how he got in this position.

Bromise shut his swollen eyes and envisioned the person who betrayed him. His chest heaved. His breathing became erratic. "You muthafucka!" he bellowed and roared with pain.

Then he opened his bloodshot eyes and stared into the darkness. He was already seduced by an irresistible thirst for blood—already fully manipulated by an anger that placed him under a hatred-induced spell that only the sacrificing of Fontane's life could break.

As he sat there against his will, fury surged

through him like a sudden burst of electric current, causing a single tear to escape from the corner of his eye.

Bromise was starving to see panic animate Fontane's unsuspecting face when he greeted him with his .50 Caliber. He was determined to give life to his fear of death, but above all, he looked forward to seeing the life in Fontane's eyes slowly fade away as he blinked one last time.

"Fontane!"

# CHAPTER 1
## *The Point of No Return*

*Present Day . . . February 17*

Two days ago, Bromise and Chasidy hit a lick on Future, taking three bricks of cocaine, thirty thousand in cash, and his big body white-on-white BMW 760Li. They also forced him to remove every stitch of clothing and piece of jewelry that he had on, including his trademark chain and medallion.

Although the loss was only pocket change to Future, his reputation was in jeopardy, and he couldn't overlook that. To do so would be equivalent to him inviting every fuck-boy to his glass front door. Plus, the wounds on his pride were fresh, and only fragments of the culprit's head would do the patchwork. When news of the lick made it back to the hood, Future knew he had to silence the messenger and cease any thoughts of him being an easy mark.

Future was an ultimate hustler. Many men only leased such status like rappers leased vehicles, but very few owned it. However, he was a street professor in the class of finance. And though he lacked the killer instinct himself, he had a team of goons that had goons, and all of them were on the call of duty. Similar to how the government drafted men from the land, the city was well aware of the certified killers that Future drafted to his roster. For one to question the heart of these men was almost never. Bromise could vouch

1

because he was one of Future's goons.

He was abruptly taken away from deep thought by the tunes of "My Niggas" by YG. He quickly reached for his iPhone #2 and placed it to his ear.

"Wudup, Joe?" The caller's name wasn't Joe. Joe was a term used throughout Chicago streets to keep from saying actual street or government names in any given situation. It was Future, and he sounded rattled. "There's some hardcore fugazi shit going on." Future breathed heavily. "I don't know who the fuck is guilty, so I'ma need to see you and the rest of the Convolution on the east at two o'clock sharp."

"Say no more," Bromise said and ended the call. Although *that* very summons was previously written in Bromise's phase book, he didn't expect for it to come in the form of a direct call. Not on that particular iPhone. That's not the way they did things. Bromise bolted upright from his king-sized bed. His train of thought quickly jumped over to the express rail.

If the two o'clock meeting was a set up, then he'd be walking into a trap. But maybe the lick wasn't the *only* issue that had Future shook up.

At nineteen, Bromise was young in age. But it isn't age, its experience and what a man learns from his experience that defines what he is. His young life was spent in the presence of professional drug traffickers, shiesty fuck-boys, and double-crossing murderers. People that spent years perfecting their poker faces, and had lifelong guilty consciences that they took in stride. Bromise was trained not to have a conscience. His experience taught him that a paranoid man didn't think logically. Future would point the finger at anyone that made him feel nervous or uncomfortable after a vile act had been committed against him. Something as small as missing *one* meeting a week ago, would not go unanswered this week. So he had to be smart about this. *Why did he call directly on iPhone #2, though? Is there a chance he knows something?*

Bromise ran his fingers through his fro and silently began to weigh his options. If he bailed on his entire plan and didn't go, he'd come off as liable. And the roster of certified killers would be covering ground in his direction faster than a shark swam to bloody raw meat. Not even an option. Future had contacts at both the O'Hare and Midway airports. One of his kids' mamas and her ratchet blabbermouth crew worked at the train station, and the bus stations were definitely off limits. They sat smack-dab in the Gangster Disciples' territory, an opposing street organization that stayed gunning for his head, and the bus stations were overrun by them. A totally unrelated shootout with the oppositions or *opps* wasn't exactly a smart alternative.

He was sure that his known spots were currently under Future's surveillance, as well as his house in Lincoln Square. But he was prepared for that. In advance, Chasidy used her real estate license to close on a foreclosed, four-bedroom two-bath brick home that sat tucked away in Blue Island. Bromise paid cash, enabling her to close on the home fast. She fudged the title information, making sure that no parts of the home deed could be traced back to Bromise. He was safe there.

Going to the two o'clock meeting would undoubtedly open him up to be pressured by Future and the rest of the Convolution. But again, he was prepared for that.

"Shake it off," he said to himself, knowing the unscripted call contributed to the paranoia, and not a botch that he may have overlooked. Deep down he knew that if he was a suspect he'd be dead by now, and so would Chasidy.

"If he wants me there at two o'clock sharp, then I'll be there, front and center," he thought aloud and leaned his head back against the headboard, preparing his mind for what lay ahead.

With one click from his bedside remote control, the intro to "Dreams and Nightmares" by Meek Mill started to play. He stared into the man's eyes on a photograph that hung perfectly from the wall. The solid gold frame complimented its prestige. It was a photograph of Brisco Balducci, his deceased grandpa. "Forever immortalized, Grandpa," he said with a smile. He missed him with a passion. Since the day Bromise's dead-beat dad had left while his mother was in her second trimester with him, her beloved father, Brisco, vowed to be the father Bromise would never have.

In his heart, he knew that his grandpa would be proud of the way he executed the beginning parts of his two-day-old plan. All he had to do from here on out was keep his head leveled, remain intimately in tune with the chain of events, and maintain steady advancements until the conquering of his scheme was fully realized.

Still staring at the photograph, he fixated on Brisco's Giorgio Armani necktie. It was his favorite and currently hung alone in Bromise's walk-in closet.

# VENOM IN MY VEINZ

He imagined what Grandpa would say if he were there right now. Although Brisco was gray with age, he was a gangsta's gangsta. Amongst close family and friends, Bromise still would boast about how he died, threatening the US Marshal that shot him:

*"You faint-hearted sonavabitch you!" Grandpa yelled, lying on the pavement in a puddle of his own blood. Three bullet wounds to his chest. A mob of Federal agents appeared as a moving backdrop to the scene. They were rushing in to relieve the overzealous marshal that stood over Grandpa, his banger still aimed and smoking. "If I make it outta the hospital I'm gon' kill you wheresoever I see you, pig!" Brisco fumed. "At your church praying for forgiveness, or at your daughter's music recital. I'm gon' kill you! And if I die, you sonavabitch, you can expect an ass whuppin' from the time you enter the firebox of hell, 'til the time Satan feels so bad for your ass that he sends you upstairs with your kind. You pussified sonavabitch you!" Grandpa yelled.*

Even when nearing death, Brisco was still *gangsta*. And Bromise loved it! It wasn't clear what amazed him more. The fact that his grandpa meant every word he spoke from his bloody mouth, or the fact that he immortalized his legacy as a feared tyrant with a *fuck the world* smile burning on the minds of those that watched him die.

Bromise's memory had stored everything that his grandpa said to him over the years, and he'd replay those words when he needed to hear him most. A smile touched his lips as he could hear the sternness of Brisco's voice now: *"You can't be afraid, Bromise, by the possibility of a near death situation when you're blazing a trail for your cause. Can't cross your legs now, baby boy. I molded you much better than that. Look at it this way: you're living to die any fuckin' way. Whether it's a bullet today, or a natural cause tomorrow, you still gon' die! So you might as well die taking what's yours, grandson. Remember, only in paradise is death bad for claiming the weak. Be man enough to live and die by your own terms. That way, God can at least respect you when he sends your black ass to hell! Just ask him about me. Ha! Ha! Ha!"*

Meek Mill's lyrics took a backseat to Brisco's solemn words. His hearty laughter echoed within Bromise's head. He was confident that Grandpa was watching over him, and was determined to win. "Help me fight this war, Grandpa." He was at the point of no return.

# CHAPTER 2

*Brisco Balducci*

Decades before Chicago took on its street moniker "Chiraq" for its parallel comparisons to the casualty-stricken war in Iraq, Brisco Balducci came to America from Italy sometime in the early 1950s. During a time when the FBI, headed by J. Edgar Hoover, turned their undivided attention to national security concerns, as Europe moved closer to war and World War II eventually unfolded, leaving Chicago and other major cities wide open. Several occupational drug traffickers and seasoned mafia figures had discovered the city's weaknesses and exploited them.

Chicago was deemed a goldmine. It made for an ideal location to store and traffic large amounts of narcotics through the state's highway channel. They even set up businesses to launder their messy money. Brisco monopolized the former prominent Taylor Street corridor in Little Italy. Little Italy was a community of Italian-Americans on the city's west side.

The city of Chicago was considered wide open to any person ballsy enough to put their occupation into motion. From the mafia boys to big city investors and entrepreneurs alike, they all jumped on the bandwagon.

The smart businessmen that migrated to the city, found ways to profit from opening up discount stores and Blues clubs. While hundreds of laborers got jobs in construction as they destroyed several blocks along State Street for the development of the public housing projects. Fine dining also thrived in Chicago. One restaurant in particular became by far the most popular. Its name was Fridas.

Brisco was among the savvy businessmen that contributed a great deal to the city's pace. His views on how to take control of a city under siege were tested and successfully executed in both Detroit and Miami.

Jamaican Bill held similar views that were shaped in Kingston, Jamaica and New York. Jamaican Bill had come to America soon after Brisco had. The two crossed paths at a local chess tournament in Chicago, where Brisco took home the gold while his soon to be business partner and closest friend earned a respectable third place ribbon. For the next two years they would meet at Murray Park once a week and play chess. It was at that metal, two-man table that their plan was formulated.

Together, they swiftly took control of 50% of Chicago's streets by the mid-1980s. But Brisco would not be satisfied until he gained complete control of the joystick that regulated the city's entire dope trade.

Half of said joystick was in the possession of Carlos and Hector. As far as the mentalities of the four mob bosses were concerned, Hector and Jamaican Bill were both hotheaded with an inordinate desire to be the head man in charge. They were 80% action and 20% thought. To them, the answer to any problem was always a body count. If they could have it their way, a street war would commence, and the last mob standing would take full ownership of the city's joystick. Grandpa and Carlos, on the other hand, were thorough thinkers. In their weighty opinions, a war would be detrimental to their businesses. They thought it to be rational to maintain their cordial relationship and hold back on any bloodshed. Hence, keeping the city peaceful at a 50/50 split. This arrangement lasted another twenty years, and the first decade of Bromise's life was exposed to the ground floor of it all.

By the time Bromise had met with his twelfth birthday, he learned just how shrewd his grandpa was. On a quiet fall night at 1:00 a.m., Brisco stopped by his daughter's, Abagail, home to visit his grandson. It was exactly 56 hours and 32 minutes before he took full ownership of the city's joystick.

"Get up, baby boy," Brisco said, waking Bromise up out of his sleep. "You have business to handle."

Bromise turned over to face him. When his eyes adjusted to the lone nightlight in his bedroom, he saw a chrome .45 automatic lying on the pillow next to him. Brisco sat on the edge of the bed, also next to him. He sat upright. His posture was perfect.

"Men are the dumbest sonavabitches walking this planet, Bromise," he said in an undertone as not to wake Bromise's mother, who was sleeping in the next room. "If you can't convince men to believe what you tell them, you can always convince them to believe what you show them. So fuck what people tell you, and fuck what they show you. Always follow your own instincts. Do you understand me, grandson?" he asked.

Brisco was consistent with asking rhetorical questions that didn't call for an answer. The only problem was Bromise didn't know if this was one of those questions. So instead of responding verbally, he simply looked into his eyes with a partial smile and nodded in agreement.

"At nine o'clock this morning, Carlos and Hector will be driving a midnight blue Porsche 911. They'll be heading to Frida's restaurant on South Michigan Street. Do you know where the place is located?" he asked.

Again, Bromise nodded in agreement.

"The two of them won't be armed nor escorted by security. Furthermore, I know the police in this city well. Well enough to know that if a kid your age is riding his bike to school and just happened to leave them both asleep, they won't work overtime at solving the cases. And everything that Carlos and Hector owns, just may fall into the lap of an old man who deserves every fine bit of it," he said as he firmly grabbed hold of Bromise's knee and gently shook it.

He understood exactly what his grandpa was asking of him, and he winked his eyelid to make him aware that he knew.

"I left you a present in the backyard, Bromise. Make sure you get to my house right after school and no later," he said. And without as much as another word, Grandpa was gone, leaving Bromise alone with his chrome .45 and a million thoughts.

With his chest stuck out, he was proud that his grandpa trusted him to accomplish such a feat. In the past, Bromise demonstrated his gratitude by refusing to let him down, ever. Instead of going back to bed only to rush to get the job done once he awoke, he raised up right then and began to prepare for the job.

After he ate a bowl of Frosted Flakes, he brushed his teeth and then got dressed. For jobs like this, Brisco taught him to dress a lot younger than his actual twelve years. His mother thought the age-inappropriate clothing Brisco would often buy for him was just bad taste on his behalf. She even thought it was cute.

He looked inside his closet and found an over-sized T-shirt that Brisco had got him a few weeks prior. The shirt was all white, with a large purple dinosaur blowing bubbles on either side. He also found some plain blue jeans, a pair of off-brand sneakers and his old backpack. He topped it all off with an over-sized Chicago Bulls cap. After he stuffed his backpack with a change of clothes, he considered himself ready for work.

From his mother's house to Frida's restaurant was a thirty-minute bike ride, so he had some crazy pedaling to do. To kill time, he sat around watching cartoons until 8:00 a.m. Before he left the house, he grabbed the chrome .45 and pulled his baseball cap down as far as it would go over his head. Not only to shield parts of his face, but also to make sure that his ears stuck out to help project the innocent child-like image that he was aiming for.

After his moms Abagail kissed him and sent him off for school, Bromise walked out to the backyard and saw a beat up Diamondback bicycle leaning against the side wooden panel of the garage. He instantly turned up his nose. Bromise wanted to ride his own bike, but he knew Grandpa chose this bike for a good reason. Even if he didn't tell him what that good reason was. Whether he liked it or not, he was going to ride that raggedy old bike. He grabbed a hold of the rusted handlebars, aimed the bike toward the alleyway, and pedaled off to Frida's.

# CHAPTER 3

*Molded by the Mob*

*Adolescent years . . .*

T he second Bromise sat on the bike's thin seat he knew he was on the clock. He increased his speed when he made it to the end of the alleyway and pedaled at a fast and steady pace. Bromise had nothing on his mind except finding the *midnight blue Porsche 911.*

Although the bike ride was long and tiring, he was calm along the way. Anxiety didn't set in until he made it close to Michigan Street, and realized that he underestimated his travel time. His wristwatch read 9:05 a.m. In spite of pedaling his ass off, he was still over a block away from his destination. "Grandpa is going to kill me!" he yelled and stood up on the pedals. Bromise could pedal faster standing up, and at that moment he definitely needed to push!

Now he was riding along the right side of a street. As he passed an intersection, he decided to turn into an alleyway that was coming up a few feet ahead. It was a short cut that would save him a few needed minutes. He pedaled the bike with as much force as the strength in his legs would allow. Suddenly, he smelled the aroma of well-seasoned Mexican food. He knew then he was getting closer.

He forged ahead at top speed. The surrounding garages and houses were nothing more than a blur. His focus was on the building that he could only catch a fleeting glimpse of between the slits of each house that he sped past. Frida's! He was only a half block over from the place. Instead of riding to the end of the alleyway and back around, he decided to look for another short cut. "Ah yes!" Bromise discovered a deserted gangway coming up on his right. The exit would place him directly across the street from Frida's. He took the vacant yard and pedaled through the gangway of an occupied house, quietly, as he heard voices coming from within.

Now he could see Frida's clearly just ahead. Bromise slowed the bike's pace and rolled down a short flight of concrete stairs before his front tire awkwardly hit the sidewalk and jumped the curb, placing him in the epicenter of Michigan Street!

Tires screeched, but before he could react, a car crashed into the bike, knocking him to the pavement. *Ouch! I fucked up!* Was all he could think. The thought of failing outweighed any physical pain he was feeling. He massaged the ache in his left leg when he heard two doors slam shut.

"You dented my fender, you little faggot!" the driver fumed before he and his passenger started speaking to each other in their native tongue.

Upon focusing in their direction, Bromise saw two Dominican men staring at the dented front end of a midnight blue Porsche 911.

*This can't be Carlos and Hector, could it?* He thought and heard a man yell from the sidewalk.

"Give the little punk fifty dollars and c'mon, will ya? Brisco and Jamaican Bill have been inside waiting for you two for over an hour now!" He was a burly man also of Dominican decent. He stood in front of

Frida's entrance.

"I wouldn't give this bum kid fifty cents. He just wrecked my beautiful car. Look at her!" Hector ranted and pointed to the damaged Porsche. "And the nigger-lover, plus the nigger inside aren't going anywhere. Let 'em wait!" Hector yapped and turned to Bromise with a cold, intimidating stare.

Bromise knew then that he would be his first victim. If the fact that he hit him with his *beautiful car* wasn't a good enough reason to be angry, his obnoxious and disrespectful mouth was more of a reason to be.

"Get up, you little nigger faggot!" Hector said and snatched Bromise up by his collar.

"Release him, Hector!" Carlos demanded as he stood aside the Porsche.

"This fuckin'—"were the last words to exit Hector's foul mouth. Bromise leveled the chrome .45 and squeezed the trigger. The slug that waited attentively in its chamber knocked down the fronts of Hector's disrespectful teeth, and all of the irreverent thoughts that he had in mind. Brain matter expelled from the back of Hector's head, splattering across the Porsche's windshield. His lifeless body plummeted to the ground. Bromise blazed his eyes at Carlos as he cowered on all fours at the rear of the vehicle. He glanced over at the burly Dominican man that remained in front of Frida's, and inadvertently spotted Jamaican Bill, who looked in awe from inside of the restaurant. Bromise's heart raced with adrenaline as he watched the Dominican man panic with fear, after realizing the banger in his hand had jammed. He faced him, and with both elbows locked, Bromise squeezed off three rounds. Two of which hit the man square in the chest.

Michigan Street converted into pandemonium as a mass of people screamed and ran for their lives. The scurrying rush awakened the running rabbit in Bromise, but he couldn't bring himself to abandon the scene. Not before he had completed his mission. He calmly walked over to Carlos, who was still at the rear of the Porsche, attempting to hide his trembling bones from his worst nightmare come true. He shook uncontrollably and pissed his pants. His hands were joined in a praying manner as he babbled in his native tongue. At this point he hadn't a snowman's chance in hell of surviving this. So maybe he was asking for repentance.

Bromise didn't care. He looked him in the eyes and met Carlos' forehead with the tip of the shiny banger. Without hesitation, he banana'd his split with one squeeze of the trigger. Then he let loose a barrage of slugs that ricocheted off the Porsche's bumper after exiting the side of Carlos' head.

With his mission accomplished, he ran five blocks down and crept inside a gas station bathroom. He got undressed and put the bloody outfit in the backpack with Grandpa's banger. Then he slipped on a change of clothes that he brought along. He took a deep breath and vacated the space. He casually walked to the bus stop and blended with a crowd of people who waited patiently to start their morning commute. He had to take a total of three public buses to make it from Michigan Street to school. His bus rides went smoothly, and it was just another day in class.

By the time Bromise made it to Brisco's

Kenilworth estate later that day, he was already looking outside his front window, awaiting his grandson's arrival. Never before had he witnessed his grandpa smile as brightly as he did as he approached his front door. It was rare that he smiled at all, so to see him touch his ears with the sides of his mouth was an incredible sight to see. Bromise knew he did well.

"Never send a man to do a boy's job," Brisco said as he welcomed his grandson into his home.

"Who's at the door, Brisco?" Bromise's grandma yelled from the back of the house.

"Come on in and talk business with me, grandson," he said and locked the door behind him, totally ignoring his wife's inquiry. He hated when she yelled through the house. He and Bromise sat down in his plush living room. After they both got comfortable, Bromise passed him his backpack, and he blessed Bromise with another one of his valuable lessons. "What you did today made it possible for me to take full control of this great city, and isolate the drug market, baby boy," he said with a childish grin. "What I want you to understand is that there's five levels to the dope game that you should be aware of.

"The first level is where all of the problems of stupidity and trivial beefs stem from, Bromise. I refer to it as the nickel and dime level. It's crowded with nickel and dime hustlers that have million dollar dreams that they would kill to bring to life. They only handle small amounts, chump change, and the pressure of vast competition only makes them more reckless than what they were before.

"The second level is the small weight level. It consists of small-minded men that believe their money and balls are larger than what they really are. Delusional is what I call them. For

The most part, they handle a few ounces of product and employ the nickel and dime level to push their product.

"The third level is the featherweight level. Men on this level are holding a few pounds. Only the dumb ones sell weight by supplying the men on the small weight level with ounces they need or the occasional pound. The smart ones employ others to push only nickels and dimes to increase their profit margin, and to escape any unwanted attention. Very seldom do they sell weight. Those are the men like Future. Do you understand?

"Yes, Grandpa," Bromise responded solemnly.

"Well, okay then," he said and readjusted his sitting position. "The fourth level of the game is the middleweight level. Men on this level are really starting to get their foot in the door. Whether they're getting it cash on delivery or by consignment, their packages come by the kilos, and they sell packages by the pound. This is where silence and secrecy are extremely important and must be practiced in order to survive. This level of men keeps their business amongst their tight-knit circle of a chosen few. Paranoia of the Feds and fear of losing everything they've worked for causes them to be very discreet. The smart ones are not flamboyant like others on the lower levels. By appearance alone, you may never know who's holding what. Now pay attention!" he spat with sternness. Bromise shook from the abrupt change in his tone. "Because this level is also the *'you can't trust your friend, double cross/main indictment level.'*

These men have much to lose should they take a fall, so they're always on the watch to use someone else's ass to save their own. An exit strategy, if you will. Many of them are money hungry. They continuously seek ways to take out the men who are either on, or close to their level to secure their own position in the game. One day you're going to reach that level, Bromise, and when you do I want you to remember that your biggest threat is the person that is closest to you. Do you follow me so far?"

"Yes, Grandpa, I follow," Bromise said just as solemnly as before.

"Now the last level is the heavyweight level," he said, leaning forward and placing his hand on his grandson's shoulder. "That level and the men on it are the real plug on product that supplies entire cities. It may seem as if everyone in the city is selling product for themselves, or for the man on the level just above them, but truth is they're selling product for the men on the heavy weight level. Even if they never get a chance to meet the man, he is the true employer of the game. That level, my favorite grandson, usually could only be claimed by four men or less, at any given time. The product goes down from the heavyweight level to the nickel and dime level, and back up again in the form of currency, and those men get it by the barrels. To the nickel and dime men, the dope game is just a hustle. To those higher up the food chain, the drug trade is the most profitable business nationwide, truly the American way. Nickel and dime men use their limited money and influence to keep their blocks under control. Whereas, heavyweight traffickers use their power to keep entire cities under wraps. The only way

# VENOM IN MY VEINZ

to grow in this business, grandson, is to understand it. To know when and how to use the strengths of your affiliates and prevent their weaknesses from hurting your mob. Carlos, Hector, Jamaican Bill, and myself were the heavyweights of this great city. Jamaican Bill receives his directives exclusively from me. With Carlos and Hector gone, the city is mine, grandson, all mine," he said and rubbed the top of Bromise's head roughly. "As long as you understand this business and how it's played, one day this city will be yours. Right now I won't allow so much as a tenth of product into this city that doesn't have my stamp on it. Why is that?" he asked.

Caught off guard by his question, Bromise took a deep swallow and answered, "So that everybody has to buy from you personally?" He leaned forward in his seat, anxious to see if his answer was the correct one.

"Not necessarily so they can buy from me personally, no. Listen, I never touch anything myself, or do direct business with anyone except Jamaican Bill and my long distance friend. I made this move to isolate the market, so I and only I can supply what the city demands. What I'm going to do next is take down the prices on kilos and flood the city one good time. After the flood subsides I'm going to shut down sells momentarily. Now why is that?" he asked.

This time Bromise was better prepared and was confident he would get this question right. "If you take down the prices, a lot of hustlers will be able to buy more product than usual and that'll make flooding the city that much easier. But Grandpa, I'm not sure why you'd want to shut down sells," he said with riveting curiosity circling the rings of his pupils.

"Because if I shut down sells momentarily, that would ensure a drought. Let me explain. If I flood the city first, that gives everyone ample opportunity to inflate their prices on the product they had previously purchased before the drought, and sell out of everything that they may have put up. It not only gives them the chance to profit immensely, it also gives me the likelihood to see to it that everyone sells out of product. Even if they don't sell out completely, which they probably won't, they'll still be in dire need of product, and they'll have more than enough money for it because of their drought sells. And that, my boy, would open the door for me to return to business with a richer and hungrier market awaiting me," he said and stared into Bromise's eyes, sensing how amazed he was. "Besides, I need a vacation anyhow.

"From this point on I want you to pay close attention to the way that business is conducted, and I want you to keep a portion of each of my drug shipments in a safe place for me. I also want you to do any clean-up work that my men cannot take care of, just like you did today and have in the past. Do you understand all of what I am saying to you, Bromise?"

"Yes," he said, and only then did he display a smile. The both of them talked for quite some time thereafter, and during their conversation, Bromise realized how it was possible for him to hit Carlos and Hector so easily.

Brisco manipulated the tension between Jamaican Bill and Hector, and used it to his advantage. He suggested a sit down with Carlos to renegotiate their latest terms. After Carlos' acceptance, he agreed to meet with him but only under specific conditions. The conditions were as follows: Carlos and Hector and Brisco and Jamaican Bill had to come to the meeting alone and unarmed. Both mobs were permitted to have only one security member to stand guard. He also had to come alone. The two security members were allowed to come armed, however, both had to wait outside until the meeting was adjourned. Not under any circumstances were either to enter Frida's.

The old man, Mo, that owned the joint was an overweight Mexican who did business with both Brisco's mob and Carlos' mob, so both sides trusted him well. They used his restaurant as the meeting place and agreed that only Mo's security guard would sit in, armed, as an unbiased party to guard the safety of all four of the mob heads. Understandably, Mo was afraid to secure the meeting because he was weak in both finances and soldiers to go to war with either mob, should something go wrong during the meeting and he was to blame for it. To comfort him, both sides agreed that Mo would be held liable only if something were to go wrong inside the restaurant, and he failed to provide the necessary protection. If anything were to happen to one of the mob bosses outside of the restaurant, then it was of no concern to Mo or his security guard. Both mobs further agreed that if either mob sought to penalize Mo for a disturbance that occurred on the outside of the restaurant, the opposing mob would form an alliance with Mo and declare war against the mob that breached the agreement. The compact satisfied Mo enough to offer his assistance, and that's what made it possible for Brisco to hit Carlos and Hector, and to persuade them to agree to such conditions in the first place.

Brisco's personal security was missing from his outside post when Bromise arrived. He was sent to get cigarettes, although Brisco was a non-smoker. In the process, he was to call Abagail and ask if Bromise had left for school already. Unbeknownst to his security person, Brisco sent him away to avoid the possibility of someone assuming that he'd ordered the hit. This was his way of killing two birds with one stone. Ordering his security to call Bromise's mother was a ploy to avoid having to tell him what was to come, but also to check on Bromise's departure at the same time. Jamaican Bill wasn't even hip to the plot.

But Bromise never thought that his grandpa and Jamaican Bill would actually be inside of Frida's when he showed up on his bike blazing.

He felt that his grandpa's plan was ingenious, but even at such a young age he saw a flaw in it. In his opinion, Grandpa placed Jamaican Bill and himself in a position of sitting ducks. Not to mention, open season targets inside of the restaurant that resembled a fish bowl.

"Why did you leave Jamaican Bill and yourself open like that?" he asked.

Brisco leaned forward from his high-back chair, planted his hands on both of Bromise's shoulders, and gave him an answer that he'd never forget. For it explained what he meant that morning when he told him never to believe what people tell or show.

"Hector believed what he saw, Bromise," he said in a calm but confident tone. "He saw me being weak enough to fold, so his intention was to attend the meeting solely to apply pressure. He saw that I would break, and that illusion persuaded him that he could take what he wanted from me.

"Carlos, on the other hand, believed what he heard. He heard me say let's make a deal that works out for everyone. Therefore, he was coming to the meeting with the intentions of closing the deal, and hoping to persuade me into giving him a little something extra, with Hector's help of course.

"I only believe in my instincts," he said, "and my instincts said that those two racist sonavabitches had to go. I believed that with all of the tools that I've instilled in you, you'd be capable of taking care of them both before they knew what was coming. Bromise, it's vital that you understand that the wind carries secrets. If you keep your eyes open and refrain from having a million no-good men block the wind, you'll give those secrets the opportunity to blow into your ear. You see, I found out yesterday that Hector had planned to have Jamaican Bill hit at 10:00 a.m., right after the meeting was over, to try and weaken me. That's why I instructed you to show up at nine and hit them both before the meeting even began. At 9:05 a.m. I got a little uptight because you were nowhere to be found, and I didn't have a contingency plan. You were my only ace in the hole, the one warrior that I had to depend on. So I'm elated, baby boy. That you managed to pull it off as I knew you could." He smiled and winked at Bromise one last time.

Before Bromise left Brisco's estate, he instructed him on which parts of the city to avoid for the next few days. He further informed him that he'd have his first shipment brought to him soon for *safekeeping*. On the night of Carlos and Hector's murders, the streets were shocked that someone had the guile to shoot them down, and in broad daylight at that. The gossip lines were in full swing, and the news was, "a killer-midget posing as a ten-year-old kid." The outfit worked like a charm! It went down as one of Chicago's highest profiled double-homicide cases to date, still unsolved.

On the following day, the South and Westside streets were both high in death toll. Twenty of Carlos and Hector's lieutenants were found dead in a short series of systematic hits, causing their subordinates to either flee the state, or work for Brisco through his subordinates.

Six weeks following the murders, the city befell to a calm. Jamaican Bill took control of the South and Westside, previously owned by the late Carlos and Hector, and Brisco controlled the other half of the city with an ironclad fist. He was now satisfied, for he owned the joystick to the city.

Brisco shared with Bromise many lessons, but seeing him thrown to the wolves, only to return leading the pack was what benefitted him most. He showed his grandson that a man could take control of the world if he formulated the proper plan of action and executed it to its fullest.

When he said that the city was his, Bromise heard him as clear as a summer day. But witnessing him in raw action convinced the young boy of just how dangerous one man's mind can be. Although he was viewed as a loving man by his family, his heart pumped pure venom through his veins, making him the most lethal man Bromise had ever known. His only wish was to be as cunning, calculating, and powerful as his grandpa when his time came.

Bromise stayed under his wing. Through him, he

learned as much as he could and emulated his image. To be certain that his molding process was strictly done by the *G-code*, Brisco made sure that Bromise was a boy doing grown man things on the regular. He was the heir to Brisco's throne.

# CHAPTER 4
### My Ticket In

*Two years later . . .*

After Brisco was killed, streetgossip.com went into full swing. The streets turned into a big chat line. The rumor was that Jamaican Bill set him up for the US Marshal that killed him.

Bromise's mother, on the other hand, believed that it was his uncle, Cigar (Bromise's dad's younger brother) who knew something about something. Yet, there was no way of being sure of either allegation. Mainly because Cigar conveniently disappeared just before Brisco was killed, and hadn't been heard from since. Both stories carried some weight, but it was hard for Bromise to believe either. Cigar was his favorite and only uncle, and the only other family member that Brisco did business with.

Jamaican Bill was a probable suspect, but he was also extremely close to Brisco. He trusted Jamaican Bill enough to work hand-to-hand with him. Considering Brisco's philosophy of *the game,* it was mad difficult for Bromise to fathom that his grandpa would be so foolish as to put himself in a position where he would be slumped by his right hand.

Due to people's outward façade, it was nearly impossible to differentiate their respect from fear, and either of the two from envy. In one form or another, everyone appeared to have love for Brisco. They even paid their last respects at his funeral and expressed heartfelt condolences to both Bromise and Abagail, Brisco's only daughter. Needless to say, that made it more difficult for Bromise to figure shit out. And if matters weren't already at its worst, Bromise's mother had lost her battle with cancer one week after her father's funeral. After that, Bromise went to live with Chasidy and her older sister, Porsha.

The biggest part of Bromise was missing now. Without true family, he felt like the only other person he had in this world was his girlfriend, Chasidy. The pair were inseparable, and without his grandpa around to lean on, she became his other half. Brisco molded them equally, and in many ways she was a female version of Bromise, just three years his senior.

Post Brisco's death, Jamaican Bill took full control of the city's joystick, thus, Brisco's operation. He refused to go into business with anyone in the Convolution except Future. And as expected, Jamaican Bill's younger brother, Rudeboy, was promoted to his lieutenant. After he strategically lined his ducks in a row, Jamaican Bill made his presence felt right out of the gate. He raised the price tag on dirt-cheap kilos that Brisco made available during his reign. He also did away with most of the middleweight hustlers that hesitated to comply with his *new order*. Subsequently, he was honored as King and his position was secure.

His next course of action was to release a heavy flow of heroin throughout the city, and scout out the best of the middleweight hustlers that he left alive for the purpose of working for him.

Future was the pick of the litter. Brisco had allowed him to keep his six blocks on the Eastside after Carlos and Hector's murders. The way that Brisco organized the drug trade enabled Future and a few other hustlers to claim their positions. That opportunity contributed a great deal to Future being Jamaican Bill's number one draft pick. During this time, Future was young and greedy and would do anything for self-gain. From afar, Bromise watched as he pulled one shiesty move after another. Future befriended the leading competitors around the way, and before long, they were all pinched by the Feds while he managed to slip through the cracks when the indictments were handed down. The shocking part was the streets turned the other cheek to his methods. Since his name could never be found as a "confidential informant" in black and white, or court documents, it was just assumed that he had either more luck or more connections than the average Joe, and maybe he's not a snitch. Then he assembled a team of young guns that he'd either known for a while, or saw potential in. He put all their asses to work and sat at the top left of Jamaican Bill, while Rudeboy sat secure on the right.

Brisco once told Bromise that what blinds men the most is lust, money, and getting so wrapped up in what's going on around them that they can't see what's really going down in front of them.

The men that weren't blinded by those things were blinded by the ride that Future was taking them on. They didn't pay attention to how he got into position. They didn't suspect his treacherous ways, but Bromise suspected the fuckery all along. With Jamaican Bill backing him, in just two short years, Future went from having six blocks, to supplying 30% of the city with highly addictive narcotics, while other middleweight hustlers suffered loss after mysterious loss.

It wasn't a coincidence, but it was what his grandpa had warned him about years ago. Precisely at the time when he explained to him the different levels of the game, and the type of men that thrived on those levels. Even though Bromise saw the street politics and knew firsthand how dirty the game was, he still wanted in. But Future stood in his way. In his defense, in honor of the late Brisco Balducci, he made sure that Bromise didn't want for anything. But he still wouldn't risk letting him make any major moves, or get his own paper. *Fuck that!* Bromise didn't want any handouts from him, or anyone else. Yet, over and over again, Future would dwell on Bromise's age, and how he needed to study the game before he entered it.

Future didn't realize that Bromise spent the better part of his life studying under one of the best teachers that the game had to offer. There was no secret as to who his grandpa was, only the integral part he played in his big scheme of things. Brisco never told a soul of the work Bromise put in, and neither did he.

Although Bromise was capable of doing a lot more than what was expected, everyone still treated him like a snotty-nose little brother. The fact that he was fourteen and only five-feet-inches tall and weighed less than ninety pounds didn't help his cause much either. Moreover, he had a smooth baby face and big innocent brown eyes to compliment his dimples, along with a soft-spoken demeanor and dark chocolate complexion that he inherited from his father's Nigerian background. His mother's Italian blood caused his hair to look and feel different than his peers. As a result, the boys often teased him, while the girls seemed to like running their fingers through his naturally tight curls. Everyone that he socialized with was older, a feat that he worked hard to achieve. Yet, no matter how much he tried, there was no way of hiding his youth. Bromise looked foolishly young. That earned him the nickname, "Youngin." Oddly enough, his kiddie appearance made it so his nickname fit him like the Rag & Bone denim on Nicki Minaj.

Future had no idea what Bromise was capable of. At least not until he tagged along one day to check on one of Future's trap houses that had been repeatedly coming up short with cash.

Bromise must've been on a million of these trips with Future in the past. To collect money, drop off product, and watch while he threatened his workers for being delinquent with his currency. But unbeknownst to either of them, this routine trip would prove to be anything but routine.

It was a late Friday night. Bromise was riding with Future, carrying his Glock in his waistband while they made round after round to his various trap houses. He had one situated in what they called K-Town, which is arguably the most dangerous section on the west side. As they pulled up to a curb, he parked his S550 Mercedes Benz. Bromise was busy bobbing his head to "Money Trees" by Kendrick Lamar. He stared beyond the car window, watching the trap house carefully, when he noticed the lookout, John-John, was not on his security post and nowhere in sight.

Future exited his Benz like a ghetto Don, with Bromise following close behind. As they walked up the stairs, a strange sensation came over Bromise. This specific trap house was one of twenty handed down to

# VENOM IN MY VEINZ

Future by Jamaican Bill. Once they made it inside, Bromise copped a seat on the armrest of an old beat-up couch. He watched as Future rounded up Goldie, Fats, and John-John. He lined the three of them in the middle of the front room and circled them like a drill sergeant, scolding his cadets.

Goldie ran the trap house. Fats and John-John were his nickel and dime workers. Bromise never liked John-John, or that dude, Goldie. To him they were both *in the game-in the way* and should've been forced out a long time ago. Fats, however, stayed to himself, quiet and focused on the hustle. He was also the closest in age. For those reasons, Bromise liked him.

After Future finished with his first drill of threats, Goldie and John-John began to complain about an up and coming clique that were calling themselves the BB (Bogus Boys). These dudes were living nightmares. Although they dabbled in the drug trade, the bulk of their pay came from jacking their competitors.

During this time, a large number of inner city cliques started to populate Chiraq streets. The BB was the talk of them all. They were extremely ruthless and quite comparable to the Taliban. The BB had earned an intimidating reputation, and it was common knowledge that wherever they set up shop, they shut down the neighboring competition by force. In short, these dudes took blocks. They were at the very top of everyone's robbery and homicide suspect list, including the jakes; Chicago's Police Force. Those that they didn't rob or kill were the cowards that folded under their pressure and joined their clique. And now here they were, in K-Town, inside of their own trap house, directly across the street from Future's trap house. Shortly after they moved in, they began to take clientele from Goldie, which in turn took cash out of Future's pockets. And he wasn't having it.

Bromise sat on the armrest looking at Future. He could tell by the glare in his eyes he was pissed. He made the reason behind his anger clear as he yelled at the three men for the third time.

"So you tellin' me that I'm comin' up short on my ends because you nigga's pussy!" Future shouted angrily.

"Ain't no pussy here? Future, you already know we buck shots with the best of 'em," Goldie said. "It's just the way the game is right now. The only way to move dem fools around is to out hustle dem, and we need better product for that." Goldie tried to make his case. Because he ran the trap house, it was his ass that was in the sling.

"Better product my ass!" Future yelled. "Do I look like a fuckin' new jack to you, nigga? We got the purest shit in the city. What you need is some fuckin' heart, and what I need is some real niggas runnin' this fuckin' trap!" Future continued to circle their stiff, nervous bodies.

"I'll get this shit together in less than a week, word is bond," Goldie said with a stride of confidence that fell short mid-sentence. "Just lemme figure out a way to handle those BB niggas."

"If you couldn't stop this shit from gettin' outta control, how in the fuck am I supposed to believe you can get it under control?" Future asked rhetorically. "What you need to do is get my cash together now, and get the fuck outta my trap! I'll be better off lettin' this lil nigga, Youngin, run the show!"

# VENOM IN MY VEINZ

Suddenly, all eyes in the room were on Bromise. He knew a prime opportunity when he saw one, and this was definitely it. He thought about what Brisco would do in this situation: *"Shock those that don't believe."* He heard his grandpa's voice, and that was his cue to chime in.

"Listen, Joe, if you give me this trap house to run, I'll make it so the BB disappear. Plus, I'll have your money right in less than five days." Bromise was thirsty for a chance.

Future knew he was serious. All that shit about him being too young to run his own trap house was his opinion. If he was closing it down anyway, he had nothing to lose with trying the kid out. But instead of seeing it that way, a chorus of laughter filled the air. Every man in the room, with the exception of Fats, held their guts as they guffawed at Bromise's expense. He was livid!

Bromise bolted from the armrest in Goldie's direction, pulling the .40 Glock from his waistband. He stepped to him and touched the tip of his nose with the front of the barrel. Frozen in place, Goldie stared cross-eyed at the banger. The laughter was then consumed by bone-chilling silence.

"Put the banger down, Youngin," Future said nervously.

Bromise ignored his request and gradually pushed the .40 forward, smashing it against the bone that held Goldie's nose in place. He was beyond scared, and looked as if he wanted to cry like the bitch he was. "This is how easy it is to shut niggas up," Bromise said, looking square up into Goldie's fearful eyes. "And squeezing this trigger is all that it takes to move

33

any fool that's standing in my way, out of my way. And right now, you're definitely in my way," he said, intending for all to hear. "I don't care how powerful a man is, or how many other men ride for him. A warrior doesn't need a storm to perform. Even alone, he can do what one hundred toy soldiers won't. Push one hot copper tip into the head of his adversary. Then another slug through the heart of his main man, and many more through the bodies of every man still standing, until he subtracts his whole clique from the city's population count, permanently. And then, toy soldier, your problem is solved." Goldie's eyes became misty. Bromise was sure he could smell the gunpowder. He squeezed the double trigger, sending Goldie's lifeless body crashing to the floor. Red specks of his DNA dotted Bromise's face and True Religion tee. He was pissed about his tee.

"What da fuck!" Future looked over at the other two men before training his eyes back on Bromise. "What da fuck did you just do, Youngin?"

"I did what needed to be done, Joe," Bromise said, shoving the Glock back into his waistband.

Future stared at Bromise in total disbelief. Then suddenly, a slight smirk pinched his lips.

"Well, you heard the lil nigga," Future said in the two men's direction. "He runs this trap now. Give him the house keys, and let's count my muthafuckin' money so I can get up out dis muthafucka!" Future demanded.

"But, but, Future . . ." John-John stuttered.

"But Future my ass," Future interjected. "Didn't you just see what da fuck just happened?" he asked, gesturing toward the bloody mess on the floor. John-John nodded yes. "Do you want the same shit to happen to your ass?"

John-John, still silent, shook his head no.

"Well then, I suggest you get with the program. Ain't shit to talk about. Youngin is runnin' this trap now, so take your problems up with him," Future said. He walked out of the front room and toward the back of the house. Fats followed closely behind. John-John reluctantly tossed Bromise the house keys before stepping over Goldie's corpse and joining them in the back.

Bromise hated the name Youngin, but at the moment it didn't seem to bother him as much. He held tightly onto the house keys and walked over to the front room window. It was boarded up with a small carved-out section, allowing vision outside. He stared at the BB trap house. His thoughts were mixed. Half, wondering how in the hell was he going to get rid of the Bogus Boys in under twenty-four hours, while the other half mused in disbelief of earning his first trap house.

A few minutes later, Fats and John-John came out from the back and began to wrap Goldie's corpse in oversized blankets. They exited out the back door with it, just as Future joined Bromise in the front room. He sat in a chair holding a small grocery bag filled with cash.

"Listen, Youngin," he said, causing Bromise to face him. "I left you thirty-nine 25-gram bags of Al Capone (heroin) in the back room, and four bangers with a vest under the mattress. I'll send you a team when you call for them. Right now this is officially your problem. All you have to do is sell the product and re-up from me, and only *me*. How you sell it is your business, but as of now you owe me  $31,200. Not thirty, not thirty-one and some change. You owe exactly $31,200. You my lil nigga, Youngin. Don't fuck that up. 'Cause although I might like you—I *love* my money. So I'm coming for it seven days from now. When I arrive, I wanna hear the sounds of that money machine counting my bread, or you gonna hear the sounds of burners poppin' at ya head. Are we clear?" Future asked, after putting forth his best stone-face.

Bromise didn't bother to answer him verbally. He just nodded in accordance, which Future was used to by now.

"What else do you need?" he asked sincerely as he rose from the chair.

"John-John dead, and Fats back here when I call for my team," Bromise said bluntly.

Future looked at him with a comical expression. "Anything else, Don Grown Ass?" he asked sarcastically.

"As a matter of fact, yeah," Bromise said with an arrogant tone. "When you hear about what happened to the BB niggas, don't ask me silly questions of how I got it done. And please, shut *my* door on your way out." Bromise wore a straight face.

Future shot him the look and said, "Now don't get all cocky and shit. That was one vital mistake your grandfather, Brisco Balducci, made. You just make sure you do whatever you have to do to keep air inside your body long enough to pay me my bread. You wanted to play with the big boys, well, here you have it." He stood to his feet. "And oh yeah, there's some bleach and other multi-purpose cleaners in the kitchen." He looked over at the bloody mess on the floor. "You gon' have to clean that disgusting shit up yourself. One." He turned away, exited the house, and shut the door behind him.

Bromise didn't like what he said about his grandpa one bit. Hell, he wasn't a quarter of the man he was, and he knew it. *Fuck Future*, he thought, and reclaimed his position back at the boarded window. He wrapped his fist around the plastic grip of the .40 and freed it from his waist. "Come out, come out, wherever you are, Mr. Boogeyman," he whispered as he scoped out the dark and gloomy trap house across the street. It's time to get active!

# CHAPTER 5

*Adrenaline Rush*

Bromise stood in the window until his legs began to cramp. Twenty hours had passed since Future left, and his eyes had been glued to the BB trap house the entire time. It was a duplex that sat far back on the lot that it was built on. The front door was approximately twenty feet behind the other existing houses that were constructed on either side of it, thus, giving them a rather large front yard to work with.

The sky was a canopy of pure darkness that overlapped the already shadowy area, yet, Bromise's keen observation noted five men and one woman that currently occupied the duplex. The only light came from the moon.

Three of the five men were stationed on the outside of the duplex. Two of those three men were security detail, while the third one focused on pushing their packs of product to dozens of cluckers. He was considered their bag man.

Bromise watched incognito, as they solicited customers with aggressive tactics. They ran up to every vehicle that drove by. The product they were selling was wrapped in aluminum foil packaging and kept hidden between the wood siding on the left side of the duplex.

When the bag man ran out of product, he didn't have to leave his outside post to retrieve more from the inside. He would simply whistle, and one of the two men on the inside would toss him a new bundle out the window. His body language conveyed that he felt safe out there. He wasn't armed, but he was comfortable for sure. From where Bromise stood, he held in view a sizable bulge in both the front and back of the other two men's shirts. They were holding heat. Not to mention the two choppers (AK-47s) he saw stashed in the front yard, just inches away from the security men. Bromise understood exactly why he felt safe.

The two men on the inside of the duplex never came out to assist the other three men with their assignments. They held their positions in front of a downstairs window at the back end of the duplex, accommodating clientele that drove up the alleyway like a fast food drive-through joint. "They got a decent operation going on," he admitted to himself.

He assumed the woman was a mere runner because she left the duplex every two hours with an empty plastic bag that dangled loosely from her hand. Only to return in under ten minutes with the same plastic grocery bag filled to the rim with what he suspected to be their highly demanded product.

Her first trip caught Bromise off guard, and that alone made him curious. Her second trip caused his instincts to flare with suspicion, so he timed her. Now, her next trip would be expected.

Just a few moments prior to when she would make her move, Bromise noted that the bag man would receive a call on his cell. He would then signal for the security men and direct them to walk around the house and back, as if to secure the perimeter. By the time the two men would make it back around to the front of the duplex, the woman would have reached the front door, while all three men stood guard on the front stoop as she made her exit.

Bromise figured they had some type of security protocol that prevented their front door from opening without all of them knowing first. He loved routines. Because of their little ritual, he was able to predict the woman's third departure, moments before she actually committed to her journey. And this time he was ready.

After he secured the trap house door, he ducked into the alleyway. As she walked along the street, he kept up with her pace, peering through every gangway that split each house they passed. She stopped at a red and white house two blocks down from their trap house. He crouched in the shadows between two houses across the street from her, and watched as she pulled out a set of house keys, unlocked the door, and entered.

Bromise started his Nike stopwatch. He lit up a Kool cigarette and leaned his backside against the aluminum paneling of an abandoned house. He released a billow of blue smoke and took another pull, and another, before tossing it aside.

She stayed inside for five and a half minutes. To his utter surprise, she exited the house without the filled plastic bag like the two times prior. Bromise maintained his position as she stepped off the front porch and began walking.

When she was out of view, he cautiously headed for the red and white house. His curiosity was at its max. He jogged up the stairs and rang the doorbell. Had someone appeared on the opposite side of the threshold, he was fully prepared to act as if he had the wrong address in search of a friend. After several rings there was still no answer. He lowered his head and cupped his hands on either side of his face, and peeped through the window. The curtain was heavy and black, with wear patches that allowed him to see small sections of the front room. Just as he expected, the house was completely empty.

He took the steps to the front porch and started back for his trap house. To avoid the front route, he cut through a vacant lot a quarter of a block away, and used the same alleyway to get to his back door. Once inside, he reclaimed his space in front of the boarded window and continued to spy. He was almost certain that the red and white house was indeed their safe house. He just needed to confirm it.

It was now 2:15 a.m. With his eyes still peeled, he jotted down notes in a notepad. *Snap it up, grandson.* At once, Bromise raised his head and noticed something wasn't right. "Why are all six of them standing in their front yard now?" he uttered as they scurried about.

The men were locking the doors and the downstairs' windows, while the woman turned away the last of their clientele that were still coming by the flock. *They must've run out of product,* he thought. It appeared as though they were closing shop. After the last man rechecked the secureness of their duplex, they all piled into a conversion van that was parked a couple of houses over.

Bromise watched as they pulled away from the curb and bent a corner. His instincts told him to get active. He secured his trap and retraced his steps through the alleyway. He caught up to his destination quicker than before, and his hunch was confirmed. "Ah ha, what do we have here?" He grinned when he saw the BB conversion van parked in front of the empty red and white house. At that very moment he considered the six of them dead.

He headed back to the block with rapid steps and rushed around to the back of the BB duplex. *C'mon now, that ain't going to stop nothin'*, he thought, after noticing they left every light on inside the duplex. He proceeded to case out the joint until he located a weakness in its structure.

Then he quickly walked over to his trap. His mind was on nothing but the position he'd been craving for. Once inside, he covered his hands with black leather Peccary gloves and rushed into the bedroom. He came out of his Carhartt winter coat and pushed the mattress off the box spring and stood over the four bangers Future left behind. He took time to strap on the vest. Then he grabbed hold of the .454 Casull and a fully automatic Bushmaster ACR. Next, he went throughout the trap, gathering all the tools needed for the job.

The streets were extra quiet, and under the current circumstance that wasn't exactly a good thing. Any uncommon sound could be heard way off into the distance, and that made him a bit uneasy. There was a back porch attached to the duplex, and a window aside from it that he perceived to be the structure's weakness.

He jumped up and grabbed a firm hold on the support beam that held the top porch in place. Then he pulled himself upward, and climbed from the bottom beam to the top porch. The duplex was an older model. It had double hung windows with sliding latch locks that could open from the outside, if only one could

# VENOM IN MY VEINZ

manage to slide something small, yet sturdy, over the latch. The wooden frame that outset the window wore a thin crack that was too small to get anything through. But he came prepared. He reached in his coat pocket and pulled out a butcher's knife. He slid the tip of it into the crack, and wedged that sucker just enough to maneuver his trusty clothes hanger through. Brisco taught him this trick a good while ago, when he had to sneak back into his mother's home one late night after doing a job for him.

He forced the hanger through and up the crack. After some precise maneuvering, the hanger met the latch. *Bingo!* The window was unlocked. With just a few moments of work, he was now walking inside of the notorious BB trap house. The upstairs part of the duplex was totally vacant. He found the door that he was looking for, opened it, and took the stairs that led to the lower level. Upon making it downstairs, he was confronted by a huge mess of garbage and whatnot that he had to navigate through. He walked around calmly, observing every nook and cranny while breathing in through his mouth in a failed attempt to avoid the foul smell that dominated the entire space.

With the Bushmaster ACR precisely aimed, Bromise slowly approached a closed door and gently pushed it open. "Ahhh shit!" he yelped and threw his hand over his nose and mouth. Apparently, this was the bathroom, and the odor was vile, similar to sewage. He felt nausea creeping up the back of his throat, and he swallowed it back down. He walked inside and shut the door gently with his foot, not wanting to touch anything inside of the germ-infested bathroom. The space was small. He paused for a minute to look around. He never saw anything more disgusting, and he wondered did the lady of the house ever use these quarters to freshen up. *If so, damn she's a triflin' cunt.* Bromise stepped inside the bathtub and lay on his back with his head against the bacteria-coated cast iron wall. His finger caressed the trigger of the Bushmaster. The weapon slowly rose up and down atop his abdomen from the rhythmic tempo of his breathing.

*SHIT!* He didn't realize he fell asleep until he woke up. He clutched on to the Bushmaster. *They are here.* He heard a female's voice just beyond the bathroom's door.

"I need to wash my hands before I eat. You greedy niggas bet not eat my Italian beef, neither."

In seconds, Bromise bolted from the tub and stood to his feet. Just as he slipped behind the bathroom door, it opened. She walked in. It was the same female that he followed to the red and white house. She walked to the sink and began to wash her hands. She reminded him of a young Stacy Dash, brown skinned, standing about 5-feet 3-inches tall, with one of the most amazing asses he'd seen, aside from Chasidy's.

He made one swift motion and got behind her. Quickly, he covered her mouth with his leather palm and pressed the .454 Casull against her temple. "Don't say a fuckin' word, you Bogus Boy bitch," he whispered into her ear. The inches of physical growth he acquired over the past two years, allowed her back to weigh on his chest. He could feel the rapid thump-thump of her heart. "When I remove my hand, I want you to yell out that you have to use the bathroom, and not to eat the Italian Beef that you like so much." He caught her eyes in the filthy mirror and locked on.

# VENOM IN MY VEINZ

"Please don't kill me," she mumbled into his hand. Bromise squeezed her vocal chords with the tip of his thumb and fingers, and nudged her head with the front of the burner. "That's not what I said to say. Don't fuckin' play with me!" He loosened his grip, and she went through her breathing drills to replenish the oxygen supply to her lungs. Then she yelled out, "I need to use the bathroom, y'all, so don't eat my damn Italian beef. I'm serious!"

She stared at Bromise through the mirror and asked, "Are you happy now?" He stepped around her and locked the bathroom door. "Pull your pants down and sit on the toilet," he whispered with a serious mug.

For Bromise, she was an easy read. The muscles in her face revealed what she was thinking and feeling. Her thoughts spoke clearly without having to say a word. He decided to ease her worries. "Look, I'm not here to rape you. I need you on that toilet just in case one of those dumb niggas decide to look under the door. Trust me, my plans do not include involuntary sex." An instant show of relief fondled her face. But before Bromise allowed her to get too comfortable he whispered, "Now open your fuckin' mouth." She reluctantly parted her lips. He gently placed the nozzle of the Bushmaster on her damp tongue. Then suddenly he heard the sound of urine streaming into the toilet water below her. He had her right where he wanted her. Terrified.

"What's your name?" he asked, slowly pulling the nozzle from her mouth.

"Benita," she said in a broken tone.

*Benita Westbrook? Nah, it couldn't be. Could it?* He thought and took a step back as if to get a better look.

Jamaican Bill's younger brother, Rudeboy, had a bounty out on a female named Benita Westbrook. The bounty was still active and the instructions were *'wanted dead or alive'*. And the more Bromise looked at her, the more she fit the description. If this was her, then he was standing next to the most infamous female setup artist Chiraq had ever seen. Word is, she setup Rudeboy to get robbed, and his captors left him for dead. He took two slugs like a champ and lived through it. And he'd been after her head ever since.

"Your last name wouldn't happen to be Westbrook, would it?" he asked.

She hesitated, looked down at the floor, and swallowed deeply. It was written all over her face. She didn't have to say a word.

"Don't even lean on it." Bromise said, easing her anxiety. "I'm not here for you. You're just in the wrong place at the wrong fuckin' time." In truth, right now he needed her. He needed her calm and overly confident that she stood an excellent chance on living through this. He couldn't afford for her to jeopardize his mission. He was expecting five BB niggas to be in the next room.

"Do you have any kids, Benita?"

She nodded yes and sniffled as tears dropped into her lap.

"Would you like to see them again?"

"Yes," she replied while trying her damnedest to control her emotions. Her hands trembled with fear. Her face began to ball-up, and she started to breathe abnormally. It was only a matter of time before she broke completely, and possibly even sobbed out loud.

# VENOM IN MY VEINZ

That, he didn't need. Brisco once taught him that when challenging most men, one would need to apply physical pressure to make him bow down. And when challenging most women, one would only have to apply a certain mental pressure that would force her to heed to one's demands.

"You have two choices, Benita," Bromise uttered softly. "I could kill you and every Bogus Boy in this muthafucka, take what I came for, and leave your kids in the custody of the state. Or you can choose to go the simple and smart route, which would work out better for you and your little ones in the end, and that brings me to your second choice. Do what the fuck I say and you'll live. It's that simple."

"I don't wanna die," she whispered, and a man's voice yelled out from the next room.

"Benita, where the fuck is the Drake CD?"

She shook at the call of her name, as he got closer to the door.

"Benita Westbrook, don't make me bust this door down on yo' ass."

"It's in the CD changer already," she yelled back. "Disc number three!"

"Your food is gettin' cold too. You betta hurry up fo' we eat dis shit!" he yelled and left the door.

"How many niggas are in the next room?" Bromise whispered.

"Two. Tip and Corey." She wiped what was left of her tears.

"How many bangers are they packing?"

"Two. A AK and some type of handgun."

"Which one of them fools really about that life?" he asked.

47

"They're both crazy, but Tip is the one you need to watch out for. He's a trigger-happy nigga for real," she whispered truthfully.

"Which one is Tip?"

"He's the light-skinned one with the long French braids. The one you just heard at the door."

"Where are the keys to the safe house, Benita?" Bromise asked in a tone that was a couple of notches above a whisper, as the sounds of Drake "Started from the Bottom" blasted from the other room.

"What safe house?" she asked, dumbfounded.

Bromise swung impulsively, hitting her across the face. He tried to hold back some, but the impact to her jaw was more like a punch than a slap. "Do *you* remember now, or do I have to knock your thoughts back on track?"

"I don't know what—"

Bromise shoved the nozzle past her teeth before she could finish her lie. "You want to live, right? Well, playing games with me is the quickest way to get your ass slumped. I know what you're thinking. You want to leave here alive and take the money for your damn self, but that's not happening. You need to be thankful that you're leaving at all. Now where the fuck is the key to the safe house, bitch?" he fumed without yelling, and stared into her eyes with pure fury.

Benita reached down into her pants pocket and pulled out two house keys. Neither key was on a ring. She held up the round one and made a gesture to speak. He removed the nozzle from her bloody mouth, and with a calm demeanor she said, "This is the top lock key." She then raised the other and said, "This square key is for the bottom lock."

# VENOM IN MY VEINZ

Bromise grabbed a tight hold of the keys and pushed them inside of his True Religion's. Surprisingly enough, she reached into her vagina and pulled out a small plastic bag. Before he had the opportunity to inquire, she unfolded the bag and removed a small key from it. "Safe key," she said and held it up for him to see. "Now can I go please?" Bromise took the key and put it with the others.

He purposely ignored her last request and said, "Last question. Why are there only three people here today, including you, when six of you muthafuckas work this trap regularly?"

"It's not even eight a.m. *Me,* Tip, and Corey get here at around seven to set up shop. Everybody else usually comes in at nine."

Bromise glanced down at his Nike wristwatch, 7:35 a.m. He still had over an hour before the rest of the BB showed up. It was time to get active. "Call Tip and tell him to bring you some of that good smelling Italian beef in here. When he gets to the door, you let him in. Got it?" She nodded yes. Bromise slid behind the bathroom door, and opened it slightly. The toilet that she sat on was less than three feet away from him. Yet, from the outside there was no way of seeing him. She called out to Tip three times, but the music was so loud it took him a minute to catch on.

"Did you call me, Benita?" Tip yelled.

"Yeah, boy, bring me my Italian beef!"

"Too late, we ate dem shits. Corey went out to get some more though. He'll be back in a minute!"

*Shit!* Bromise shut the bathroom door and locked it. "Get the fuck up," he said, waving the banger in her direction. She didn't hesitate in pulling her panties and

49

pants up. She shook her legs one at a time to get the blood circulation flowing, and fastened the top of her pants.

Bap, bap, bap, was the unexpected sounds of Tip banging on the door. "Open up the door, gurl!" he said playfully.

"Wait a minute! Damn!" she said and looked at Bromise with a fat question mark across her face.

"Hurry up and freshen' that thang up so I can beat it up! C'mon now, before your baby-daddy comes back. It's been so long since I hit that ass from da back. I damn near forgot how good that snap-back is!" Tip said frantically through the door.

She looked at Bromise and hung her head, as if she was ashamed of what he just heard. He eased his way over to her and put his lips close to her ear. "Sit back down on the toilet, and when I unlock the door you tell him to come on in."

She did as she was told. With his free hand, Bromise unsecured the lock and took a couple of soft backward steps. His finger was steady on the trigger. Biting his bottom lip from sheer anticipation, he aimed the nozzle at the door, trying to estimate where Tip's head would appear once he came in. He gave Benita his grandpa's signature wink, and in a very seductive tone she said, "Come in, daddy."

The doorknob turned. Benita buried her head inside her lap to avoid witnessing what was sure to come. The door swung on its hinges, and Tip was standing there butt-ass naked, and at Bromise's mercy. Just his luck, he estimated Tip's height just right. "Pop goes the weasel," Bromise said with a tapered grin and squeezed the trigger. The rapid slugs started at Tip's hairline and ended at his chest cavity. The impact threw him against the wall and onto the vile trap house carpet.

Benita remained in her ostrich position with her hands covering her ears, hoping to detach herself from her surroundings.

"Let's go," Bromise said, tugging on her arm.

She stood up and looked at him with a face drenched with crocodile tears. "You're lettin' me go, right?" she asked. Rather Bromise wanted to or not was beside the point. Fact is, he couldn't and she knew it. She turned to make a run for it, but the Bushmaster made Swiss cheese of her body. Bromise calmly walked up to both Tip and Benita's bleeding bodies. He pulled out the .454 Casull, aimed, and fired twice. The slugs were so powerful, that each one went through the floor and into the basement upon exiting their craniums. One shot each to their heads. Execution style.

Over the course of the next two hours, Bromise waited in hiding for the rest of the BB clique. He snuffed them out clean. They never knew what hit them.

After the job was complete, he went to their safe house and ransacked the entire place. He emptied the safe, found their stash spots, and even took the pocket change from their dirty clothes. If there was a penny to be had, he had to have it!

Bromise made it back to his trap and sat alone, totally ignoring the clucker's desperate knocks at the door. When nightfall came, he set fire to both the BB duplex and safe house and watch as the flames leveled the building. A few days later, after the jakes bombarded neighbors with questions to no avail, the smoke had cleared, and he conducted a trap house grand opening. He sold dime bags the size of twenties, with a buy one get one free deal. With no competition on the block, it was only a matter of time before Bromise had a soup line of cluckers at his back door. Now it was time to call for his team.

# CHAPTER 6

*Squad Assembly*

F uture sent Bromise a team two hours after he called for them. Although he didn't stop by to see how things were moving, Bromise knew he had a watchful eye on him.

Chasidy, her older sister, Porsha, Fats, and Bromise were all sitting in the front room of his trap discussing unrelated murders that they caught on the local news. It was a drive-by in the Englewood District of Chiraq. Seven people, which included young black males and females were killed.

"Who does drive-bys in the damn winter time, the day after a foot of snow hits the ground?" Chasidy said to the group. "Where they do that at?"

"Well, obviously Chiraq," Fats spoke up. "Niggas playin' for keeps out here."

The four of them had just made it back from an afternoon of shopping. In Bromise's absence, he left the trap in the care of Trent, BG, Jay, and KO.

BG and Trent were two of the workers that Future sent. He initially sent four, and Bromise personally requested Fats, which gave him a total of five. Bromise, however, got rid of the first two workers the same day they came. They were both lazy, didn't follow instructions too well, and quite frankly, he didn't trust their demeanors. So he personally replaced them with Jay and KO.

Jay and Bromise grew up cutting elementary

53

school together and stealing cars for his uncle Cigar, who in turn would strip the cars and sell the parts for a profit.

Jay's younger brother, KO, was pretty good with his hands, the true boxing type for real. That's how he earned his street name. After the three were escorted to juvenile detention for getting caught inside of a stolen car, neither of them broke under the pressure of good cop, bad cop interrogations. So on that note, Bromise trusted them to a certain degree.

Bromise was comfortable with the three men he selected. The two that Future sent appeared to fit in also, but he kept a close eye on them. They were all around the same age with Bromise being the youngest, and they were hungry for the dough.

Jay and KO were the young guns of the team. On the very first day of their arrival they cased out K-Town, starting within a ten-block radius, and worked their way in. They scoped other trap houses that Bromise didn't know were in the area. They counted four in all. Upon filling Bromise in on their discovery, the two of them disclosed a tactic that only confirmed that he had the right men on his team.

Though he really wanted to tag along and join in on the fun, Bromise knew it was best to sit back and evaluate their performance. With his approval, by nightfall Jay and KO had shot four men at two of the trap houses, killing three and wounding one. The very same night they robbed and intimidated the soldiers in the other two traps, sold their product back to them, and now they were copping exclusively from Bromise. When Jay and KO finished terrorizing the hood, Bromise had the only trap that was up and running in

# VENOM IN MY VEINZ

K-Town. He was now the undisputed king of Komensky Avenue.

The other half of his team, Trent and BG, were around-the-clock hustlers. They'd been in the trap now for three straight days, living off microwavable burgers, chips, and other gas station edibles. Bromise wouldn't have it any other way.

Without warning, Bromise stood to his feet. "After the shit we've accomplished as a unit these past few days"—he glanced over at Chasidy, and then his right hand, Fats, and the two young guns that sat comfortably on couches as Porsha looked on—"I think we deserved to be called something else other than a *team* or a *clique.*"

"What you have in mind, bae?" Chasidy smiled and stood with her man. All eyes on him.

"I know that typically, squads consist of soldiers. But soldiers are expendable, and we're anything but typical," Bromise said.

"So what'chu sayin', Joe?" Fats asked, sitting on the edge of his seat.

"We are a squad of warriors," Bromise said and looked around for everyone's reaction. The room fell silent. Then Fats stood up and raised his glass filled with peach Ciroc and mango.

"Now that's dope, my nigga," Fats said and everyone stood up, meeting their glasses in the middle when Fats intervened. "Wait," he said, "before we toast it up, I just wanna say something. I was taught that a true gangsta should never name himself—his peers should. And it can't just be no any name . . ."

The effects of the liquor caused KO to chuckle involuntarily, interrupting Fats.

"I'm serious!" Fats said, regaining the floor as Trent and BG walked up and joined the group. "The name has to have meaning and purpose, something like a tattoo," Fats said, realizing how good that just sounded. "Anyway, what I'm saying is this . . . Joe," he looked at Bromise. "You got straight venom runnin' through your muthafuckin' veins. And because of that, I vote that your new and official street name be *Black Mamba*. Squad, what say you?" Fats extended his half-filled glass out in front of him, and everyone met him in the middle.

"Salute," they all said in unison and clanged their glasses before turning them up, and then they all *shook-up* with one another, one shaking the hand of the other with their signature handshake.

A couple of minutes later, Trent and BG bustled about, pushing packs to a hasty clientele when Bromise heard a voice coming from the back room. "Yo, Black Mamba!" Trent yelled. "Future just pulled up out back!"

Bromise was caught off guard by the call of his *new* name, but admitted to himself that he kind of liked the sound of it. He hadn't seen or heard from Future in six days, but he was more than ready to stand behind his achievements, and remove the debt from his shoulders at the same time.

"Tell him I'll be out in a sec!" Bromise yelled back to Trent. He turned and leaned in, planting one on Chasidy's soft lips. "I'll be back in a minute, baby," he said, and then headed for the back of the trap. Chasidy watched his backside until he disappeared.

He had the $31,200 that he owed to Future, already counted and packed inside the floor. It was protected by a Macy's plastic bag. He grabbed it and headed out the back door. The second he made it outside, he regretted not putting on his coat. February weather in Chicago was beasty, and the hawk was out big time. He spotted Future sitting inside of his Viridian Green Aston Martin Rapide S. Brand spankin' new and it looked mean sittin' on factories. Real grown man shit.

Even in the snow, Bromise projected a proud stride as he approached the high-priced vehicle in his Timbs. He was feelin' himself, not only because he was about to be out of debt, but a day early to top it off.

"Listen," Future said as Bromise sunk comfortably in his ivory, sport bucket seat. "Before we start, I just want you to know I took care of John-John for you, as requested." They locked eyes and without saying a word, they shook-up. "So now that, that's behind us, what's really good, Youngin?" he asked with a sudden burst of energy.

"Same building, just a different floor. I'm movin' on up, big homie." Bromise chuckled. From time to time he'd refer to Future as the Big Homie because he reminded him of Big Worm from the movie *Friday*. Same dark complexion and husky build, with the Gucci Mane belly. "I believe this is yours." Bromise tossed the Macy's bag on his lap.

"What's this?" Future asked curiously.

"That would be not thirty, or not thirty-one and some change—that right there is your thirty-one bands, plus two big faces. The new ones, by the way," Bromise boasted before he reached into his Affliction jeans pocket and pulled out a neat bundle of crispy one hundred dollar bills. He removed the rubber band and peeled off twenty from the top. "And this is the two bands you left behind," he said and handed him the rest of his cash.

"You gotta be kiddin' me!" Future was astonished after peeking inside the bag. "I leave you for six days, and the BB niggas are history. They shit is burnt to the ground, and you toss me my bread in full like it's pocket change. I've got to know, how did you pull it off?" he asked with burning curiosity.

"Within those same six days John-John got slumped, I wonder how was that pulled off?" Bromise said sarcastically.

"That's not important," Future said bluntly.

"My thoughts exactly," Bromise responded, implying the same.

"Point taken," Future reasoned and decided to shift the subject. "I see someone has upgraded." He tilted his head, gesturing beyond the vehicle's interior. "From what I know, you and your lil team didn't exactly leave any hustlers alive in these parts that could afford a brand new Challenger SRT. Shit, that bitch wet!" he exclaimed, talking about Bromise's new whip.

"Yeah, I got her today. She's a year old with only 8k miles on it. And does she fly!" Bromise said enthusiastically.

"You paid cash, lil nigga?"

"You know it."

"You must've reached out to Brisco's car dealer connect. That's wusup, Youngin. Your grandpa would be proud of you, even though your young ass ain't got no L's."

# VENOM IN MY VEINZ

"I got dealer's plates. Fuck a driver's license!" he proclaimed.

"You remind me of Brisco more err'day," Future said as Macklemore "Can't Hold Us" played in the background. "I can't believe how much you've grown. I'd be the first to admit," he said, "I've been sleepin' on your skills, Youngin. But all of that is about to change. I have a serious position open that I designed just for you. Somethin' much better than workin' a trap house all day."

"What can be better than that?" Bromise gestured toward the soup line of cluckers that started at his trap's door, with a single file line through the backyard, and continued for the length of the alleyway. And they were still coming in droves. Future could *act* unimpressed, but Bromise knew for a fact that none of his other trap houses rocked like this one.

"You're thinkin' small, Youngin," he said as he shifted in his seat and lowered his voice. "I'm talkin' a whole 'nother level. A level that slims the chances of you gettin' pinched in a jake raid or robbed. A level where you command when the bread comes, and not having to wait on some sick ass clucker to need a fix."

"I hear what you're saying, I do," Bromise said and glanced at the trap. "But I put in some serious work for that trap, big homie. I'm not ready to just give it up like that. Look at the numbers we're doing." Bromise hinted toward the growing soup line as more vehicles pulled up. "Look at that shit, Joe. And this is just the beginning."

Future furrowed his brows and said, "Who said anything about you having to let the trap go? If you can manage to pay your consignment on time, meet your quota, while supervising from a distance, then you can keep your trap and your team.

"You don't even have to pay me to rent the trap. I'll sell it to you for twenty-five bands, just to show you its love here. To add to that, I'll let your bricks go at fifty bands even, and you don't ever have to worry about paying shit upfront. That's the cheapest I'm lettin' 'em go to anybody, so feel special," he said, looking Bromise square in the eyes. Bromise showed no reaction. "Right now, all you have to focus on is movin' three bricks a week, that's your quota. I take the quota up two bricks every month. If you can't keep up then you don't have no business being a part of my roster. But after what you've accomplished these past six days, I'm willing to take a chance on you."

Bromise sat quietly, listening to his own thoughts. Future sounded convincing, and maybe the offer was too good to pass up, but he knew there was more to what Future was saying. He just wasn't saying it. His instincts told him that it was more behind the smoke and mirrors. The more he thought about it though, the more it didn't matter.

"What's the catch, Future?" he asked harshly, as if he knew what he was holding back.

Future reached in his middle console and pulled out a brand new iPhone. "I head an organization called the Convolution. The tan church down from Crane High School is where we meet and talk business from time to time." He handed Bromise the iPhone. "This is your cell now, Youngin. Your code of summons is #666. There'll never be a phone number, or any tracking number associated with your summons. When you get that triple six alert, you have exactly one hour to report to the church or your ass is left out in the cold," he said seriously.

"But I already have this exact iPhone," Bromise said.

"So keep it, but that one there"—Future pointed to the new iPhone—"will only be used for the Convolution. Never make a call period, and you'll never receive a call. And don't text outside of the Convolution. Understood?"

Bromise nodded and glanced down at this new iPhone. "You don't think I'll be getting one of those alerts tonight, do you?" he asked unassertively, in hopes that this Convolution mess wouldn't come between what he'd already had planned with Chasidy for the day.

"That's every time you see that code: #666. Rain, sleet, or snow. This is your verbal and only warning, so there'll be no exceptions, Youngin. If you're on the verge of bustin' a nut, jump off that pussy quick, and get to the church. If you're about to die when you get that alert, you betta hold your last breath until you report to the church. You gotta stay in tune. You gotta stay on top of what's shakin' in these streets. Are you hearing me?"

"I hear you, Joe."

"After you hear the initiation sermon at your first meeting, you're going to view it as a blessing and a curse in one. You'll find yourself neck deep in the game, and everybody there including me, would rather see you die, than to see you walk away from the Convolution. This is where the stakes go up. You play big, and receive bigger. So are you ready to elevate your game and link up with the untouchables?" he asked and they locked eyes again.

"Real grown man shit, huh?" Bromise said.

"Grown man at its finest, so get your team prepared," Future responded without hesitation.

"Send me the three bricks, Future." Bromise gently swung the Aston's door open and paused to say, "And with all due respect, Joe, they are not my *team*. We are a squad. I think we've all earned that right." Bromise stood to his feet and walked to the driver side after shutting the door. Future magnetically let his window down with a light tap of his finger. "Another thing, big homie . . . I no longer go by the name Youngin. I'm the one and only, Black Mamba," Bromise said with authority. A slight smile creased Future's face. He reached out his right hand and the two shook up. Then he earthquaked "So Sophisticated" by Rick Ross from his four, 12-inch subwoofers before he peeled off. Bromise turned and headed for his trap.

When Bromise opened the safe in the BB red and white safe house days ago, he couldn't believe his eyes. He recovered over ten kilos of Al Capone from there alone, and the unexpected discovery of their two-stash spots amounted to $103,000 in cash money. He now had seven kilos with an additional three coming from Future.

However, Bromise felt uneasy. The hairs on the back of his neck stood at attention the second he sat inside the Aston Martin. He was sure Future was up to something. He just couldn't put his finger on it.

# CHAPTER 7
## A Typical Day in Chiraq

Once he made it back inside his trap, he searched for Chasidy until he found her near the pantry tidying up. Bromise vowed to never have his trap filthy like the BB had theirs, and with Chasidy's OCD-like behavior, he was sure to keep to that vow.

He stood there for a moment, admiring her sex appeal. She was fly in her skinny jeans, pink hoodie, and matching blue and pink Retro Jordan's. Her hair was a rich shade of raven-black. It flowed in waves to adorn her glowing, dark hue. Her eyes, framed by long natural lashes, were a bright, almond-brown and seemed to illuminate the entire trap house. A straight nose, full lips—she seemed the picture of perfection.

Bromise hugged her from behind and kissed the nape of her neck. She spun around. Her big brown eyes melted his heart. He was excited to tell her the good news. "Baby, *Chiraq* is going to be mine."

She slid her tongue in his mouth, and he grabbed her fatty with both hands. Her ass was so round, he needed a third hand, but he managed.

"Are we still going to the Wild 100's, bae?" Chasidy asked, batting her long natural lashes.

"No doubt. Let's get active," Bromise said with a smile.

Chasidy was excited to go to the Wild 100's, which consisted of a Southside neighborhood that was notoriously known for its violence. But it was also home to the most rocking roller rink, and tonight was the skate off competition. Chasidy and Porsha had friends competing and wanted to go and support.

She scurried toward the front room to retrieve Porsha and her Gucci Abbey handbag, while Bromise rounded up his squad and dished out last minute directives to Trent, BG, and KO.

Everyone else met outside. Fats hit the automatic start to his '71 Chevelle SS454. The stainless tips attached to the dual Flowmaster exhaust bellowed a cloud of white smoke against the frigid cold. He got inside and Jay joined him on the passenger side.

Chasidy and Bromise filled the backseat of his Challenger with Porsha at the wheel. She waited until Fats pulled away from the curb, and then trailed him.

Without saying a word, Chasidy, in one swift move, yanked both Bromise's pants and boxers off. She tugged them over his feet after he kicked off his Timbs, and tossed them in the front seat.

Porsha quickly caught on and replaced the rap song they were listening to, with "Ghetto" by August Alsina and maxed the bass.

They had only been in the car for three minutes before Chasidy started ripping at Bromise's clothes. He was completely turned on by her sudden authority. He sat bare assed on heated leather seats.

"I wasn't expecting all that, baby," Bromise was pleasantly surprised.

"I know, right," she purred. "Blame it on the peach Ciroc and August Alsina's sexy ass voice," she said and flicked her tongue across the very top of his dick head. Her hands kneaded his thighs and her fingers were inches from his balls.

Bromise gasped when her French tips gently scratched his sac. With her free hand, she started to jack him off.

"You like that, daddy?"

"Daddy like," Bromise confirmed with a relaxed expression on his face.

Porsha maneuvered the whip to Lake Shore Drive, testing the SRT HEMI engine, but her passengers hadn't a care, for they were lost in each other.

Chasidy brushed her long black hair against Bromise's bare thighs for a few seconds, making sure to get some of her long silky strands all over his balls and hard dick. She paused to push her dress straps over her shoulders and remove her black lacy bra.

"Touch my titties, bae," she said and Bromise took a handful. He felt her up while admiring the fullness of her titties. He put his second hand to work. Chasidy savored the attention and the sensation of his hands squeezing her breasts. Her nipples were super hard as Bromise tweaked them just right.

Chasidy returned to her kneeling position and made sure to rub her immaculate tits across his lap, then roughly spread his legs as far as the space would allow. The wider Bromise's legs were spread, the easier it was for her to access both his erection and balls. He was turned on by her abrupt aggressiveness. She spent some time kissing on his thighs, edging closer to his happy area.

"Shit, don't tease yo' nigga," Bromise encouraged.

"I gotcha', daddy," Chasidy assured him.

Bromise let out a loud moan when Chasidy put

one of his balls into her mouth. She gently swished it around then switched to the other one. Surprisingly, she managed to put both balls into her mouth at once, and Bromise nearly had a fit. His lips curled with pleasure.

"Daddy can get used to this, ma," Bromise breathed.

"Hmm . . ." Chasidy continued to tenderly lick his balls while warming them up with her mouth. She further used her tongue to move them both around. Her lips were completely enveloping his sac, up to the root of his manhood. Her hands began to stroke his shaft.

"Oh shit, Chasidy!" He didn't seem capable of saying much else. She liked that. Turning Bromise on to the point where he couldn't really say much besides, *"Oh Chasidy!"* appeased her. She loved hearing her own name shouted in pleasure.

She removed his balls from her mouth and spat on his dick. Then licked the length of his shaft with the tip of her tongue. She drenched his lap with saliva. Starting at the root, she worked her way up to the sensitive underside of his dick, right under the head. She gave that area some licks, and then teased him a bit with some long, slow licks up and down the shaft. When she knew he really needed some direct stimulation, she finally put her lips around his whole dick head and started to gently suck him off. Fondling his balls with her French tips, she slowly lowered her mouth over his entire organ, getting it deep inside her mouth.

Bromise squirmed in his seat and held onto the sides of her head with both hands, trying his damnedest to hold on. "Whatever the fuck you doing . .

# VENOM IN MY VEINZ

. don't stop!" he shouted and aroused her more.

"Mmm." She slowly bobbed her head in his lap, getting her hands under him and squeezing his butt. Bromise's breathing became heavier. She had no doubt he was enjoying his first blow job. Then unexpectedly, she stopped and said, "Daddy, when you feel close to your nut, don't worry . . . I swallow." Chasidy looked up at him, slapping her face softly with his throbbing hard-on. "Don't even hesitate. Just let your load out in my throat."

Bromise could neither believe his ears, nor her skills. He thought to be in heaven that very second and not on Lake Shore Drive speeding in excess of ninety miles per hour. He twirled her long mane into his fist and began to fuck her mouth.

This was Chasidy's seventh time performing oral, but what she hadn't learned from hands-on experience, she learned from watching her mom's pornos. She even had the chance to see her mother in action on a number of occasions. Her mother, Brooke Berry, was at one time, the Queen of her sport and had true talent in pleasing a man.

Chasidy loved to swallow cum, because her mother glorified it. She didn't understand why girls were squeamish about swallowing. To her, it was perfectly natural, and niggas fucking loved it! The only time she didn't swallow was when she wanted a man to give her a facial, like she saw in porn movies. Since then, she'd allowed two johns to cum all over her face and hair just for the experience, and extra cash.

Bromise began to buck his hips up and down. Still holding on to either side of her head, he relaxed a little and allowed her to regain control. She stroked the root of his dick with both hands and swallowed his shaft. Swirling her tongue wildly around the underside of the head of his dick, she drove him insane with desire as his lips began to curl again. He was sweating. She could feel it on his thighs, brushing against her face. He kept moaning and groaning with pleasure as she became firmer with her sucking. Then she drooled and slobbered all over his lap, making the blow job as wet and messy as possible.

"I love being your cocksucking slut, daddy," she said and ran her French tips up his abdomen.

"I love that you love it, baby . . . just . . . don't . . . stop . . . what . . . you're . . . doing," he said and dropped his head back.

"Your wish is my command." Chasidy returned to his dick, sucking like a slut in heat. She made sexual sounds to excite him more. "Hmm . . . Oh . . . UMM!" she moaned and stretched her mouth to its limits. She swished his hard organ inside her cheeks, getting it as deep into her throat as possible while breathing through her nose. She was buried in his lap; his dick completely inside her mouth, his thighs pressed up against her cheeks. Her nose and eyelashes were butterfly kissing his pubic hair.

"Oh fuck! Nothin' has never felt better!" His groans were getting louder, and his breathing more desperate. She firmly grabbed his dick with strong suction from her mouth and fondled his heavy balls. His sac began to draw closer to his thighs, a sign that his orgasm was imminent. She knew that. Chasidy intended to drink him dry. She sucked and licked him lovingly while stroking his balls. Then she looked up, his eyes were shut tight and his hands were at his sides, clinching the supple leather seat. With her mouth firmly around all of him, she took his hands and placed them on her tits, letting him have something softer, more pleasant to hold on to while he came.

"Fuck! Fuck! I'm about to nut soon . . . I can't hold it much longer." Bromise began to speak in tongues.

Chasidy sucked him faster and amplified her moaning noises as she prepared to finish him off. Her pace and intensity grew with each trip up and down his shaft. She made loud slurping sounds on the way up, and secreted more saliva on the way down. His dick was rock hard and throbbing. She could feel it shaking.

"OH shit! OH fuck! OHHHH!" The contractions began, and his erection flexed. She focused the muscles of her mouth and tongue intently on the head of his dick while tightening her grip around his balls. She felt the pre-cum that she'd tasted throughout the blowjob, start to ooze out even more. Then the explosion came.

The rush was just as intense for Chasidy. She had never seen a load so big. The intensity and amount of cum was difficult to handle. She bobbed her head up and down and quickly swallowed it all up, not losing a drop. He grabbed her tits tightly. Chasidy didn't mind the pain. She knew his orgasm was really intense, and he needed something to grip onto.

Spurt after spurt of hot cum shot down her throat. She was able to gulp most of it down quickly, but some filled her cheeks. With his cum mixed with her saliva, she licked the tip of his shaft and bravely swallowed it all down. She struggled to breathe through her nose, which was now buried in his pubic hair, as she finished him off, milking even more cum out of his balls with her fingers. Just when she thought it was over, his dick quivered with involuntary aftershocks, and yet more creamy juice trickled down her throat. She kept his stiffness inside her mouth after the main part of his orgasm ended, while drop after drop of cum dripped from his dick.

Bromise completely collapsed, spent and drained. She lovingly stroked his thighs with his manhood still in her mouth. She refrained from further stimulation, as she knew his dick would be extra sensitive. Slowly, she let him withdraw, and gave the head a soft little kiss, licking off the last remaining drops.

"Pass that shit, sis," she said and reached her hand over Porsha's shoulder. She took the Garcia Vega between her fingers and planted her back against the supple leather backseat. Chasidy inhaled the Irene Kush and looked over at Bromise's sleepful face. She felt empowered by her talent. "Here ya go, daddy," she said and placed the cigar between his lips.

They saw the multitude of teenagers surrounding the skating rink as they drove up. And that only excited them more.

"Hey!" Chasidy danced in her seat. "Hurry and park, sis, and let's get active!" she said excitedly and licked across Bromise's lips. He smiled at how she suddenly used his vocabulary, and quickly got dressed.

"There they are," Porsha spoke up when she saw Fats and Jay already outside of his whip and holding an open parking space for her to drive into. It was a perfect fit. She parked and they all took a turn rising out of the whip.

"Hey, that's my shit!" Chasidy started twerking in

the parking lot to the Drill music that came from within the skating rink. Drill music is one of the most prominent contemporary facets of Chicago Hip Hop.

"That's that Lil Herb featuring Nicki Minaj!" Porsha joined the parking lot show her younger sister was giving and they danced to the song "Chiraq."

"Let's move," Bromise said, looking around. "Y'all will have more than enough time for that inside." He wasn't feeling the sudden male attention.

It had been all of five minutes and the line of people going inside wasn't getting any shorter.

"Man, Joe, I ain't feeling this," Fats said and blew warm air into his freezing hands.

"It's cold den a bitch out dis mafucka," Jay added as Bromise looked down the length of the line and shook his head in disappointment. His iPhone read twenty-nine degrees.

"Wait!" Chasidy sensed that Bromise was about to call it off and head back to the whip. "My bitches already inside. I just texted one of them to come to the front door. I'll be right back," she said and stepped out of line. They looked on, before losing sight of Chasidy amidst the crowd.

"Wusup, lil mama? You bad as hell," Fats said to a chick in front of him. Porsha immediately rolled her eyes, pressing her lips together. "Yeah, I'm talking to you." He attempted to gain her attention once more, and she refused to acknowledge him, keeping her eyes forward. "Bitch, I know you hear me." Fats became aggravated. "That's what's wrong with you pretty bitches today . . . can't even pay you prissy 'hos a compliment."

The teenaged girl turned on her heels and raised

an index finger. "My man is stupid-crazy and he's older than y'all. So if I were you I'd leave me the fuck be."

"Well, you ain't him," Jay chimed in and slapped her hand down. "Don't talk with yo' hands, ma. That can get you fucked up. And we don't give no fuck about yo' man."

"Yeah, you heard him," Fats said. "Your man might be *stupid* for leaving your fine ass standing here alone, but we'll humble his craziness if he run up on the squad." He chuckled.

"We'll slump his ass and forget about it," Jay added. "And if he run, that's what the lasers are for. Where his crazy ass at anyway? It's target season for us," Jay said seriously.

"Let's move." Bromise broke their attention. "Chasidy just texted, saying to meet her at the front door." With Porsha leading te way, they stepped out of line and started to make their way to the front. Fats looked back at the chick he just embarrassed and blew her an antagonizing kiss.

Once they made it up to the front of the line, they were forced to stop short at the mob scene of teenagers that gathered like bees at the entrance.

"I'm right here, y'all. C'mon." Chasidy grabbed Bromise and Porsha's hand and forcefully made her way back to the entryway with Fats and Jay close behind, dishing out stiff elbows through the crowd.

"Damn, bitch!" a female shouted. "Who da fuck you think you is . . . Katie Got Bandz or sum' shit?" Katie Got Bandz was a popular local female rapper who was regarded as VIP to the Drill scene. She hardly waited in line at public events such as this. Chasidy turned to the voice and recognized the loud mouth teenaged girl to be a senior at Percy L. Julian High School.

"What the fuck you say, bitch!" Chasidy did a 180-degree turn back into the girl's direction.

"Hey listen," the doorman sounded off. "If you want to come inside with your friends, then this is your only chance."

"Fuck that 'ho!" Porsha said, shaking from the cold. "That bitch ain't worth our time." She tugged Chasidy's hand and Bromise gently squeezed the other.

"Let's get in here, baby, before this dude changes his mind," Bromise said.

Chasidy winked at the girl before turning to face the doorman.

"So it's you and these four, right?" the doorman asked.

"Right," Chasidy confirmed with a smile and led the way inside.

"Damn this heat feels good," Fats exclaimed, after he walked inside the building.

"I know, right," Jay said. "I feel like it's hugging me." They laughed and followed Bromise to the coat check.

"Hey, bae," Chasidy said. "We'll be over there chatting with my bitches."

"Wait." Bromise reached for her arm as she handed her and Porsha's coat over to the coat check person. "I don't think that's a good idea."

"What?" Chasidy asked, looking confused. "Talking to my friends?"

"Checking your coat in," he said and darted his

eyes around the rink.

"That's how you feel?" She was skeptical.

"Yeah, this shit don't feel right," he said. "I ain't feelin' it."

"What's wrong, Bromise?" Porsha asked, sounding concern.

"Sis, ain't nothing wrong," Chasidy cut in. "He just don't want to be here. He always want to leave early when he come out with me." She displayed her sad face, not comprehending Bromise's reluctance.

"Aw, let's just stay for a little while," Porsha insisted. "Let's get turned up!"

"A'ight." Bromise caved in, and Chasidy rewarded him with a juicy kiss. He smacked her bubbled ass and watched as she and Porsha walked over to their female friends. They greeted one another in excitement and started doing the Dlow Shuffle like it was choreographed.

Bromise turned to Fats and Jay. "Don't check y'all coats, Joe," he said solemnly.

"Wudup, Joe?" Fats inquired.

"I doubt we'll be here long. On the low, look over at the north side of the rink."

Fats followed his direction and spotted eleven rival street gang members. "I see them mafuckin' opps."

"Now glance at the east side of the rink."

"Shit." Fats was taken by surprise as he spotted thirteen more. "These opps err'where, Joe."

"Man, fuck an opp," Jay said, ready for whatever.

"I feel the same, Jay," Bromise said, "but we have to be smart. They got the numbers, and there's hundreds of eyewitnesses in this place. Breathe easy," he said and walked over to the concession stand.

The three of them ordered Maxwell polishes and sodas and sat at the table with the oppositions in view.

"Y'all brought y'all burners in, right?" Bromise asked and bit down into his polish.

"Hell yeah," Fats said with a mouth filled with food.

"You know I keep the ratchet." Jay confirmed that he was also armed.

"Okay cool." Bromise sipped his Pepsi. "Let's see what they do."

Chasidy and Porsha stood near the floor with a team of girl skaters who were about to take the floor. She was friends with two of the team's members. The team had on airbrushed R.I.P. T-shirts in remembrance of LA Capone, a talented local rapper who was shot and killed at the young age of seventeen.

"This is the competition take over!" Chasidy cheered. "Bring home that prize money ladies!" She and Porsha clapped, and the team of girls rolled to the middle of the floor. They all froze in place as the entire rink fell silent. So much so, that you could hear the flick of a cigarette lighter somewhere in the crowd. Then "Round Here" by LA Capone blasted through the club speakers, turning everyone up and the girls started their performance.

"I see the way you look at Fats." Chasidy turned to her sister. "Why don't you go after him?"

"I'm not thinking about his player ass," Porsha replied.

"What you mean? Fats is a good guy."

"Good to who? Bromise?" she said. "He was flirting with some girl outside right in front of me."

"Well, what you expect? He's single and you ain't checkin' for him, so . . ."

"So . . ."

"So, all I'm saying is that it'll be fun to go on double dates and whatnot." Chasidy turned her attention back to the skating performance. "Woohoo!" she cheered.

"Um, excuse me." An unknown young lady approached Chasidy. "You don't know me, but I recognize a real bitch when I see one."

"Well, you know what they say: real recognize real," Chasidy said, hardly taking her eyes away from the skating floor.

"Exactly, and us real bitches gots to stick together, ma," she said. "Anyway, I saw what happened outside the rink earlier and that shit was foul."

"That 'ho don't want any trouble. That's why she yelled from the crowd. She wants to remain anonymous."

"Anonymous, umm . . . I wouldn't say all that." She rolled her neck. "*That* 'ho ain't had enough of your name on her mouth."

Chasidy stopped her view of the skating performance and fixated on the face of the chick in front of her. "What did you say?"

"That same bitch that called you out is in the bathroom right now talkin' shit about you."

"And why are you telling me this?"

"Because I hate a hatin' ass thot," she said and casually walked off.

"Sis, don't pay that shit any mind," Porsha reasoned.

"Girl, I'm not going to let that 'ho fuck up my

day." She smiled. "I'ma go to the concession stand real quick, though. Do you want something?"

"I'll go with you."

"Nah, sis, there's no need," Chasidy insisted. "I'll bring you back a Dr. Pepper. I'll be right back," she said and left Porsha's side.

Chasidy saw Bromise and the squad sitting at a table near the concession stand. They appeared to be in deep concentration as she walked passed them unnoticed. She made her way around the corner and to the restroom area. The skating rink was a very old building with outdated facilities. There were only two commodes inside the ladies' restroom. It's a wonder there was not one person waiting in line. Chasidy quietly walked up to the door and put her ear to it in time to hear what was being said.

"That nut-guzzling 'ho. Fuck her. How that bitch gon' walk up and get in before me when I was out there freezing my fucking nipples off. She lucky the doorman was there to save her ass. The bitch think she's all that when really she's just a backpage.com 'ho!"

Those words were like needles in Chasidy's ears. She was livid and wanted to get at the chick right then. She tugged on the doorknob, but it was locked.

"Wait your turn, 'ho, whoever you is!" the same voice yelled from inside.

Chasidy stormed off, heated. She walked over to the concession area and pulled up a chair close to Bromise. "Let me borrow your rachet."

"Huh?" He was both caught off guard and preoccupied with his current surveillance of the opposition.

"Let me borrow your rachet," she repeated.

Bromise reached beneath the table and wrapped his fist around the handle of his Glock .40 and looked at Chasidy. "I'm not going to ask why. But are you sure you want to do this?" he said and looked both ways. "There's a lot of people here and the blast from this canon is loud."

"You know what," she said. "You're right." She placed her handbag on the table and reached inside, pulling out a razor blade. Then she placed it under her tongue. "Watch this for me." She pushed her handbag toward him. "I'll be right back."

"What's that all about, Joe?" Fats asked.

"I 'on know, but you know she ain't fuckin' with a full deck," Bromise said and watched her walk away until she disappeared. "Fats, you get Porsha. Jay, secure the front entrance. And by all means"—he looked back and forth between them— "Keep an eye on the opps."

Bromise rose from his chair, and with a brisk pace he walked toward the restrooms with Chasidy's handbag in tote. He turned the corner in time to see Chasidy kick down the restroom door. Bromise sprinted to the opening and looked inside. "Damn," he muttered as Chasidy came down over again upon two teenaged girls with the sharp side of her razor. Suddenly, three girls turned the corner as the victims' screams turned to low grunts. Bromise quickly shut the restroom door.

"Um, this bathroom is out of service," he said with a straight face.

"You cannot be serious." The girls were clearly aggravated by the news.

"My bad, but I hear there's another one on the other side of the rink," he lied and watched as they left his sight. He threw the door open. Chasidy hovered above the now motionless girls, exhausted but still ripping away at their skin with each slow strike of her razor. "That's overkill, baby. Let's move!" Bromise grabbed her hand and quickly guided her to the sink. He placed her hands under the running faucet, ridding the blood. Then he took his hands across her face and removed more visible DNA. A dry paper towel absorp the dampness, and he drapped his coat over her shoulders, concealing the freash blood on her clothes. He tossed the razor in her handbag and they vacated the facility.

As soon as they made the corner, he saw the three girls that he'd just turned away, standing with armed security and pointing in their direction. "Shit!" He looked around for Fats and Porsha, then Jay. He couldn't spot them. "Take this." He handed Chasidy her handbag as they were getting closer to the three girls and armed guards. "Just stay close," Bromise whispered and squeezed Chasidy's trembling hand tighter. They walked past the guards when a voice spoke up.

"Ay, ain't you Black Mamba?"

Bromise turned and found himself face to face with four rivals. They had the ups on him. The guards purposely looked the other way. Bromise pushed Chasidy to the floor and reached for his Glock when deafening shots rang out. Fats dropped two of the rivals from behind as Bromise managed to hit the other two after they fired several shots back and forth. The rink turned into an uproar and the crowd stampeded the front exit. Bromise grabbed Chasidy's hand and rushed for the door.

Once they made it outside, more gunshots rang out as Jay ate up the rival's whips with the projectiles from two blazing Desert Eagles.

"Let's move!" Bromise yelled out and hit his automatic start. Porsha climbed in and Chasidy followed. Bromise squeezed off shots just above Jay's shoulder, covering him as he made a run for Fats' whip. Fats screeched his tires in reverse and swung open the passenger door, allowing Jay to dive in as the rivals returned fire, penetrating the whip's metal. Bromise was the last to break away. He exchanged shots, then replaced the empty clip with a full one, and started up again.

"Bae, let's go!" Chasidy cried out from the Challenger.

Jay popped up like a Jack-in-the-Box from the passenger window of Fats' whip with his reloaded Desert Eagles, blasting with a passion.

Bromise threw himself into Chasidy's arms and Porsha stomped on the gas.

Fats peeled off in the same direction as his whip continued to get hit with gunfire. His back windshield burst and the hood of his trunk flew open.

"Agh!" Jay yelled in pain and reached for his bloody eye.

"Are you hit? Are you hit!" Fats shouted while ducking.

# CHAPTER 8
### The Psychology of the Game

*February 1*
*Two weeks before the robbery . . .*

Bromise's twentieth birthday had passed a month ago, and he'd been a part of Future's roster for a little over five years now.

He set the cruise for seventy-one miles per hour, coasting up I-57 in his Audi RS7. He was headed back to Chiraq after a late night/early morning menage with a couple of sorority girls from SIU, out in Carbondale, Illinois. It's a six and a half hour drive one way, but they were well worth the trip. *What a nigga won't do for new pussy? College chicks are the best!* He put a flame to his Garcia Vega stuffed with Irene Kush, and inhaled the taste deeply. Big Sean's "Control" bumped mildly from three 15-inch subwoofers, but neither the music nor the steamy scene he left behind played any part in his current mental.

His fingers were clinched together as he rested his forearms on the heated steering wheel to stretch his lower back. Bromise thought extensively about his life, his past, his present, and where he wanted to go from here.

For a split second his eyes darted from the road when he caught a glimpse of iPhone #2. Suddenly, he recalled the very first meeting he attended at the church years back. There was no secret about the fuck boy antics *he* suspected Future of, but he really had no idea of the true extent of Future's trickery until after he became a member. Upon initiation onto Future's roster, aka the Convolution, Bromise fastly became convinced that he had made a deal with the devil.

Future's reason for recruiting him wasn't only to elevate Bromise's game, as he put it. It was for his own selfish gain: 50 percent to help increase his profit margin and 50 percent street politics. Future wasn't just impressed by the way Bromise eradicated the BB clique and set a hood-record for most bags sold during a trap house grand opening, he was also threatened by it. Bromise had an unmatchable skill set to execute swift and quietly and always hit his mark. Future needed his skill set and that was the politic side of it.

In 2012 alone, 512 people were slumped as a result of gang violence. And for the past five plus years, Bromise had been putting in work exclusively for him. Nothing beats a cross like a double-cross. And in one way or another, Future was blindly double-crossing everyone he was doing business with, while he kept outsiders guessing. At his direction, the Convolution performed several different strategies that enabled them to walk away clean from *licks*. They'd been known to do whatever they had to do to execute successfully, including killing women and children. No one was exempt from their terror. All the while, outsiders had no clue that Future was in fact the mastermind behind the majority of homicides and licks in Chiraq. And it was the Convolution that pulled off each lick with precision.

It didn't matter if Future sold someone thirty kilos or thirty ounces, he would send the Convolution to take back every crumb before that person had a chance to bust down the package that the product came in. Bromise witnessed him sell the same kilo five different times, to five different people. His hustle was the ugliest, but to the outsiders, it was well respected and trusted just the same. To date, no one had ever suspected Future of any dishonorable deeds. The only skeletons he had were the Convolution. They were one another's skeletons, and they all were just as guilty.

Two years ago, the Convolution committed to two things:

1. No more consignments. Meaning, each member had to bring his own capital to the table.

2. Cocaine distribution only.

During the "*bad heroin*" epidemic where Fentalyn was mixed, cluckers were dropping like raindrops during a thunderstorm from fatal overdoses. Before long, the streets and whoever was associated with *Al Capone* became as hot as an Arizona desert on a blistering summer day. The transition was smooth, though. It was business as usual for them. No matter the product, they were getting it sold.

Then suddenly it dawned on Bromise, as he pressed on the gas and switched to the fast lane, taking the Audi to 101 miles per hour and counting.

Before each robbery, Future would make it clear, "Just bring me back the product." The money, jewels, and whatever else they decided to confiscate was theirs for the taking. After Macklin got slumped and Kill-Kill was sentenced to two consecutive life terms, Future, Freeway, Fontane, and Bromise were the only Convolution members left. And Bromise carried the load. The Convolution wasn't shit without him and the others knew it.

In truth, being a Convolution member had its benefits, so it seemed like a fair exchange. But that was the overlay for the underplay. The fact of the matter was that none of them were eating like Future.

"So," Bromise spoke out loud to no one in particular. "You let me keep the money and jewels from each robbery, huh? But the jewels are damn near worthless, and the money, well, that's eventually invested back into the product. And who has the product? You, that's who! It's the product that's valuable. It always has been, and all the product goes to you!" he yelled as if he was confronting Future face-to-face, and not sitting in an empty cabin of a fully loaded Audi. He floored the V8 twin-turbo charge and merged onto I-94 West Dan Ryan Expressway and continued to rant.

"If I take a brick and seventeen bands from a lick today, you get the product while I stuff my pockets with the seventeen bands. Meanwhile, when it's time to shop, I place the same seventeen bands right into your greedy fuckin' hands and walk away with the dope that I handed over to you to begin with. Where's the risk in it for you, muthafucka? Where's your investment!" He struck his steering wheel with his hand and headed toward the Chicago Loop.

Admittedly, he'd somehow lost sight of what Brisco set out for him—the countless man-hours he spent molding him. And the past five plus years had been nothing more than a blur. While he was busy recognizing it being done to others, he fell blind to the ride that Future had been taking him on. But that was about to change. At twenty, he had eight trap houses and $200k to his name, with all the toys a young baller could want. Yet, he was due so much more. And if it wasn't for Future *robbing* him with finesse, he'd have more to show for it.

Jamaican Bill, who was now at the wise age of fifty-six, was rumored to be approaching retirement soon, and everyone expected Rudeboy to be next up. But on the low, Bromise knew that Future intensely desired that position and would be next in line had Rudeboy taken a fall.

In truth, it wasn't about the money as much as it was the power that Future was focused on. He had more money than he knew what to do with. Thanks to the Convolution, he could literally retire today and live off his residuals for the rest of his natural life. There were many so far in debt that they'd be paying Future for the rest of their days. He had a debt scroll that could streak the length of Highway I-90.

He accomplished most of this in the early days when he promoted the convenience of consignment to all the middleweight hustlers. Being able to obtain any amount of product without having to pay a dime up front appealed to them. Future was a known regular on the night scene. He frequented the most popular nightclubs and received VIP treatment wherever he'd go. Strip joints were his favorite, and he used this distraction to get over on naïve hustlers. Without speaking a word, Future entranced them with the idea that it was better to make it rain than it was to stash away for rainy days. They partied every weekend and frequented King of Diamonds on Mondays.

Future would tear down the club with bundles of one-dollar bills. He wasn't stingy with the bands. Strippers would often fight for his business, and his entourage of hustlers would do what they could to keep up with him. But Future's money was too long. Brand new whips and paper tags on a monthly basis became the new fad—all the while he fed them a steady flow of product on consignment, his victims falling right into his hands.

Before long, the men lost their sight of entitlement, and lacked the accountability they once had as they suddenly found themselves continuously dependent on Future's next move. Similar to whores and a pimp.

Then whenever Future was ready to pull a tactic that he saw done to perfection by Brisco, but with different intentions for a totally different end game, he would inflate his prices. The hustlers that didn't have a stash saved at that particular unpredictable moment, rather they liked it or not, had no choice but to comply with the new demand. They were stuck paying for overpriced product.

For the smart hustlers that did have bands on deck during these unpredictable droughts, they were pretty much doomed also. Future would have the Convolution, with Bromise leading the missions, to hit their safe houses at a moment's notice and cripple them financially. When the victim of the robbery came back to Future spilling a sob story about how he was jacked, Future would sell him whatever amount of product the hustler could afford, plus, he would front him whatever amount he was comfortable with accepting at the inflated price. Then he'd have him robbed again. That was the ugly residual game that Future played on countless middleweight hustlers. Instead of getting all riled up like they would expect him to, he would sympathize with them and recite his famous lines.

*"I've been playing this game for a long, long time now. It's not always a straight rise to the top. Sometimes you might fall off and hit the bottom, and sometimes that's needed in order to make you that much stronger. So I understand your present position. Right now I'm not trippin' on the bread you owe me. I know you'll repay me in due time. So relax. You already at the bottom, so there's no other place to go but up. In fact, just to show you that it's all love"*—Future would tap the left side of his chest to clarify what he meant—*"Order another three bricks from me, and just continue to shop at my store, and only my store. Visit me six times, and I'll squash your debt to me, as long as we keep doing business. That works out for the both of us. You need to get back in position, and if I put you there, it'll be your continued business that will help me maintain my position. A favor for a favor."* He got them every time.

Bromise also fell victim to this scheme at one time, and found himself down one hundred bands and counting. He quickly wised up and paid his debt in full to Future. Then he became an active voice against consignment. Shortly thereafter, the Convolution came to the table and heard his argument, and that's when consignment amongst members was eliminated.

Finally, Bromise pulled his Audi into the driveway of a 5,000 square foot home in Lincoln Square, one of the most desirable Chicago neighborhoods. He shared the property with his lady, Chasidy.

He had one thing on his mind: dangle the crown in front of Future's face, and just when he reached for it,

# RUMONT TEKAY

snatch it away from his reach. To accomplish that, he'd have to get rid of Rudeboy first. Only then could he focus on Future.

Brisco once told Bromise, *"No man is untouchable. Any man with desire and the heart to kill another man could do it. Squeezing a trigger is the easy part, grandson. How to get in and out unscathed as the victor, now that takes thought.*

*"Wars are expensive. Squeezing a trigger doesn't cost a penny, but the repercussions could cost a man everything, even his life. Some men can't be touched without first declaring war against them. If the contender has enough money to withstand a war, cover damages, and lost wages, he'd have a probable chance in defeating his opponent. But you must have your ducks in a row. The funding alone can be a burden.*

*"Take into account the shooters from your side that are bound to be casualties and the heat from law enforcement. That equals time spent away from the grind and large amounts of money being missed. Not to mention, the purchase of weapons and ammunition, bunkhouses, travel fees, freelance soldiers and legal fees, will also cost a pretty penny. Petty street wars are as simple as aim and shoot. Mob wars are more complicated than that."*

Bromise knew that Future fell into that mob war category. With Jamaican Bill supporting Future, he knew that he was going to need a group of men that weren't afraid to die, and die-hard for the cause. Men without a conscience. He had that covered.

Slumping Future was going to take more than just a squeeze of the trigger, and much more than a simple set-up plan that the average man would concoct.

Future, himself, was not only aware of this, he thrived on it, which was his core reason for designing his *debt hustle* to begin with—to keep niggas at bay.

But Bromise had an advantage that the outsiders didn't, and he was sure to use it to his advantage. For him to commit an effective act of war against Future was to first, ambush him from a blind corner. To disturb his foundation was to divide his team, so that he stood alone. His finances had to be cut off, so that he would grow weak. Only then would he be touchable, and that's how Bromise would get in and out unscathed as the victor. It was going to take time, patience, and a vexed determination to go all out and turn-up in the worst way imaginable.

Before he exited his whip, he looked up and noticed Chasidy looking beyond their ripple fold drapery. Even from his obscure view, she was definitely a sight to see. He secured the Audi and headed for the front entrance. It was time to let her know that the wait was over. She was his better half, his partner in crime, and played an integral part in his plan since day one.

He was confident that if anyone could set Future up for a fall, it would be the one female whose pussy he couldn't resist. And it just so happened that she was still his boo.

# CHAPTER 9
*Behind Every Boss there's a Chasidy*

Chasidy was as angry as the Taurine bull she was. Her normally calm demeanor quickly changed, and her face contorted into a grotesque sneer as she watched Bromise walk from his whip.

"I'm Chasidy," she yelled into her iPhone. "So tell me why this doggish ass nigga acting like he done lost his fuckin' mind and forgot who the fuck I am," she shouted angrily while her sister, Porsha, asked irrelevant questions. "You ain't no help. Let me let you go, girl. His ass walking up to the door now. Bye!" she hissed and tossed the cell aside. She couldn't believe Bromise had the audacity to stay out all night, and with some white college bitches at that.

Chasidy knew it was a better way to handle this, but she was on some real *fuck some rational shit* right now. She stood there with her arms folded, dead center of the foyer waiting for Bromise to appear. And when he did she went ham sandwich on him.

"Are you tired of living, Bromise Balducci? Or Black Mamba, as you like to call yourself!" She could tell she caught Bromise off guard. He had the nerve to stand there with a confused look on his face.

"Baby, what are you talking about?" Bromise shut their rustic mahogany door and reached for her waist.

"Look at the time! What time is it, Bromise?" Her nostrils flared. She denied his touch and pointed to their wall clock.

"It's a little past three o'clock in the afternoon, and your point?" He shrugged his shoulders.

"My point?" *What!* Her eyes narrowed to slits as she gave him a once over. He had some nerve waltzing up in there, looking every bit as sexy as Akon's fine ass, like wasn't shit wrong. "Where were you at last night?" Chasidy spewed.

"Listen, first of all, lower your voice in my house," he said, walking past her and going into the kitchen. "Whatever it is, I'm sure you're just overreacting as usual. So calm down, relax, and let's talk about this like adults." He placed both of his iPhones on the granite countertop and noticed a sealed enevelope addressed to him. He tore threw it and began reading a day old letter from Kill-Kill. His brows furrowed the more he read.

She walked over to him and calmly said, "Where. Were. You. Last. Night?" He didn't respond. Instead, he became more engrossed in the yellow sheet of paper directly in front of him. His lips moved when he read in silence. She snatched the attention-getter from his hands and pounded it on the granite countertop with her palm. He peered down at her with those sexy bedroom eyes. A slight, mesmerizing smile touched his lips. His teeth were so white against his pitch-black skin.

"Baby, like I told you before I left, I headed out of town on biz."

"Why didn't you mention that you were going to Carbondale?"

"Did it matter?" he asked, wondering how she knew.

"Yes, it mattered that you felt the need to keep it a secret." She planted her hands on her hips.

"Since when do I report my every move to you?" He gently removed her hair from her face, before tracing it behind her ears. She loved his touch. He softly took her face into his hands and said, "Listen, and relax a little. Everything will be fine. Why all the questions? I travel all the time."

"I know you were with some lil prissy white sluts last night. One of the thots called my phone," she said, holding back tears.

"Whoa, whoa . . . she what?" Bromise raised her chin with his finger. "Listen, as a favor to my mans Fats, I went out to Carbondale on biz. That's it. After biz was handled, neither one of us was in a hurry to make that long drive back. So naturally we found something to get into, a college shindig. Yeah, bitches were there. A lot of flirting was going on, but nothing happened. I recall allowing a young lady to use my phone. She came off as desperate, so I figured why not. Apparently, she went through it and probably picked your number because it showed up so many times. She's just a little bored white chick playing a college prank, nothing more. Do you believe me?" Bromise was impressively quick on his toes.

*Shit!* She hated the effect that this man had on her. And his One Million cologne wasn't helping matters either. The masculine scent matched his personality to a tee, and it did something to her every time he came around. Chasidy was certain that it was more to this story, but she wanted to believe him. Like Porsha told her, at the end of the day, she's the bitch living on the top of the hill in Lincoln Square with red bottoms that cost more than most bitches' rent. He took care of her, he protected her, and no matter what, she knew he loved her.

"So are we on the same page, baby?" he asked with sincerity, as he searched her eyes with his, managing to reach her soul. He patiently awaited her response.

Chasidy looked at him and thought, *Jackass!* Then she answered, "Yes, bae, I believe you." And without warning, Bromise swept her off her feet and placed her on the countertop. They paused for a short interval, taking each other in as he began to undress. He started with his Pelle Pelle leather jacket. Then he freed his chiseled chest and abs from his Polo Tee. As he reached for his Gucci belt, she removed the only item that shielded her curvaceous frame, his Derrick Rose, authentic Chicago Bulls jersey.

She tossed it aside and ran her tongue across the top of her lip, slowly. His eyes widened when he saw she had nothing else on. He shook his leg free of his Polo denim, and rushed to meet his passion with hers. He took her in his arms and they kissed fully as she ran her hands over his bulging back muscles. She could feel his strength. The anticipation stimulated her, as they both breathed heavily.

Bromise laid his mouth on her neck and began to tease her skin with his tongue. His hands continued to travel her body, and just before his finger entered her soaking wet pussy, he placed his lips against her ear and whispered, "No other bitch matters to me." She stiffened as the tip of his finger slid between her wet pussy lips, then entered her, and began to probe the inner regions of her tight pussy.

His touch was paralyzing. "Oh, daddy, I love your strong hands." She reached down and found his erection and seductively inched her way to the edge of the counter. Then she guided the tip of his massive dick to the front entrance of her pearly pink gates.

"Oh yes," he moaned and initially stretched her walls slowly. Then he began to fuck her the way he knew she liked it.

Somehow they made it to the hallway. Bromise planted his back against the wall and continued to long stroke her pussy. He was relentless with his thrusts, and she loved every bit of it. She pressed her perfect breasts against his pecs and held on to his neck while her fatty continued to pop, midair, placing Bromise on another galaxy. She loved watching his fuck faces as she twerked on his pole.

Then Bromise carried her into the dining room and gently set her curvaceous frame on their eighty-inch rectangular table. It was solid rosewood and sturdy. He pulled out and spread her legs more. He brought his mouth and nose close to her juicy wetness. She licked her lips in anticipation of pleasure. The tickling sensation from his hot breath on her pussy lips made her giggle with delight. He kissed them lightly. Chasidy took a short loud intake of breath. Bromise's arousal intensified. He gave her pussy a tight French kiss and started eating her out. She grabbed the back of his head and shoved his face in it. He vigorously licked her wetness and she gasped for air.

"Uh shit, yes, YES!" she yelled in ecstasy, giving him clear indicators that she was enjoying herself immensely.

He put in a finger along with his wet tongue into

her tight walls, and she shouted out in pleasure. Then he increased the pressure by inserting another finger. She squirmed and said, "Oh daddy, what are you doing to me?" Bromise kept on with his job, and she continued with her exclamatory remarks of pleasure.

He stiffened his tongue and increased his pace. She grabbed a hold of his fro and began to throw it back in his face more. "Bromise! Bromise! Yes! Fuck! Ewggg," she shrieked in pleasure as she gushed out her juices.

He kissed her flat stomach and made his way to her nipples. He fondled her tits while he licked and sucked on them both. He slightly bit down on one, and she let out a moan.

"Ohh daddy, I like that," she said softly.

He kissed her shoulders and breathed down her neck. She whimpered and shivered. His organ was now poking and rubbing against her dripping wet clit.

"Please get inside me," she said and kissed him.

"Be patient," he said and climbed onto the table, straddling her. He rested his stiff dick in the middle of her enticingly deep cleavage. She caught on quickly and wrapped her tits around it. They felt soft and hot around him. He fucked her tits slowly. She loved it.

He climbed back down, placing his soles on the hardwood floor.

"Now," she said. "I need you inside of me."

Bromise put her right leg on his left shoulder and rubbed his dick head against her fat pussy lips. She took her fingers and slightly parted her pearly pink gates in anticipation of the fun to come. She was burning with the desire of being fucked hard. He pushed his dick in and she gasped. Thrust after thrust, he seared through her soft flesh, jabbing her ovaries.

"Harder," she said, "HARDER!"

Bromise slid his forearms behind her thighs and picked her up, with her legs spread eagle. In this position he was sure to give it all to her. Chasidy held her breath in preparation. In midair, he grabbed two handfuls of her fatty while she hung on with her hands wrapped around his thick neck. Long stroke after another, Chasidy bounced, going buck wild on his dick. Without pausing, not even for a breath, they aimlessly found themselves now in the living room. He set her sidewise on the edge of their plush sofa, grabbed her small waist and increased his pace. He buckled down, gripped her waist tightly and pounded the face of pussy repeatedly, with his pelvic bone.

"Yaooowww!" she howled in ecstasy as he punished her tight walls. Sexual tremors swept over them like mini-earthquakes, shaking their bodies, as she came violently all over his dick. Bromise wasn't far behind as he blew his load inside her.

Spent, he pulled out and climbed over her, and flopped on the cushion. Chasidy straddled his lap. They gazed in each other's eyes.

"I love you, Bromise." She wrapped her arms around his neck and they kissed completely. Suddenly, his erect penis commanded their attention, and they fucked again. This time they shared two orgasms and ended up in their master bedroom for the finale. But all the sex in the world couldn't stop the troubles from penetrating Bromise's mind.

*Two hours later . . .*

Bromise couldn't believe the college chick called

# VENOM IN MY VEINZ

Chasidy's cell. *At what time exactly did she get inside my locked phone?* He rubbed his chin, in deep thought, and then quickly shook his head to rid himself of them. He just didn't have the time to wreck his brain figuring out how some gadget savvy, college girl found a way to break into his iPhone's security code. *Whatever.* Plus, his baby was doing okay now. He smiled and looked over Chasidy's flawless naked body. She lay angelically on their California King mattress, draped with thousand-count Egyptian cotton sheets. After he put the dick on her and clued her in to the plan, she fell fast asleep.

Bromise walked inside their master bathroom and stepped into the glass shower. The warm stream of water was invigorating. He turned to let it massage his back as the daylight caught his attention from the skylight window in the ceiling. He looked up and began to reflect.

Future had a fetish for young, sexy exotic dancers, and Chasidy, at the tender age of twenty-three, fit the bill flawlessly. Chasidy wasn't just a stripper—she was an entertainer that had the ability to steal the room at a second's notice. That's how she got her paper. She traveled to different clubs across the U.S. on the regular. She did this solely to peep out their setups and different angles on how to manage, in order to implement them into her own club back here in Chiraq. Bromise fronted her the cash, and just recently helped her open up a pole dancing fitness studio.

While on the road, she'd scout new girls that would be a complimentary addition to her club's lineup. Both her fitness studio and gentlemen's club were named *Reflections*. Chasidy was on her shit.

Future had shamelessly tried to come up with Chasidy behind Bromise's back many times in the past. And last year he got his wish. Shortly after he and the Convolution returned from their trip to Cancun, Future left on a business trip to Richmond, Virginia. During his stay there, he encountered Chasidy at Amnesia's, a strip club that she visited when in town.

When she returned home, she explained to Bromise how she bumped into Future. She further said that once he witnessed her perform on stage, for him it was love at first sight. On that night alone he threw away $3,500 in fifties on exclusive lap dances from her back in the VIP room, while boasting, "I can give you somethin' that Black Mamba can't."

"And what is that, hun?" Chasidy had asked, uninterested.

"I can buy you the world if you let me."

Bromise quickly recognized the opportunity. He talked it over with her and encouraged her to pursue him subtly. At that moment, her mission was set to start.

Their second encounter took place in Miami. Future landed on Friday, and Chasidy flew first class, arriving that Saturday. She returned home to Bromise on Monday morning after a day of sexcapades with Future. She blew his mind and left him pussy whipped. On that occasion she returned with $9k in cash and $4k in sexy apparel, compliments of him. And the amount of financial gain grew with each visit. The cash and gifts for her were just an added bonus. Their end goal, however, was as clear as spring water as she kept him on a short leash, waiting on Bromise's next command.

Since then, Bromise allowed her to *get away* with

him at least once every two weeks. Each time in a different city. She kept him posted on every detail, leaving out all explicit sex acts. Bromise didn't care to know about it.

In the meantime, Future never once as much as alluded to the possibility of Bromise's girl committing the ultimate betrayal against him. No, as wickedly smart as Future was, he really thought he was getting over, fucking Bromise's girl behind his back for the past year, and smiling in his face at the same damn time.

While he lathered, Bromise took a second to ponder a reason that men deceived themselves for the sake of a piece of ass. They're so busy trying to manipulate situations to their favor that they overlook the subtle signs before the situation has been flipped on them, making them their own victims.

Future was so convinced that he manipulated Chasidy into betraying Bromise to the point where he had total control of the woman that was rightfully not his. Never once did he stop to think maybe this situation wasn't his to control. His alter ego made it impossible for him to fathom that manipulation itself was actually what was manipulating him. While he was creeping around expensive suites and sending for her across state lines, he didn't consider that maybe his relationship with her was in fact, under Bromise's thumb. Sadly for him, Bromise controlled the woman that controlled him, which meant that Future's life expectancy was ultimately Bromise's to predict.

# CHAPTER 10
*Benita Westbrook versus Chasidy Berry*

*Three Days Later . . .*

When Bromise had encountered Benita five years ago inside the Bogus Boys clique's duplex, he viewed her as a *bad bitch* right out the gate. He was young, but mature enough to know that she was physically his type for sure. Even before that day he knew she was a down chick, just from the stories that were circulating. But as scandalous as she was sexy, she couldn't hold a candle to Chasidy on either front. In comparison, she was a panther leading her pack, while Chasidy was a lioness leading hers.

Bromise always wanted a stomp-down bitch like Benita Westbrook, and as fate would have it, he wound up with a bitch even better. Brisco once told him, *"She's a black widow, sure, but she loves you, grandson. She may not know it, and I know you're too young to foresee it, but you two will end up together in future years. Protect her, baby boy, but only to the degree that she protects you."*

To date, Chasidy's accessory to murder rate with Bromise was at eleven and counting. Brisco was a strategist who taught Bromise how to be a sharp thinker, and he did it well. But it was the brutal use of force that fit him best. Chasidy would stress it's the easy way out, and he was just being a lazy bully at times. So he accredited her for having taught him that it was more than one way to skin a cat.

Judging the book of *Chasidy* by the cover alone, would be a tragic mistake that Bromise had seen many men make time and time again. Although she was riveting with physical beauty, and one of the most intelligent, wittiest females he'd ever known, like him, she was dangerous and loved the game more than anything or anyone.

While unsuspecting men looked at her and saw what they only wanted her to be: *wifey, baby mama, fuck buddy, whatever.* Bromise saw her for what she really was: a cold-blooded killer who had the ability to turn into a double-edged sword at any given moment, thrusting remorselessly in his direction. He vowed to never get distracted by her *cover* and lose sight of how treacherous she really could be.

Bromise sat at the wheel of a private rental SUV with Fats and Jay in tow. Jay had finally become accustomed to the eye patch he wore, having lost his left eye years prior during the roller rink shoot-out. They were currently making their rounds and picking up cash from Bromise's traps.

"I got a letter from Kill-Kill a few days ago," Bromise said while "Commas" by L.E.P. played in the background.

"That's wusup," Fats said. "Besides you and Macklin, may he rest in peace, Kill-Kill was the hardest gangsta wit' the Convolution."

"How long has he been down, anyway?" Jay asked from the backseat.

"Three years," Bromise answered, keeping his eyes on the road.

"I know he sick wit' dat double-life sentence over

his head," Jay said, "but fuck 'im. I never liked da nig anyway."

"Watch your mouth," Bromise said and blazed his eyes at Jay before turning back to the road. "Have some fuckin' respect, Joe. He put in a lot of work in these streets."

"How is he holdin' up, anyway?" Fats said, purposely taking the attention off Jay. "I mean, considering his circumstances. I'm sure he's gucci, right?" he asked, inquiring about Kill-Kill's mental and physical state. Gucci was another street term for *good.*

"Yeah, he's more than gucci," Bromise said. "Apparently, he's about to come from under that double L." He gripped the steering wheel just a little harder.

"How so?" Fats asked curiously. Both he and Jay were all ears, waiting on the answer.

"The courts granted his appeal. He has a new hearing on the eighth of this month," Bromise said. "And it's looking like it's going to go in his favor this time."

"That's this Friday, Joe," Fats said. "Is you saying dat nigga will be free come this Friday?"

"I'm saying it's a high possibility. Everybody's talking about it," Bromise confirmed.

Jay frowned in contempt at the unexpected news.

Fats looked out of his window and then back to Bromise and then out of the window again, and silently pickled his thoughts.

Bromise knew why Jay felt some type of way about Kill-Kill, because deep down he felt the same. Kill-Kill was a typical OG that looked down upon the generation that came after his. He was a part of the older group that talked negative about the younger generation as if they had nothing to do with them. *"Disloyal. No honor. No respect. No sense of structure or street ethic,"* were some of the words that Kill-Kill would often speak in reference to the young and wild. Instead of doing what it takes to teach them, pass down the knowledge that the preceding generation did for them, he thought it better to complain and ostracize them.

When Kill-Kill was on the streets, he and Bromise hardly saw eye-to-eye. But Kill-Kill's position during that period influenced him to hold his tongue, time and time again. Bromise was younger then, and Brisco had taught him to always respect another man's earned position. And Kill-Kill had definitely earned his stripes and bars.

Never once in the entire three years that Kill-Kill was down did he reach out to Bromise via snail mail, or in any form for that matter. *So why now?* Bromise wasn't exactly positive, but he was sure to show up at the hearing and support the team as requested.

Bromise drove through an intersection when his phone chimed. "Talk to me," he said.

"Are you around, bae?" Chasidy asked.

"Well, that depends. Where are you?"

"I'm at the Trio Salon gettin' dipped. Come up here quick. I got some news."

"Say no more," Bromise said and ended the call. "We're making a slight detour, fellas." He accepted the Kush from Fats and bent a corner. After four stiff hits off the blunt and several coughs in between, he pulled up to a stop light with Trio Salon in view. He called

Chasidy.

"I'm pullin' up, baby. C'mon out," he said.

"K, comin' out now," she said and showed up on the sidewalk as he pulled to the curb. She climbed into the backseat aside from Jay, looking like new money with her mink coat and red bottoms. She leaned forward and met Bromise's lips as he leaned his head backward. They kissed fully. It wasn't until she released his lips that she acknowledged the other men in the whip.

"Hey, y'all," she said and waved with a coy smile. And they reciprocated.

"Talk to me, baby," Bromise said and adjusted the rearview mirror on her face.

"K," she said, "Rudeboy will be at Antoine's tonight."

"Antoine?" Bromise said, seeming confused. "Who the fuck is that?"

"He's that retired basketball player that used to play in the NBA," she said. "Anyway, he be hosting private craps games at the Resident Club Lounge on the 32nd floor of the Optima Chicago Center. Hella bands." She rubbed her thumbs and fingers together. "Well, anywho, they're doing an exclusive set tonight and Rudeboy will be there for sure."

"How do you know this?" Bromise studied her face through the rearview.

"One of the girls that dance at my club is dating him. Her name is Tasha. You know he's married, so the only time he dips with her is when he's out at the casino or hosting exclusive craps game."

"And she valid?" Bromise asked.

"One hundred proof." Chasidy put her stamp on it.

# VENOM IN MY VEINZ

"They'll be there at around elevenish."

"Okay, baby, good lookin'," Bromise said and rose up in his seat. "Where are you parked?"

"Right ahead, bae." She climbed out of the SUV, stopping at the driver side door. Bromise quickly let down his window. She reached in and put her hand atop his. "You be safe now, you hear." She kissed him and told the squad goodbye.

Bromise watched as she climbed into her Range Rover Supercharged and sped off. He immediately received a text from her saying, *"I'll be at home waiting on you to get there. So please come to me when you're finished. I've missed you and I love you."*

Immediately, Bromise got on his cell and put the plan into motion. He used his contacts to reach out to someone that knew someone that knew the housekeeping staff at the Optima Center. He paid the Mexican male a band to ajar a side entrance of the building. The plan was simple: get inside, take the back stairs, and by all means slump Rudeboy. Spare the others. Get in and get out.

Later that evening, Bromise, Fats, and Jay sat across the street from the Optima Center in the rental SUV. They passed the blunt of Kush around, scoping out the scene. On their laps sat two burners each as Meek Mill spit "Heaven or Hell" through the factory speakers.

"Who the fuck is this?" Bromise said, after screening an incoming call. He didn't recognize the number. *Should I answer?* Typically he wouldn't give it a second thought, but the fact that he was, told him that maybe he should.

"Who dis?" he spat through his cell.

"It's me, Chasidy," she said.

"Why aren't you calling me from your phone?" Bromise asked, extra curious.

"I accidently left it in my Range. I'm on Tasha's phone," she said, placing her finger in her ear to block the noise.

"Where are you?" Bromise asked.

"Bae, you won't believe this," she said. "Apparently, Tasha's bum ass baby daddy took off with her whip and left her stranded at the beauty salon. So, of course, she calls the only reliable bitch she knows," Chasidy explained, "So after I pick her up, tell me why the first nigga she calls for help decides to give her a call back hours after the fact?"

"Who?" Bromise asked impatiently.

"Antoine's doggish ass."

"The retired basketball player?"

"Exactly," she confirmed. "Anywho, he asked her to come where he was, and I let her convince me to take her there, and I'm here with them now. And Rudeboy is here also."

Bromise rose in his seat and turned down the music's volume. "Wait, you're where? And with who?"

"I am with Tasha, Antoine, and Rudeboy, and some of their male friends. We are at the Sky Bar," she said. "We are about to part ways, though. They are headed to the Optima Center, and I'm heading home."

"No, wait!" Bromise blurted and looked over at Fats and Jay.

"What is it?" she asked.

"You can't leave now," he replied.

"Why?" she asked.

"Because you've been with them for hours now and have been seen with them by a host of people. You leaving minutes before this goes down won't be a good look for you," he explained. "Rather you like it or not, you're stuck with them until this is over." He ended the call without bothering to give her a chance to speak. He was pissed.

"Damn, Joe," Fats said after he hit the Kush. "What we gon' do now?"

Bromise wanted to abort the mission. He wanted to put the Optima Center in his rearview and gear up for another day. But he knew how exclusive Rudeboy traveled, and it could be weeks, maybe months before he'd get this opportunity again. *Damn, why did she let herself get pulled in by Tasha's thot ass!*

"We're moving forward with the plan," Bromise said, answering Fats' question. Then he increased the volume to the song "Levels" by Meek Mill.

"But, what about Chasidy?"

"What about her! She can handle her own!" Bromise barked. "Ain't nothing stopping this hit. This shit goes down tonight," he said sternly.

"If it comes down to it," Jay chimed in, "she gotta take one for the squad."

Bromise swallowed hard at his words and raised his left wrist. His Backes & Strauss diamond watch read 10:43 p.m. "Jay, go double check that side door, and make sure it's still unlocked."

"I'm on it." Jay left the SUV and crossed the street inconspicuously.

Bromise knew that Fats wanted to say something in Jay's absence about proceeding, but he knew he wouldn't.

They watched Jay cross the street and get back inside. "Yeah, Joe," Jay said, "it checks out."

Thirty minutes later, three Maybachs drove up and parked in front of the Optima Center. Three valets approached the vehicles simultaneously, opening the back doors first. Even from where he sat, Bromise could see the uneasy expression on Chasidy's face as she tried to keep up with the upbeat tempo of her surroundings. *She's not holdin'. Damn!* It dawned on Bromise that she was unarmed and therefore unable to protect herself. That was the only other explanation for the vibes he was picking up. He started the countdown on his Nike wristwatch that wrapped snugged around his right wrist.

The watch sounded off at 11:53 p.m.

"Let's get active," Bromise said and steered the SUV around the building and up to the unlocked side entrance. Bromise and Jay bailed, and Fats switched over to the driver seat. Once inside the building, Bromise and Jay started off taking the stairs by twos. By the time they reached the 30th floor, they were forced to stop for a breather.

"You underestimated these stairs, Joe," Jay said, and all Bromise could do was smile in agreement.

***

Chasidy sat alone at a table with her legs crossed. The lounge was sizable at 3,000 square feet. She rolled her eyes at the back of Tasha's head, who'd been joined at Antoine's hip since they got there. She took a tiny sip of Louis XIII and sat the glass back in front of her while most of the room's attention was on the dice game.

"Hello," a very tall handsome man stepped up,

108

interrupting Chasidy's thoughts. "May I have a seat?" He gestured toward the empty seat at her table.

Without looking up, she waved her hand and said, "Whatever." She couldn't believe how her iPhone had no reception in such a high-end place. She wanted to call Bromise, but couldn't. Her gut wasn't sitting well. Something wasn't right about this hit. She could feel it.

"Why is it that someone as gorgeous as you is sitting alone in a room filled with rich men, such as myself?" he said and extended his hand. "My name is Michael Sutton."

She shook his hand and quickly realized how massive it was, as it appeared to take up the size of her entire forearm. Then suddenly she recognized him as a back-up center for the Chicago Bulls. She gently pulled her hand back and darted her eyes at the entrance, clearly paying dude no mind. *I hope Bromise decides not to go through with this, because something ain't right!*

"Excuse me," he said, clearly getting impatient. "Don't you know who I am?"

"No, I don't," she lied, "and why should I?"

"Why should you?" He laughed. "Because I'm Michael Sutton, bitch!"

At that moment, Bromise stormed through the glass double doors in all black with a ski mask to match. Two fully automatic burners filled his hands.

Jay secured the lounge from the outside.

"Everybody stop what the fuck you're doing and get up against the wall! NOW!" Bromise bellowed, catching everyone off guard and terrifying them with his intimidating image. Everyone, including Chasidy, rushed to comply with his demand. It had to be twenty people there.

Bromise visually swept the lounge and quickly spotted his mark, Rudeboy. "You!" Bromise pointed both of his Steyr TMPs directly at Tasha. The TMPs were light and compact, machine pistols that could be emptied in one burst. "Check the bathrooms," he said, and out of shock, she moved like a snail, slow and confused. "Now bitch!" he yelled. She snapped out of it and got to the rest room door in a jiffy. He trained one of the burners on the group and watched Tasha from his position.

"Is it clear?" he asked in a stern tone after she peeked her head into the men's rest room.

"Yes," she said.

"Check the other one," he ordered, and she sprinted to the women's rest room.

"No one's in there either," she said.

"All right, get your ass back over here," he hissed and addressed the group. "If you do exactly as I tell you to do, this will be over in under three minutes and thirty seconds. If anyone of you decides to be a hero, I promise you tonight you'll meet your maker. Again, do as you're told, and you'll live through this. I want everyone to strip down to nothing. NOW!" he barked, waving both burners in their direction. Bromise recognized some of his favorite NBA players in the room when he realized that Chicago would host Miami tomorrow night, and from the looks of it, a few of the Heat players had already made it to the city.

"Wah yuh a duh? Duh yuh know who I am?" Rudeboy broke his silence, speaking Jamaican tongue. "I get naked fah nuh mon. Yuh tink yuh cyan dweet to mi! Yuh want mi naked den yuh cum fah—come for it!"

"I'll come for it all right!" Bromise charged at Rudeboy and struck him in the throat with the top of the burner. He fell to the ground, struggling to breathe. "Quite frankly, I don't give no fuck who you are, chump." Bromise stood over him and quickly aimed a burner in two Rastas' direction. "I wish one of you muthafuckas would," he warned through his teeth.

"You don't have to do this, man, please." Antoine wept in fear.

"Shut your big scary ass up!" Bromise seethed and trained the other burner on him. Antoine stood there, all 6-feet 9-inches of him, shaking in his alligator boots. Bromise took a few steps back, regaining control of the room as Rudeboy remained on the floor gasping for oxygen. "Now again"—he turned his attention to the rest of the group— "I don't want to have to slump none of you, but I will," he said, as he didn't want to turn one homicide into twenty. "Everyone strip the fuck down now!" They frantically did as they were told, and in the process revealed concealed weapons, money, jewels and other personal items. He directed Tasha to round it all up and place it inside a large empty garbage can that sat aside the craps table.

Twenty men and women all stood against the wall butt naked and obedient.

"You." Bromise gestured toward a Rasta. "Do the honors of strippin' your man down to absolutely nothing and place him in a chair." The Rasta cooperated and began to undress Rudeboy, who was still disorientated while Bromise watched. It was revealed that Rudeboy was also holding heat. Bromise directed the Rasta to toss it in the can with the other confiscated burners. "Now, I want everyone to find a seat in one of these nice, comfortable chairs," he said, and they quickly found their spots in one area.

"You, bitch," Bromise said and pointed the burner at Chasidy. "Here." He tossed her several zip ties. "Get your ass up and tie everyone to their chairs, now."

"Yes, sir," she said. "Please just don't hurt us." Chasidy caught most of the zip ties with her lap, and picked up the rest from the floor. She stood to her feet and got busy.

Bromise glanced over at the craps table and what he held in view was a heap of cash that could've easily resembled an athlete's signing bonus. *Man I love hittin' licks.* He tapped the double glass doors with the back of his Air Jordan heel to get Jay's attention.

"Watch them, Joe," Bromise said after Jay peeked his head in.

Jay quickly let go of the door handle. He swiftly pressed the butt of his assault rifle against his shoulder. His offhand gripped around the plastic covering of the barrel. He held the group in his sights from the opposite side of the glass.

"Hurry up, bitch!" Bromise yelled and sprinted to the craps table. He freed his hands of the burners and allowed them to hang loosely from his shoulder straps. He swept the heap of cash into the same can with his forearm.

"I'm moving as fast as possible, sir," Chasidy said as she approached the last one to be zip tied. It was Michael Sutton.

"See, bitch," Michael said in a hushed tone as she approached. "If your punk ass wasn't acting all bougie,

I'd be somewhere else right now fuckin' your brains out. You high-siditty bitch!"

That was it. Chasidy lost her cool. She dropped the zip ties and wopped him with a right hook followed by her left, catching the large man in his mouth and chin. Before either Jay or Bromise could react, he wrapped her arms up with his large hands and put her in a chokehold. Then he locked his knees, lifting Chasidy off the floor by her neck.

Bromise quickly raised his burner at eye level, as he aligned his front sights on his target.

On the opposite side of the glass, Jay's index finger was physically twitching around the steel trigger. Beads of sweat developed on his nose but were immediately absorbed by the ski mask. Through his sights, he watched as Chasidy's feet dangled in midair, kicking wildly to get away from her captor's tree bark like arms.

"I'll break this bitch's neck!" Michael yelled in a manner that was meant to be taken seriously as specks of blood flew from his mouth. He hoisted Chasidy up like a rag doll after tasting his own DNA. "I'm telling you. I'm not joking!"

"Why would I care?" Bromise said, keeping the burner steady. "That bitch was here when I came," he said and threw his left hand up behind him, gesturing Jay to stand down. *I got this!*

Jay placed his index finger under the trigger guard and took a deep breath.

Bromise was an excellent shot under normal circumstances when he could implement a rule of thumb: always shoot for the center mass. But with Michael using Chasidy as a human shield, that rule was not an option. He looked up into Chasidy's drained face. She was on the verge of passing out. He couldn't wait any longer. He squeezed the trigger and spurted over a dozen shots, catching Michael in his jaw.

He released Chasidy and his body plummeted to the ground. Bromise walked up behind Rudeboy and took a fistful of his top dreads, pulled them roughly, and met the back of his head with the burner. Bromise blew his brains across the floor-to-ceiling window as everyone looked on in horror. He grabbed the drawstrings of the garbage bag and pulled it from the can. Then he ran up on Michael's dead body and glanced over at Chasidy, who lay unconscious and bleeding from the shoulder.

He bolted out of the lounge and down the back stairs with Jay on his heels. Fats was on point with the SUV's engine running. They escaped the building and piled inside. Sirens and a sea of blue flashing lights pieced the night sky as cop cars were quickly closing in.

Fats calmly pulled the SUV out of the alleyway and joined the vehicles on the road, fleeing the scene.

"FUUUCCCK!" Bromise yelled at the top of his lungs as he pounded the dashboard with a closed fist. He dialed Porsha's number. When she answered, he simply said, "Wait about fifteen minutes then call Northwestern Memorial Hospital. Chasidy will be there with a gunshot wound. Go see about her and get back to me ASAP."

# CHAPTER 11
## *When Life Throws You Lemons*

*February 7*
*Lincoln Square*

Porsha rushed to the hospital the second the receptionist confirmed that Chasidy was there. Upon arrival, one of the doctors explained to her how lucky Chasidy was for only having sustained a minor flesh wound to the shoulder, while the other two guys on the scene were dead on arrival.

After a couple of detectives from the Chicago Homicide Division had questioned Chasidy, they were convinced that she, along with the other nineteen guest of the Resident Club Lounge, were victims of that fatal night. The doctors ran a few more tests and saw no reason to hold her. She was cleared and released in Porsha's care. She was exhausted and sore and just wanted to go home. Porsha followed her request.

From their California King bed, Bromise had a clear view of the glass shower in the master bath. He could see the plastic wrapped around Chasidy's bare shoulder, protecting her wound while she showered. It had been almost three days since the shooting incident, and Chasidy moped around the entire time, torturing Bromise with the silent treatment. However, he didn't take it personal. Instead, he remained home with her and cared for her in ways that she'd only allow him to, which wasn't much. As a result, he was forced to masturbate a couple of times to relieve his pain from blue balls.

He sighed heavily after reflecting on how his breakfast in bed routine didn't work this morning. Then suddenly, Bromise had an idea. He jumped out of bed in the nude, and walked straight into the master bath. He joined Chasidy in the shower and gently hugged her from behind. Startled, she looked back at him with blood-shot eyes. She had been crying. She removed his hands from her waist and gave him the cold shoulder. Bromise had no choice but to watch her vacate the steamy shower. He reluctantly glanced down at his stiff dick, and, again, he sighed heavily.

Twenty minutes later, he walked out of the master bath and into their room, barely damp with a towel wrapped around his waist. Chasidy sat comfortable in her Victoria's Secret PINK pajamas in front of their Apple iMac desktop.

He approached her and said with a stern tone, "How long do you think this shit gon' continue?"

"What shit, Bromise?" she said, never taking her eyes off the computer screen.

"You being on Twitter and Facebook and Instagram all gotdamn day, and not doing much of anything else," he said, "Especially when we got so much shit to do in these streets."

"Well, excuse me if getting shot *by you* has me feeling some kinda way, okay!" She refused to look at him.

"Look, it was a fuckin' flesh wound. I'm trying to empathize with you, but those type of unscripted acts comes with what the fuck we do," Bromise said. "Get over the shit already. You took one for the squad!"

# VENOM IN MY VEINZ

She stood to her feet and stormed out of their master bedroom crying, with Bromise closely behind, attempting to defuse the situation. He finally found her balled up in a corner of one of their five guest rooms. He went to her and joined her on the floor in nothing but his towel.

"Baby, what did you want me to do?" He gently took her face in his hands and looked deep into her misty brown eyes. "That muthafucka was on the verge of killing you. I couldn't lose you, Chasidy. I had to do something," he said sincerely.

"I know," she said, feeling vulnerable, "but I'm only just a girl. I'm not as strong as you."

"No, that's not true. You're the Queen of my chessboard, baby. The most powerful piece." He stroked the side of her face. "Bullets are scary. So I apologize for minimizing what you just went through. But I need you to understand this . . . What don't kill you makes you stronger." Bromise stood to his feet. Chasidy waited about ten seconds before she took his extended hand, and with his assistance, she also stood.

"I'm sorry for being such a bitch to you these past couple of days," she said, looking up into his eyes.

"Apology accepted." He playfully threw his arms around her, and accidently brushed up against her injured shoulder. "Oops, my bad," he said with concern and quickly dropped his arms, attempting to tend to her bandage.

"It's okay, it doesn't hurt," she said with a smile hinting at her lips. "It's healing faster than I thought." Chasidy reached under his towel and grabbed his ass. "Now kiss me, daddy."

"Now there goes my girl," Bromise said, and they

kissed.

After spending the entire day inside watching *Breaking Bad* on Netflix, and eating Chinese takeout, the two retired to their room and were currently cuddling in bed in the spoon position.

"Do you know why I call you 'bae'?" Chasidy asked.

"Umm, because it's another ghetto ass way of saying 'babe'?"

"No silly! It's because you come *Before Anyone Else* in my life."

"Awe," Bromise uttered and kissed her shoulder.

"Do you see that right there?" He pointed over her shoulder to his Marc Jacobs messenger bag atop their marble dresser.

"Yes," she said.

"There's seventy-two bands in that bag. It's yours," he said without hesitation.

Taken aback by the sudden news, Chasidy initially choked up on her response. "I don't mean to sound ungrateful, but why?"

"Well, the hit on Rudeboy ended up turning into a fine lick as well. After it was all said and done, we left up out of there with over four hundred bands," he said excitedly, as if he was reliving the rush. "After we split it three ways, I brought my share home to split with you."

"Aw, thanks bae," she said and slowly started to turn to him.

"You deserve it." He met her midway and pecked her soft lips with his own.

"I love this," she said.

"Love what?" he whispered.

"This," she said. "Us lying here. You holding me." She caressed his arm and hand that rested around her mid-section.

"It does feels nice," he agreed. "Listen, I've been meaning to talk to you about something."

"Wusup?"

"Kill-Kill is looking to come home. His hearing is tomorrow morning at the Cook County Court House, and is scheduled for that day only," he said.

"Which means . . ."

"It means his fate will be decided tomorrow no matter what. But according to Future and his team of lawyers, his chances of coming home are more than great this time. The new evidence they have on Kill-Kill's behalf is strong. And with all of the eyewitnesses slumped, there's no way the charges or his sentence can uphold any longer."

"I read a little about it on Facebook," she said.

"Facebook?" Bromise's brows furrowed.

"Yup, they've been promoting it hard these past couple of weeks," she said. "So the letter you were reading after you came home from being out all night, was that from him?" she asked.

"Yup."

"I knew it. I can spot prison mail a mile away." She smiled, then quickly pressed her lips together. "So is that going to stop or interfere with our plans?"

"Absolutely not. We're mashing forward, and Chiraq will be mine," he said with conviction. "No one is going to stop this mission, baby. Not even the infamous Kill-Kill. We've come too far and worked too hard. I'll be damned."

"Future called me yesterday when you were in the

garage fooling with your cars," she said.

"And?"

"And he wants me to meet him somewhere tomorrow, but he wouldn't say where. He said it was a surprise," she explained. "But I know it's out of the state at least, because he mentioned a first class airline ticket."

He tugged slightly at her waist and she slid her hips back, pushing her bubble backside against his manhood. The window was cracked, allowing in just enough chill, pleasantly persuading them to cuddle closer. "Well, you know what you have to do," he said sternly.

# CHAPTER 12
### *Kill-Kill's Homecoming*

*February 8*
*One week before the lick . . .*

The next morning, Bromise rolled over and reached for Chasidy. Her side of the bed was empty. He sat up on his elbows to get a visual confirmation. She wasn't there. He noticed a sheet of paper on the bedside stand. It was Chasidy's handwriting.

*Didn't want to wake you, hun. I'm on my way to the airport. I'll text you when I land.*

*Muah!*

*P.S. There's fresh coffee in the pot, and don't forget about Kill-Kill's hearing.*

He darted his eyes toward the digital clock. "Shit!" It was nearly noon, and the hearing was scheduled for 8:45 that morning. *How did I sleep so late?* He checked his iPhone and shut his eyes in frustration. It was dead. Bromise powered up and noticed he had a total of thirteen missed calls. All from his squad and Convolution members, including Future. He quickly dialed the Convolution back, but they were all going to voicemail. Then suddenly, a late incoming text came through. It was Fats. *Meet me near The Web when you get this. I'll be around till two.*

Without further delay, he bypassed a shower and went into his walk-in closet. He quickly got dressed in his TMT sweatsuit and tee, and slid into a fresh pair of Red October Air Yeezy 2's. Before he left, he rinsed his mouth with Listerine and tossed on a leather bomber jacket. He jumped in his Audi and sped off.

On his way to meet up with Fats, he continued to call Fontane, Freeway, and Future, but all lines were still going straight to voicemail. As he pulled on the block, he noticed Fats and Jay's younger brother, KO, sitting in Fats' parked '70 Mustang Mach 1. They sat with the engine idled, getting smoked out on blunts. Fats left his whip and jogged over to join Bromise in his.

"Wudup, Joe," Fats said upon entering and they shook-up. He adjusted the seat to accommodate his 6-feet 1-inch frame. Fats was overweight but he carried it well. "You're still here, huh?"

"What you mean?" Bromise asked and pushed his gear shift into park.

"Oh, so you don't know?" Fats said. "They freed Kill-Kill, Joe. That shit was all over the noon news."

"Yeah, I didn't get around to seeing it." Bromise looked off and ran his fingers through his fro.

"I was at the courthouse when the decision came down. It was chaotic for real, Joe. I'm talkin' bitches err'where!" Fats said excitedly.

"Bitches?" Bromise brows furrowed.

"Yeah, Joe. These hoes had on *Free Kill-Kill* shirts. On err'thang I love, Joe. I'm talkin' lights, cameras, action. They made a spectacle of the shit." Fats nodded. "And err'body was wondering where you was at. Freeway got at me, though."

"What did he say?" Bromise looked him in the eyes.

**122**

# VENOM IN MY VEINZ

"Them niggas chartered a G-4 to Vegas about an hour ago, and left you with this first class ticket to meet them there," he said. Fats handed him a Frontier Airline ticket and looked at his watch. "You better hit it, Joe. Your flight leaves in forty-five minutes."

No sooner than he said it, Bromise confirmed the time on the ticket. "You're right." He tossed it in his lap and left the block with Fats with him. He knew that his whip was safe with KO.

On their way to O'Hare International Airport, Fats went on about the morning's events.

And how the chaos unfolded.

"So after the decision came down, the courthouse turned-up, Joe," Fats said. "Reporters and cameras were all over the halls and a pool of people flowed out onto the front steps."

"Straight up?"

"On err'thang, Joe," Fats continued. "And then out of nowhere these niggas pull up right in front of the courthouse in two of those big dumb-ass, um . . ." Fats couldn't seem to think of the word he was looking for. "Umm Winnebagos..."

"Are you talking about those plush, Celebrity Motor Homes they show on TV?" Bromise said, knowing how big Future could go.

"Yessir," Fats confirmed. "Them the ones. They walked up to the courthouse steps, Joe, and cherry-picked all the bad bitches and piled them hoes into them big dumb-ass motor homes. Shit, I think I even saw a couple of the reporters get in, too. Which was cool, 'cuz them bitches was bad too!" They both laughed.

They were getting closer as O'Hare was now in

their sights just ahead.

"Say, Joe," Fats said, looking around the Audi's interior. "I just realized you didn't even have time to pack anything."

"No shit," Bromise said sarcastically as he pulled to a stop at the Level 1 Terminal.

"That's the good thang about having money, though," Fats said. "You can do what da fuck you want, when you want, and how you want, ya dig. Tear da fuckin' mall down while you in Vegas. Fuck it!" he said, encouraging a shopping spree. They chuckled.

Then he got on a more serious note. "That nigga Kill-Kill didn't seem too happy that you wasn't there to support, Joe."

"Why you say that?" Bromise asked, looking eyes to eyes.

"I overheard him say sumthin' to Future about you thinkin' you're too high and mighty to come down and show support . . . like your head too big for yo' body or somethin'," Fats said. "Listen, Joe, I know you don't tell me err'thang. But I know you, and I know you got some hot soup brewing—a plan that only you and Chasidy know about. And I'm cool with that. 'Cuz I know whatever move you make will have all of our best interests in mind. I trust you, Joe, but I have just one question."

"What's that?" Bromise said and took his *Beats by Dre* headphones from his middle console.

"In regards to your plan . . . does Kill-Kill stand to be a problem? 'Cuz if so—"

"Let me worry about Kill-Kill. For now, I need you to focus on The Web, and The Web only," Bromise said and they shook-up. "I'm out. Hold the whip down till I get back." He left the Audi and walked briskly through the O'Hare airport doors.

Considering he was without luggage, Bromise made it through security pretty fast and reached the gate in time to board his flight last minute. An incoming text hit his cell. It was Chasidy: *Hey hun, I'm headed to Las Vegas, but my flight has been delayed here in Houston. Not sure at this point when I'll be back in the air. Love ya!*

Now it was starting to make sense. Future had this weekend planned for quite some time. He flew in on the G-4 with the team and who knows whomever else, so of course, he'd have her travel alone as usual. But Las Vegas was clearly their rendezvous.

The young stewardess appeared happy to see Bromise as he approached the First Class cabin door and handed her his boarding card.

She greeted him with a flirtatious smile. "Good afternoon, Mr. Balducci. My name is Angel, and I'll be looking after you on your flight to Las Vegas today. May I have your coat and show you to your seat?"

"Sure," Bromise said with the biggest grin, as her exotic features impressed him. She was Asian and Black, and drop dead gorgeous with a Hawaiian tan complexion. Her makeup was perfect and her red hair twisted into a neat bun. He handed her his leather bomber. As she turned and headed down the aircraft aisle, she couldn't help but wiggle her uniform clad body just a little more than usual, knowing his eyes were glued to her backside.

She led him to his seat. "Out of curiosity, may I ask how do you pronounce your first name?"

"Yes, you may," he said and took his seat. "It's

pronounced Bro-mise."

"Oh, like *Promise*, except with a *B*. I get it, " she said and tapped his shoulder. "Well, nice to meet you." She reached out her hand.

"Nice to meet you as well," he said and gently shook her hand.

"What a unique name . . . I love it." She smiled again, engaging his gaze.

"Thank you . . . I like yours, too," he said and gave her a slow once-over while still holding onto her. She had an hourglass figure. Her crisp white shirt tapered well near her mid-section and blended with her thin waist, as her dark navy skirt hugged her curves to no end. For some reason she smelled like cinnamon rolls, and oddly enough, Bromise was aroused by her scent.

"Would you like an adult beverage, Mr. Balducci?"

"Yeah, why not," he said, releasing her hand. He watched her ass as she walked to the galley. Bromise instantly wondered if it was real.

She took the PA system handset and held it to her mouth. She paused before speaking and stared directly at Bromise. Opening her lips slightly, she ran her tongue across them, and then winked at him.

"Ladies and gentleman, welcome aboard this Boeing 747 flight to Las Vegas. As we are about to depart, please ensure your seat belts are fastened securely. The crew will pass through the cabin to do a final safety check before departure. I hope you enjoy your flight with us today." She replaced the handset and made her way back to seat 2F.

"Mr. Balducci, may I check if your seat belt is

fastened properly?" Without an answer, she leaned forward over Bromise's lap, far more than was required, and let her hand trace the seat belt strap across his lap. As she leaned in, she could smell his cologne, Dolce & Gabbana, and teasingly allowed her hand to linger in his lap. She could see his manhood starting to pitch a tent in the front of his sweatpants. Suddenly she became thankful that the first class cabin was nearly empty for this flight.

Gently, she pulled the seat belt tighter, the motion of which made Bromise audibly gasp as his dick strained against the restraint, tight against it. "It seems you'll be nice and *safe* on the flight, Mr. Balducci." She smiled as she turned and walked back up the aircraft aisle and took her crew seat for take-off. As she strapped herself in, her gaze didn't leave Bromise's eyes. She devilishly, but purposely, hitched her skirt just a little too high to ensure he could see her stocking tops beneath her uniform skirt, and sat with her knees just slightly too wide apart.

Bromise smiled at her seduction and finally broke his gaze. He placed the headphones over his ears and shut his eyes. He reclined back as the iPhone spat "I Am A God" by Kanye West. They were now airborne and the iPhone played song after the other.

Bromise broke his doze when he heard Angel's voice over the PA again.

"Ladies and gentleman, we shall now be showing another in-flight movie. I will dim the cabin lights for your comfort." She dimmed the lights, then quickly went to the galley, poured peach Ciroc over ice, placed it on a tray, and made her way to seat 2F.

"Your adult beverage, Mr. Balducci?"

Without warning, Bromise's hand was on the back of her thigh and under her skirt. The touch of his strong fingers above her stocking top made her tremble. He looked up at her and let his fingers roam across the sheer fabric of her thong. He stroked her labia with his forefinger, and used his thumb to rub her clit. An involuntary moan left her lips. Her body was in flames for him. She bent over and tugged at his waistband while he finger-teased her soaked pussy. She could see his dick straining for release. He took a sip of his beverage.

"My favorite drink," he said and downed the glass. "How did you know?"

"Good guess." She shrugged and looked off.

"How good are you at sucking dick?" he asked blantantly.

"Well, I guess that depends on who you ask," she said in a hushed tone. "Or would you rather answer that question for yourself?" Angel smiled. She quickly looked around the First Class cabin. With the exception of a senior couple that was fast asleep, the area was completely empty.

Bromise raised his hips and she pulled down his sweatpants and boxers, and he popped an ice cube from his glass into her mouth. Kneeling by his seat, in the shadows of the aisle, she gently took his semi-erect manhood and brought her lips to its tip, allowing the ice cube to rub against the length of his shaft, slowly. She then guided his dick between her lips and, like a python feeding, slid her mouth over and around to envelope him entirely. When she kissed the base of it and back up, she gently worked her head up and down in his lap.

He moaned quietly. "Fuck, you're good."

She reached into her shirt pocket and revealed the gold package that he was all too familiar with. He stroked her lips with his thumb while she wrapped his dick with the Magnum XL. She peeled off her soaked thong and straddled him, and gradually slid down his pole. He gripped her ass cheeks and worked his hips, pounding hard with each solid thrust until he fired his load into the Magnum. He moaned quietly. Then suddenly, her body convulsed and gave in to waves of ecstasy as she creamed over the condom. They both benefitted from the quickie.

"Ohh wee, you have a tight pussy," he said, looking up at her and holding her waist.

"And you have an anaconda." She smiled and jumped off his lap. Her crewmember was hip to what was taking place and took over the PA while Angel made a trip to the bathroom.

"Ladies and gentleman, welcome to the McCarran International Airport in Las Vegas, Nevada, where it is sixty-nine degrees and sunny. We hope you've enjoyed your fight with us today."

With no intention on sticking around, Bromise grabbed his leather bomber and filed out of the plane with the other Coach passengers. He looked back one last time, and then joined the others along the air bridge. He immediately dialed Fats up and bragged briefly about his induction into the *Mile High Club*. Then after the call, the chances for such an opportunity suddenly struck him as rather odd. *"What in the fuck just happened?"*

As Bromise neared the exit, he noticed a white male driver holding up a sign that read. "Black

Mamba."

"I'm Black Mamba," he said to the white gentleman who was dressed in a black suit and sported the typical driver's hat.

"Nice to meet you, Mr. Black Mamba," he said and looked around him. "Any luggage, perhaps?"

"Not at all," he said and the driver led him outside to a black Lincoln Continental. "I got it," Bromise said after the driver went to open his door for him. Bromise pulled the handle and got inside the backseat, and the driver sat up front.

"The gentleman named Future asked that I call him once you've landed," the driver said and raised a cell phone. "Do you mind?"

"Go ahead," Bromise said and looked outside the window at his surroundings.

The driver dialed a seven-digit number and handed Bromise the cell as he pulled away from the curb.

"You've finally touch down, I take it," Future spoke from the other end.

"Yeah, I'm here, big homie," Bromise said. "All of this is kinda abrupt. What's going on, Joe?" Bromise slightly wondered what the tab was going to be for such an extravagant event. In the past, Future had been known to bill Convolution members after one of *his* spontaneous ideas: extravagant trips, parties, gifts, seasonal Club Suite tickets at the United Center, it didn't matter. If you participated as a guest, you're liable to be billed in one way or the other, later. Future had a knack of finding a way not to give anyone anything.

"As I'm sure you know, Kill-Kill is a free man,"

Future said proudly. "And we gotta do it big! All of this shit was spur of the moment."

"Yeah, I'm happy for Kill, for sure!" Bromise said.

"Hell yeah! The Convolution is here and damn near the whole neighborhood is flying down for the *I'm Finally Free* party that we're throwing at the Palms tonight," Future said. "No one has been still since we've got here. Everybody is all over the place. I know you want to freshen up and get dougie for the party. Your room is already reserved. Do ya thang and meet up with us tonight."

"Say no more," Bromise said and was about to end the call.

"Hey," Future spoke up. "Kill-Kill will be happy that you made it, Black Mamba."

"Fo' sho'. I look forward to seeing him," Bromise said. "One." He passed the cell back to the driver and sat back in his seat.

Bromise noticed a Bank of America coming up on the right.

"Stop at the BOA, quick," he said, and without hesitation the driver pulled right into the bank's parking lot.

"Give me a minute," Bromise said. He returned thirty minutes later with a small bag, after having withdrawn fifty bands. "Damn, I never went through so much red tape to get *my own* fuckin' cash," he thought out loud, in reference to how long it took to withdraw his money. The BOA in Chicago didn't take as long.

"What was that, sir?" the driver asked.

"Nothing, never mind. Just drive," Bromise said,

waving his hand forward.

They pulled up to Treasure Island Hotel and Casino and Bromise checked into the hotel. He couldn't care less about getting to his room right away. He had one thing on his mind. And when he walked out onto the casino's floor, he grinned ear to ear. He was like a clucker inside of the Carter. *Beam me up, Scottie!* He patiently scoped out all of the black jack tables, and chose whom he perceived to be the weakest dealer before sitting down.

Brisco had taught Bromise how to count cards years ago, and though it'd been a while since he played, he was still confident. His goal was to get under the other players' skin and throw them off balance.

He started off playing $100 a hand, then $200, then $500, and before long he was at $1,000 per hand and nine bands up. He was having a good old time while the other players frowned when he wasn't looking. And yet, he continued to strike gold every third hand. He'd switch it up and bet small twice in a row, and then huge the third time around. And the third time proved to be the charm for him at now twenty-one bands up.

When the waitress stopped by, he ordered everyone the total opposite of what he thought they'd drink and made jokes of it. He annoyed the fuck out of the other players, plus the dealer, pit boss, wait staff, and any unsuspecting spectators, and he couldn't get enough of it. After the manager came down to talk to him, he decided to call it quits and fold while he was ahead. In three hours, he left the casino floor with twice as much as what he came with.

He cashed out and walked over to the bar and ordered a tall Ciroc and cranberry. Then he walked out the casino's doors and hopped into the first taxi he saw on the strip.

"Where to, boss?" the cabby asked.

"Fashion Show Mall," he said and took a gulp of his drink.

Once he arrived, he took Fats' advice and tore the mall down, spending his entire winnings at just three stores.

After Bromise made it up to his suite, room service knocked on his door five minutes later. He had the munchies, and the aroma from the Porterhouse steak, candy yams, and southern-style cornbread he ordered, only influenced him to get rid of his temporary guest much sooner than later so he could smash. He tipped the guy thirty percent and rushed him out of the door. Bromise clicked the remote and the 60-inch flat screen powered up in full HD. He sat in front of it with his meal and watched the Bulls play the Thunder. Chicago was up eight points in the second quarter.

The suite's phone rang. He wiped his hands on a towel and picked it up. "Hello?" It was the driver from earlier.

"Just calling to let you know that I'm downstairs and waiting to drive you to the Palms whenever you're ready," he said.

"Good to know," Bromise said and hung it up. Instantly, he thought of Future. "Car service, too?" He shook his head. "Yup, I can see the bill now."

# CHAPTER 13
### *Social Media Pays Off*

B romise was eager to see what tonight had in store. He slid into a new pair of Polo boxers, Robin's jeans, and a Lux Trim Tee and stood in a fresh pair of Air Jordans 14, size ten. Then he slowly opened the box to the item he spent most of his winnings on. It was an elegant Cartier timepiece that was as blue as the sapphire safely nestled in its side. The case was platinum with baguette-cut diamonds, and it most definitely complemented his wrist after he put it on. He dabbed his neck and wrist with Jean Paul cologne and exited his suite.

Once he stepped outside, he paused to look up into the black sky. The stars were bright like diamonds, and the night breeze caressed his skin at sixty-five degrees. A big difference from two feet of snow with below zero temperatures. He took a few moments to take it all in.

It was 11:32 p.m. when Bromise made it to the party, and he was more than impressed with the setup. Future had rented out a two-story sky villa penthouse. It was a 9,000 square feet playground of luxury and fun! There had to be over three hundred people in attendance to celebrate Kill-Kill's freedom, and Bromise started recognizing familiar faces right away as people crowded around him, greeting him and taking photos.

Future had hired a local comedian from

# VENOM IN MY VEINZ

Chicago to host the event. As Bromise continued to make his rounds, meeting and greeting, the comedian shouted out people in the crowd. Bromise looked up and noticed Fontane standing on a loft, overlooking the entire open floor plan of the penthouse.

"Ohh shit!" The comedian spotted Bromise. "Chiraq to Sin City, the youngest nigga in charge is in the building," he said. "From the Wild Wild West, K-Town, it's Black Mamba bitchessssss!"

Fontane waved Bromise up to their section and pointed to a glass elevator on the first floor of the penthouse as the comedian kept it going.

"Now, hold ya panties, bitches, he's only here for one night. He can't fuck all you thots!" he quirked and laughter was heard over the blasting music. Bromise put forth a smile and waved, but really he could've done without the flamboyant introduction.

Bromise wasn't sure if there was a live deejay on deck or if it was Pandora, all he knew was that the entire penthouse was rocking and the songs were on point. "Happy" by Pharrell Williams played as Bromise boarded the glass elevator.

"This is some slick shit right here," he said as he began to elevate, looking down at the people more and more as he climbed to the second floor. Fontane was there to greet him along with three scantily clad ladies, as the glass door slid open.

"Man, Joe, I didn't even push a button to come up," Bromise said and extended his hand.

"That's because we control it from up here. Salutations," Fontane said and they shook-up. Then he handed him a tall glass filled to the rim. The Convolution greeted each other with the word

135

*Salutation.* To them it was a gesture of endearment and a term of respect.

"Salutations as well," Bromise reciprocated. "Is this my '*You Already Know*?'" he asked and put the glass to his lips.

"You already know," Fontane confirmed with a smile and watched as Bromise downed half the glass. Then one of the women spoke up, confused by their conversation.

"I know this is going to be a stupid question, but," she hesitated, "What's a 'you already know?'"

"There's no such thang as a stupid question, sexy." Bromise licked his lips and blazed his eyes upon hers. She quivered and became spellbound by their grip.

Fontane took the liberty of explaining. "You see, everybody who's anybody knows that Black Mamba's drink of choice is Ciroc, or preferably peach Ciroc. So when you see him in social settings and offer him a drink, well, *you already know* what he's drinking," he said in unison as the other two ladies joined in.

"Oh," she said, "that makes sense," still stuck in Bromise's gaze. He winked and her pussy moistened.

"Follow me." Fontane turned. "Everybody is enjoying themselves over this way." He led the way to another large open space that overlooked the party below. There were dozens of naked women in this section performing lap dances and working poles, as members of the Convolution tossed bundles of one-dollar bills into the air. The song "Working on the Pole" by Mac G dropped, and the females started twerking on cue.

Bromise saw Future sitting in one of the many

plush chairs, receiving a lap dance from two thick red-bones. He decided to go over to him then Freeway walked up.

"Salutations, Black." Freeway extended his hand.

"Salutations as well." Bromise met his hand and they shook-up. With no intentions of having small talk, Bromise motioned to go around when Freeway stiffened his elbow. "Future busy right now," he said.

Bromise turned his neck halfway and met his stare. His grip around Freeway's hand tightened, and then he looked over at Future, who was now receiving oral pleasure from the thick red-bones, with his head reclined.

Then Bromise loosened his grip and averted his eyes to Freeway. "Cool. I'll get at him later."

"No doubt," Freeway said and held onto his stare longer than usual before breaking eye contact and going a separate way.

Bromise took a deep breath. *In due time,* he thought and downed the rest of his drink when something caught his attention. The projected shadows on the interior walls of what looked to be a separate room reminded him of the ocean. On his way toward it, he stopped for another tall one and proceeded to walk up to the clear glass wall as the song "Make it Work" blared throughout the penthouse. His eyes widened with what he held in view. It was an all glass-enclosed Jacuzzi pool hanging off the side of the building, overlooking the Vegas strip. The pool was comfortably filled with twelve naked women and one male. That male was Kill-Kill.

A slight grin touched Bromise's lips as he looked on. "That has to be an experience," he said, and oddly enough, thoughts of his Mile High experience with Angel penetrated his tipsy mind as he downed another drink.

* * *

It was 3:37 a.m. when Angel looked at her Chanel watch. She had been at the *I'm Finally Free* party since 11pm. She was dressed to the nines, in mahogany stretch leather skinny pants, a short sleeve lace tee and six-inch stilettos. Her bone-straight red hair was no longer in a neat bun. Instead, it flowed over her shoulders. She was working it tonight.

Angel couldn't believe how she let Bromise get away without exchanging cell numbers, or at least without saying goodbye. But it wasn't the end of the world: she knew just where to find him, and her intentions were to pick up where they left off.

When he first arrived, she was able to keep up with his whereabouts from end to end of the penthouse. He was like a celebrity, and everybody knew him, all in his face and making it impossible for her to make her move. There was a moment when she thought she finally had him cornered, and out of nowhere another groupie would beat her to the punch. The last she saw of him, he and about ten other people were shooting dice in one of the secluded back rooms. She was determined to be the *one* going home with him tonight.

The atmosphere was still rocking with people and blastful music. At this point, everybody including herself was gone off of X, Kush, and Ciroc and it showed. The guys were way too touchy-feely for her taste, while she did the *Nae-Nae* on the dance floor.

They would say to her, "Please excuse my hands."

# VENOM IN MY VEINZ

Her reply, "Nigga, puhlease! You ain't Plies."

It wasn't that she didn't expect attention—it was *this* kind of attention she just couldn't get used to. Everywhere she went, men throughout the party were thirsty for a bad bitch like her. She could hardly blame them, though. With facial features like Lucy Liu and stacked with a body like CoCo from CoCo's World, how could she? She was only looking like a bag of Doritos filled with cheesy chips and everyone had the munchies, even the other females wanted a piece of what she had.

Angel got annoyed with the anonymous feels on her ass and left the dance floor. She decided to go to the ladies room and powder her nose. While there she took a few selfies in the mirror. Every angle seemed to catch her ass perfectly. *Squats paying off!* She was feeling herself, and it was only one man tonight that she wanted to feel her up.

As she was leaving the restroom, the blastful music abruptly stopped, and she heard fuck noises coming from one of the stalls. She followed the moans and groans until she came across a black spiked Louboutin heel on the floor underneath the partition. The constant pounding was causing the partition's screws to shake loose from the floor. The couple was going at it like wild animals, as one of them sounded like a wildebeest.

*Hold up, I know that heavy breathing,* she thought. She took her cell out of her purse and aimed it under the partition, and recorded twenty seconds of live footage before she left the restroom. Parts of her didn't want to see what she just saved to her memory card, but she knew that wasn't an option. Her curiosity was burning at her. She had to see it. Angel scanned her immediate area for a space that provided some privacy and not surprisingly, some guy approached her. *Shit!*

"Can I buy you a drink, ma?"

"Sure, gin and tonic will be fine," she agreed, only in hopes that his presence would stop the next dude's thirsty approach, and buy her enough time to look at the video. She followed this new dude to the bar and sat on a stool that he pulled out for her just as someone got up. "Thank you," she said with a fake smile. The bartender was busy pouring drinks and taking orders, so she figured dude would be a while. She hunched her shoulders and brought the cell close to her chest and tapped *play*. What she saw next only confirmed the identity of a man she knew. It was Future's fat belly ass butt-fucking Chasidy.

Embarrassed, she quickly put her cell away inside her purse, and suddenly heard the mentioning of Black Mamba's name. The chatter continued behind her, just over her shoulder. The music made it hard for her to make out every word said, but she was certain that the guys behind her were not friends of Bromise's. She played it off and gradually looked behind her. It was a guy she knew only as Remo, jacking off at the mouth. She watched as he continued to throw shade on Bromise's name.

*I swear I hate hatin' ass niggas*, she thought. The lights inside the penthouse became dimmer, with people still wall-to-wall. *But no sign of Bromise.* She continued to search from the bar, and spotted him outside on the terrace just as the baseline dropped from Beyonce's "Drunk in Love." She couldn't believe he was alone. It was nearly 4:00 a.m., and he hadn't left with another woman yet. This was her chance, and she was going to take it. *It would be impossible for him to resist all this.* She gave herself a quick pep talk and brushed dude off that finally came with her gin and tonic.

Bromise stood at the edge of the terrace with his forearms resting on the railings, facing the bright lights of the strip, when suddenly the hairs on the back of his neck stood. He heard footsteps behind him and quickly turned to it.

"Relax, Youngin," Kill-Kill said as he appeared only a few feet behind him. "It's only me. Why so jittery?"

Bromise collected his bearings. He didn't appreciate Kill-Kill's close proximity in the slightest bit. "I'm not jittery. I'm fast on my toes," he said. "And with all due respect, my name is Black Mamba . . . not Youngin." Bromise sized him up without breaking eye contact. Kill-Kill stood at 6-feet 6-inches tall, weighing 250 pounds of solid muscle. He was an intimidating figure to say the least.

"I heard," he said as an awkward silence took over. "Where's my manners?" He extended his hand. "Salutations."

"Salutations as well," Bromise said and they shook-up.

Kill-Kill tugged on his hand and brought him in close. "You've been eating real good," he said as he studied his diamond watch. Bromise pulled his hand back and straightened his posture. "I know this isn't the time or place, but you and I will continue this conversation," Kill-Kill said and left the terrace.

Bromise turned and reclaimed his position with a

view of the strip in front of him.

"Well, hello Mr. Balducci," Angel said as she stepped out onto the terrace. She instantly smelled the loud aroma of Kush that he blew into the breeze.

He slowly looked over his shoulder to capture a glimpse before he totally committed to fully turning around to face her. He was pleasantly surprised.

"Well, hey there, beautiful," he said, showing his perfect teeth.

"Beautiful?" She shifted her weight to one leg and shot him a glare. "Every dude in this shindig is saying the same thang to a bitch. Either that or '*Hey, can I buy you a drink, ma?*' I would expect more from you."

"Well, you know what they say," he replied, unrattled.

"No, but how about you tell me," she said, still keeping her distance.

"A million men can tell a woman she's beautiful, but the only time she'll listen is when it's said by a man that matters." Bromise turned to the sweeping view overlooking the strip and inhaled his trees.

Angel was smitten to say the least. She noticed that his Lux Trim Tee dangled on the terrace railing beside him. He had on a wife beater. She onced him over from behind, admiring his athletic build and his tricep muscles that resembled horseshoes. Then she joined him at the terrace's edge.

"Ohh la la," she said. "You have on Jean Paul. That's my favorite scent!"

"Thank you," he said. "I call it the naked man, because the bottle that it comes in resembles one."

She giggled while his cologne continued to caress her nose. *I love his scent!* she thought. And without asking, she returned the favor and took her hand to his back, stroking ever so softly. He had her open.

"How did you know to come here anyway? Aren't you supposed to be airborne somewhere in another state? Isn't that the life of a stewardess?" he asked, and his bedroom eyes descended upon her. The strip below was loud and the scene at their backs added to the clamor, but at the moment she became lost in his eyes. She wondered what he was thinking.

"It goes something like that," she said, batting her lashes. "Yesterday was actually my day off. I came in only because I had plans to attend this event. Frequent flier miles," she said with a chuckle.

"So you live in Chiraq?" he asked.

"Chicago, yes," she said, stroking his back. "Actually, a suburb near Chicago."

"I see," he said and hit the Kush.

"Wait," she said in shock. "So you don't like recognize me at all?"

"He took a second to look into her face. "Aside from the plane ride here? No, sorry, I don't."

"I'm one of your Facebook friends, and I follow you on Twitter too. That's how I knew about this event. Except, it wasn't called *I'm Finally Free* until that man you were just talking to was released from jail. I saw it on the news," she said. Bromise passed her the Garcia Vega. She hit it just barely to get a feel for it, and knew right off the bat it was some heavy shit.

"Yeah, I don't pay that social network shit no mind," he said, looking off into the view. "I think I made a page some six years ago, and probably been on there ten times total."

"Well, someone has been busy updating your pics and posting new statuses like everyday," she said. "Let me guess . . . Trent and BG?"

"Yeah, my 'lil guys are into that shit. So I let them have fun with it. But how'd you know?"

"Well, because their pages are public and they post the same exact stuff within seconds of the other. It's pretty obvious. Even your Instagram stays up to date," she said and slightly hit the Kush again.

"Oh, wow," he said nonchalantly. "I wasn't even aware that I had an Instagram." He chuckled.

She looked down at his timepiece. "That's a beautiful watch. Did you buy it here, in Vegas I mean?"

"As a matter of a fact, I did," he said and glanced at the sparkle.

"I kinda figured that. Seeing as though we flew in together, I would've noticed that much bling during our first encounter, and considering you didn't have any luggage—"

"You're very observant, I see." He cut her off.

"Well, yes, my job requires it." She smiled. "So, Mr. Balducci," she said as he turned to her. "May I call you Bromise?"

"Absolutely," he responded with his signature gaze. She caught a chill and suddenly felt like an elementary school girl standing next to her first crush ever. Without knowing what else to do, she put the blunt to her mouth and pulled. Almost instantaneously, she choked and coughed uncontrollably after hitting the Kush way too hard.

"Whoa!" he said and wrapped his muscular arms around her. "Gots to be more careful with that Irene, ma. Are you okay?" She could feel his strength and felt so secure in his arms, as he rubbed her back. Her mind was swept.

"That *Russian Roulette* you puffin' on ain't what you used to. It's killa because it forces you to respect it like any true killer would—"

She grabbed the back of his neck and kissed his soft lips. He matched her passion and their tongues met. Then Bromise took her by the waist and sat her on top of the terrace railing, ready to tear her apart.

"Not here," she said between breaths. "Meet me here." She slid a key-card with the name of a different hotel printed on its front into his shirt pocket.

He cracked a smile and took her by the waist again, but this time he gently lowered her to his chest level. Although her stilettos touched the ground, his persona had her mind so high in the clouds that she couldn't tell where the ground was.

After exchanging the longest provocative stare of her life, she went her way and he went his throughout the crowded elbow-to-elbow penthouse. For the moment, he pushed Angel to the rear of his mind and began to search high and low for Chasidy.

# CHAPTER 14

*Take One for the Squad*

A ngel was now resting sixty-two stories up, at the very top of Mandalay Bay, anxious. Just down the strip from the Palms. She was able to book The Island Penthouse Suite on the flight. Considering her occupation caused for extensive travel, she'd become a regular and this particular penthouse suite had become her absolute fav at the resort. Maybe because it put her up, up, and away from it all.

She sprawled out on the king-sized bed in the nude, bouncing her ass in the mirrored wall. All the while, envisioning how she was going to put her spell on Bromise as she anticipated his arrival. Maxwell crooned mildly from the Apple Hi Fi Stereo when Bromise walked through the door.

She sat up on her knees, and their eyes met from across the suite. *I knew he'd come,* she thought.

Her pussy tingled, watching him make his way toward her like she was the last bitch on earth. He had a swag that exuded confidence.

"This is a fly suite you got here, sexy," he said as he approached briskly. "Private elevator and all."

Before she could respond, he kissed her outright. Then he reached around her and grabbed her bare ass with a firm, strong hold. As fast as she could move, she opened his shirt, twisting each button with her thumb and third finger. When his shirt finally fell open, he stopped and studied her.

Bromise was mesmerized by what he saw. She pushed her shoulders back and flaunted her goods, enticing his touch. He began to caress her breasts, gently licking her nipples one by one. Then he moved his lips slowly down her flat stomach. His warm breathing made her body shiver. He planted light kisses above her pubic bone, and slipped two fingers inside her.

*Ahhh!* She moved into his hands rhythmically, for they followed her every move as she sat back on her feet, allowing his fingers to toy with her clit.

Then without warning, he freed her of his magnetic grip, and her lifeless body fell to the bed.

He smiled and said, "This ain't what you want," and finished undressing.

Angel loved the way his body looked. And the tattoos were everywhere, which was a plus. She was surprised to see that he was uncircumsised, and more shocked by how well hung he was. It was one thing to hear a bitch talk about it, but to see it for herself, words couldn't describe! She took a silk scrunchie from the nightstand and put her hair in a ponytail.

Bromise displayed a slight grin, as he knew what was to come.

She crawled over the bed to where he stood, and took him into her mouth. She felt the strength in his legs as he braced himself.

He shuddered as she licked his dick from root to tip. Her hot, swirling tongue stroked him crazy. He grabbed the bottom of her ponytail and twisted her hair around his fist until his knuckles met with the back her head, and she mouth-fucked him until he started squealing. She could've made him bust right then and there, but she wanted to feel him inside of her. Angel released his fully erect penis, and he covered it with a Magnum XL. She pulled him down to the bed and straddled him, surfboard style. Arching her back, she slowly came down his shaft until it completely disappeared inside of her. She gasped with delight, and the muscles in his body tensed up. She brought her ass back up slowly, giving him the perfect view of her round ass and repeated her movement over again, increasing her pace while he put his lubricated thumb up her ass. She pulled the scrunchie from her head and swung her hair around wildly.

As she leaned back and planted her hands in his chest, she twerked her pussy to and fro as he slapped her voluptuous ass cheeks. She went from moans to screams of pleasure as she came all over his condom. His size was nothing she was used to. Her pussy was sore. She slumped over with thoughts of cuddling and taking a nap with him, but that was clearly not part of the deal.

Bromise grabbed her by the waist and flipped her to her stomach.

"Give it to me, Bromise." She arched her back and pushed her ass in the air, and he pressed his large, hard dick into her wetness. She purred like a kitten. He put his hands under her breasts and grabbed them firmly.

She gasped and screamed, "Oh yes!" And moaned more as he gave deep penetration. She pushed back into him, taking in the remaining inches. "Fuck! Your dick is big!" she howled. "OMG! Fuck my ass, Bromise! I want you in my ass!" she shouted.

# VENOM IN MY VEINZ

Bromise pulled out. "Are you sure that's what you want?"

"Yessssss," she hissed. "Hurry!"

Bromise grabbed the baby oil from the bedside table. He squeezed a tiny bit onto his fingers and rubbed it all over her anus. She tensed at his touch.

"I'll be gentle," he whispered and coated the Magnum.

Angel, on her front, elevated her ass further into the air. He placed his tip at her entrance and pushed. Angel gasped with pleasure from the pressure. His *big head* disappeared inside her, as her ass slowly stretched around it with a super-tight squeeze. She shifted and settled as Bromise pulled out the tiniest bit, and pushed in again gently.

"Fuck," he whispered as he went deeper.

She tensed and arched her back more. He groaned. She moaned. The sensations to them both were incredible. He slid in further, almost to the hilt and rested there, leaning forward over her body to kiss along the nape of her neck. Her breathing was shallow. He slid out fast then back in hard.

"Ooogh . . . Ahhh," she moaned.

He reached down and massaged her clit. She pushed back against him and panted softly.

"That's it, china doll," he murmured and slid his middle finger into her sopping wet pussy. With every thrust in her ass, he matched it with finger circles on her clit. She started to buck like a horse as her left leg began to twitch.

"Yessss! Oh my God, oh my God, oh my God!" she yelled out in pleasurable pain. "Your dick is so fuckin' huge!"

Bromise continued to thrust. He traced her spine with his lips, whispering against her skin and sinking into her further. She grabbed the pillow and shoved her own face in it just in time to muffle loud screams of Bromise's name. She curled her fingers around the edge of the bed. Her booty rippled with each impactful movement of Bromise's hips.

Angel raised her sweaty face from the pillow. "Bromise!" she yelled and threw her head back, as he pounded his full length into her tight ass. She turned to lock eyes, biting her bottom lip. He dug deeper and released his nut into the condom. She continued to push back, squeezing her ass muscles, milking him until the last drop fell into the condom. Slowly, he withdrew, leaving a gaping hole. They both were spent as Bromise lay on his side beside her.

"Both of y'all. Get the fuck up!"

*What the fuck!* "Did you hear that?" Bromise looked up and around the dark room from the bed.

"I said get the fuck up!" Chasidy bellowed and briefly lit up the suite with a blast from a .38 revolver. Maxwell's twentieth song was cut short as the Apple Hi Fi Stereo rested in pieces across the hardwood floor.

Bromise bolted from the bed and turned on the lights. "How in the fuck did you get in here!" He was butt ass naked, confused, looking Chasidy square in her eyes.

Chasidy looked down at his swinging dick and replied, "Does it matter?"

Angel made a move for her clothes and Chasidy stopped her dead in her tracks.

"Ah-ah, bitch, don't you move," she uttered

through her teeth and stepped to the foot of the bed where Angel was frozen still in the most awkward position. With one of Angel's legs hiked on top of the tall bed and her other out beneath her, they stood eyes-to-eyes with only air and opportunity between them.

She could tell that Chasidy was crazy, so she didn't want to provoke her.

"Look down when I talk to you, you slanted eye thot!" Chasidy sputtered, and Angel did as she was told. That's when she noticed the black spiked Louboutin heels gracing Chasidy's feet.

"So you want my man, bitch!" Chasidy spat. "Do you want to be me too, you skank!" She took the gun and drove it into her stomach. Angel wailed and doubled-over in pain.

"Chasidy, this ain't necessary. It's not what it looks like. It's not her fault—" Bromise tried to explain as he was getting dressed, but he was preaching to the choir.

"No, see that's where you wrong, Bromise," Chasidy said, waving the gun. "This shit looks exactly like what the fuck it is. You see, let me paint this pretty little picture for you," she said and pointed the gun at Angel. "This groupie Asian 'ho right here has had you in her sights for a while now."

"Okay, where do I start?" Bromise said sarcastically. "First, fuck you mean? Second . . . who the fuck cares? And third . . . how the fuck do you know?" he questioned.

"Let's just say that this thot, *liked* one too many of your Instagram pics to go unnoticed," she said with a saucy grin. "Bitch, don't you know I police his page?" She chuckled.

"Chasidy," Bromise said with increased seriousness in his voice. "This shit better start making sense real fast."

"Bae, listen," Chasidy said in a softer tone. "It all began when I noticed the bitch stalkin' your social network pages, tagging you in her provocative pics and whatnot. I knew you hardly, if ever, check your Facebook, so I wasn't trippin' too hard on the bitch. Then I started seeing the bitch pop up at your social hangouts as of late. The bitch even fucked Future," she said and paused for a reaction.

Bromise crinkled his brows and glared down with a stare that frightened Angel. "Is that true?" he asked calmly. "Are you fuckin' Future?"

"Yes." She shook in fear.

Chasidy saw the jealousy in Bromise's face, and it silently broke her heart. "But if it's any consolation, playboy," she said, holding back her tears, "she only fucked the fat nigga just to get close to you. Sounds kinda familiar doesn't it?" she said, purposely aiming below the belt. "Fucking another nigga for you."

"Okay, just to make sure I understand you correctly." Bromise's ignored her pun. His patience was wearing thin as he ran his fingers through his fro. "You tracked this chick from Chiraq to Vegas, just to confirm your intuition?" He was still baffled.

She pressed her lips together. "Do you really not know who this bitch is?"

"Apparently not," he retorted.

"This 'ho comes from money," she said.

Angel's eyes became round circles.

"Again, what the *fuck* do that got to do with me?" Bromise was lost.

# VENOM IN MY VEINZ

"Cash, racks, stacks, bands, moolah, this bitch is about that life," she said. "Mmm hmm, she's the governor's daughter."

Angel cringed at Chasidy's words, and she walked toward her in haste. She grabbed Angel by the hair and peeled her face from the floor. "Do you see anything unusual over in that corner, thot?"

"No," she murmured.

"What in the hell?" Bromise said and removed a small blanket from a tall chest in the suite's corner. Underneath it was a camcorder with a night vision lens, aimed directly at the king-sized bed they just fucked on.

"Nooo!" Angel yelled. "What did you do!" she screamed.

"I did what any real bitch would . . . I caught your ass in a compromising situation," she said coldly. "Now, there's a hard and easy way to handle this shit. The choice is yours."

Angel listened attentively for what her choices were, as Bromise, just as curious, stood by waiting to hear what Chasidy had to say.

"You're about to make twenty-one in three days. And I just so happen to know your trust fund becomes available to you on that day. One hundred bands, and I want it all, you lil thot. Every last penny. Either that, or I will mail this video to the members of the Cabinet, your parents, grandparents, TMZ, your sorority sisters at Yale, Worldstar Hip Hop, and the list goes on, hun. It's your call."

"Hold the fuck up." Bromise broke his silence. "Are you saying this was a lick of yours the whole time, and you used me as bait?"

"You got your dick wet, nigga, so don't act like it was such a big inconvenience. Besides, aren't you the one who always preaches about *taking one for the squad*?" Chasidy said, not joking. "Well, here it is boss . . . practice what you preach."

"I can't believe this shit!" he responded. "Okay, answer me this . . . how did you know we were in this specific hotel, this particular suite, at this exact time?"

"One of my girls works at American Express. She's over customer retention. So she has access to client's platinum cards files, and this bitch's father is one of their platinum cardholders. The same platinum card she charged this extravagant suite to. Through my girl I was able to keep tabs via text alerts. And I was notified the minute she reserved this suite. After a while at the event, neither one of you could be found, and your hot dick ass . . ." She looked at Bromise and shrugged. "Just call it a hunch. And getting a key-card was easy."

"Well, at least get her off the floor," he said and kneeled down to pick Angel up from the hardwood. He placed her gently on the bed. Then he looked at Chasidy.

"Take one for the squad, huh?"

Chasidy shrugged her shoulders again and said, "What can you do?"

"Maaaaan, I tell ya, arguing with a woman is like getting arrested . . . Everything you say can and will be used against you." Bromise smiled.

Angel folded her arms and glared at Chasidy. "I bet you didn't know she's fucking Future too, did you? I have her on video!" she announced, convinced that she was dropping a bombshell.

# VENOM IN MY VEINZ

Bromise turned to Chasidy. "This is your deal. I'm out of here." Bromise left the suite, leaving Angel stunned.

Chasidy, with her fist still around the gun, turned to Angel and verbally bursted her bubble, "He already knows, thot." She raised the banger and aimed it at her head.

# CHAPTER 15
*To Crown Me King*

*February 15 (8:35 p.m.)*
*Chicago, IL*

Tonight was the night and Bromise's thoughts were in overdrive as he lay flat atop a professional massage table, butt naked. Chasidy, also in the nude, lotioned his body while massaging out the tension that he complained about in his back.

The two were inside a spacious bedroom of a north suburban bungalow. She had a john from her club rent it using an untraceable name. The joint was pretty classy with a $6,000 dollar a night price tag attached to it.

Many women claimed to know how to treat a man like a king, but over the years Chasidy had proven that she was one of the few that actually knew how. He'd never forget what Brisco said to him. "*Chasidy is the chosen one for you, grandson. Don't treat her like a bird and let her free. Treat her like she's the only companion you have in this world, and dammit, hold onto her tight.*"

He knew Chasidy better than anyone, and she knew him just the same. She knew that his grandpa, who was a calculus at heart, and strategist by default, had molded Bromise. He knew that her mother,

**156**

# VENOM IN MY VEINZ

Brooke, sold pussy, was a con artist by trade, and Brisco's secret mistress.

Bromise loved his grandma to death, but he was grateful that Brisco's ongoing love for Brooke, allowed Chasidy precious time around him as well. She got to know the real Brisco Balducci in the way that Bromise knew him, and Brisco in turn, planted valuable seeds into her.

"Turn over, boy," she said seductively.

"Boy?" He furrowed his brows. "I'm all man, baby. You know what it is," he said with a smile.

"I know. You *my* man," she uttered and ran her soft hands across his shaft and back again, stroking his limp meat into an errection. Her free hand cradled his loose balls.

"I was just thinking," Chasidy said.

"You always thinking, plotting . . ."

"No, I'm serious. Pussy is like a universal bank," she said, "that only true blue 'hos and real niggas know how to cash in on. Right now you got the black AMEX card, daddy...that titanium." Chasidy pointed to her bare pussy. "And because of that fact, you and I will never want for nothing in this world." At that moment, Chasidy bent at the waist and took his manhood fully into her mouth. She was sensual with her touch as she began to deep throat ten inches of stiff dick. When she got down to the base, she placed one ball at a time into her mouth until the both of them were snugged pleasurably between her jaws.

He could feel past her tonsils.

"Ah, yeah baby, suck that dick for daddy," he encouraged.

She began to make sucking noises. And the lining

of her wet mouth followed the length of his curve all the way up to the tip. She slowly rose from it to catch her breath, while a string of her saliva hung between her lips and the head of his dick. She smiled a devilish grin and spat on it, then started her stroke. She worked his dick more with her tongue ring and lips.

"That's it," Bromise moaned. "Just like that."

Then she incorporated the two-hand method and blew him to oblivion. She swallowed his kids and casually walked to the bottom of the table and continued his massage, starting with his feet.

He shut his eyes and the words *universal bank* resonated at the center of his mind. *It was true.* The Black Card that he had between Chasidy's dark brown, thick thighs had been worth far more than any penny he could ever scrape out of traps. It was her Universal Bank that was sure to crown him King.

Finally, he sat upright and got straight to it.

"Listen, the first part of the plan is the hardest, baby," he said calmly. "If we can get Future here, I can pull off the rest with no problem. You just have to believe that shit."

"I just can't understand why you won't clean that nigga out now, bae. Don't play with his raunchy ass. Three bricks ain't even a tip of that nigga's iceberg. So why would you take three now, then wait to get everything else that nigga got?" Chasidy asked with burning curiosity.

"Now what have I told you about that?" Bromise asked with a bit of a bite.

"I'm not questioning your judgment, bae. I mean I just don't understand why you won't just get him for everything when you kidnap his rotten ass, and leave him stankin' somewhere far from here. You already know where his main house is at."

"There's a right and a wrong way to do everything, love," he grabbed her waist, "We have to play this out precisely to the tee, in phases. That's the only way this plan will work. We've come too far. All you need to do is play your position, and right now your position requires you to get Future's ass here," he said bluntly.

"Oh, well, contrary to how *hard* you think it may be, getting him here will be the easy part, daddy," she said with a sexy and confident smile and reached for her iPhone.

As far as Bromise was concerned, the plan to lure Future to the north suburban bungalow was a 50/50 shake of the dice. No one had knowledge of this place aside from Chasidy and him. The john's liability became obsolete after Chasidy slit his throat and watched him bleed out in the driver seat of his Bentley Azure. So there were no worries as far as that was concerned. It was the fact of not having physical control that made it a gamble.

Bromise had been around Future nearly his entire life. He studied him. He learned from him. And in some ways he emulated him. Bromise knew his strengths, just like he knew his weaknesses. One of his flaws was that he would regularly detour to meet flings for a quick fuck, while in route to drop off product. That was a flaw that Bromise was banking on tonight. He knew firsthand just how tempting Chasidy's sex-game could be when it came to prioritizing errands for the day. And his bet was on Chasidy. All they had to do was text Future precisely five minutes apart. The plan wasn't totally foolproof, hardly any plan is. But not only was Bromise a fearless gambler, he was also a good listener. He remembered clearly what Brisco once said: *"Grandson, it's gonna be a time when preparation can only take you so far. After that, you have to take a few leaps out on fate."* And he intended on doing just that tonight.

"I'm sending the text now," he announced to Chasidy and activated his Nike wristwatch. The text consisted of a bogus address, his recoup-code and the numbers 1-0-8 for the number of ounces he was requesting, which amounted to three bricks.

Chasidy ran up to him and threw her tongue down his throat. He grabbed two handfuls of her fatty and matched her passion. Then she gently pushed off his chest, freeing herself from his grasp, and mouthed the words, "I love you."

"I love you, too," he responded with a smile. She grabbed his plush Polo robe from the high back chair and stepped behind him as he stood to his feet.

"Let me help you, daddy," she whispered into his ear and slowly draped the soft fabric over his broad shoulders. She looked up at him and smiled.

Minus a second thought, he reciprocated, took hold of her matching robe and covered her curvaceous temple as she scrolled down to the F's in her contact list. She tapped on Future's name.

A few months ago after he got comfortable with their *down-low* situationship, Future gave Chasidy an alert code to use whenever she had any spare time away from Bromise, in between their regular rendezvous dates. Tonight would be the first time she'd actually use it. She typed out her code and looked up at Bromise. The five-minute period was coming to an end.

"Now," he said and she pushed send as the alarm from his wristwatch sounded.

"Don't worry. He'll get back," Chasidy said flirtatiously, and batted her eyes at him. She went over to the closet and started to get dressed.

"You better hope your shit is as good as you think, heifer," he said playfully and put on his tee, followed by his boxers and socks.

"It keeps your ass around. Don't it?" she spent on her heels and placed her hand on her hip.

Looking at her from where he stood, he bit down on his bottom lip, fighting back the urge to toss her against the wall and have his way with her. She knew it too. *Damn she so fine when she does that.* Her skinny waist and protruding hips briefly spellbound him. He was able to see her backside through the stand alone, full-length mirror that was positioned behind her. She blew him a kiss from across the room then continued to get dressed. He couldn't front. Chasidy's sex-game was incomparable. His only prayer tonight was that Future felt the same.

Now fully dressed, they sat in a dim part of the bungalow in sheer silence.

Bromise had thoughts that he couldn't express to her, but reading men was how she made a living. When she stared into his eyes, his apprehension was clear.

"What's wrong, Bromise?" she asked in the sweetest tone.

"Nothing," he lied and displayed an awkward smile.

She slid from her position and kneeled between his legs, demanding his visual attention.

"You can talk to me about anything, you know that, bae." She ran her hands over his thighs.

"I'm taking a huge risk tonight, baby," he said, cutting through the shit. "If Future, for the very first time in his adult life chooses tonight to break his flawed routine, and decides to drop off the product to me first, I'd have no way of explaining why I wasn't at the location that I clearly left on his cell. It would arouse suspicion for sure, and he would see this setup a mile away. That would place me—us—in a position we can't afford. Not at this phase of the mission."

"Do you trust me, daddy?" she asked softly from her kneeling position.

"I trust my burner. And that's only when it's *my* finger on the trigger," he said solemnly. "Listen, it's not you that I don't trust—" The chiming of his iPhone #2 interrupted their verbal exchange. "Yes!" he said and waved his fist into the air and raised up from his seat.

"What is it?" Chasidy stood to her feet and took a couple of steps back.

"Exactly what we wanted," he said and walked his 5-feet 10-inch frame over to her, displaying the text. "Future just texted back the triple 0 code. That means he can't make the run right now. You see that?" He pointed to the triple 3 code that followed. "That means do not call until he calls me. This is proper formality and what we were hoping for." Bromise looked over at her iPhone. "Now all we need him to do is—" No sooner than he could complete his sentence, Chasidy's cell emitted a text alert. It was a text from Future that read: "Where am I cumming to?" With a huge smile, Chasidy quickly responded with the bungalow's street address. Seconds later he texted: OMW, an acronym for *On My Way.*

"I told you, daddy. Always bet on the Black Card, especially when it's mine," she boasted.

Bromise looked across the room at her as she stood in front of the mirror adjusting herself. Yet again, her beauty captivated him. It was all in his eyes. Chasidy filled out her metallic sequined gown to perfection. She wore it well, with knee-high metallic boots to match. She picked out the sexy little number during a trip to Berlin Fashion Week, courtesy of Future. Bromise encouraged her to bring it along for the lick.

He approached her from behind and took in her flirtatious scent before he reached around her and placed his chain around her neck. It was an eloquent 14k solid gold black rosary chain with black diamonds. She guided her luxurious black hair to one side, exposing the back of her slim neck, allowing him to attach the clasp.

"It's so beautiful, Bromise," she said, seeing it for the first time. She placed her hand over her chest where the rosary hung. He needed her to wear the jewelry tonight, for it made phase 3 of his mission possible.

Thirty-seven minutes had passed when Chasidy's iPhone chimed again. This time the ring tone was "Pour it Up" by Rihanna. Bromise nodded the go-ahead. She put forth her best smile and put the phone to her ear.

"Hey there, hun," she answered. "I bet you wasn't

expecting me to use your secret code, were you?" Chasidy laughed moderately and said, "Oh, you did . . . Hmm, I almost forgot how you can be the confident type. Well, since you have an answer for everything, big poppa, answer me this . . . Why is it taking you so long to get my dick here? Ain't no bitch in this city fuckin' with my kiwi." She chuckled and continued to flirt.

Bromise made his way to the window and peeked beyond the curtains.

"Okay. Well, where are you? . . . Oh! That's two blocks away?" she said and turned on her heels in Bromise's direction she was clearly caught off guard. "Um, um, yes," Chasidy stuttered. "You're in the right area. Keep coming straight, make a right, and then . . ." Chasidy tried to recall directions as she physically turned in circles. "Let me see, and a quick left. At that point you should see my Range parked out front. When you get here, park and come in. I got this whole place to myself, and I can't wait to show you the bedroom." She paused again, allowing Future to comment. And then she responded, "I look forward to it, hun. See you soon."

Chasidy concluded the call. She wore a blank stare. He knew that face. *Oh no!* Bromise raced over to her.

"Baby, what's wrong?" he asked and she didn't respond. He wrapped his arms around her neck and rested his cheekbone against her temple. "Baby, I need for you to really listen to me right now," he said in a semi-whisper. "We've been in this position before. Don't freeze up on me now.

"I just don't want to get shot again," she sniveled.

"Baby." He took her face into his hands. "You know I got you, just trust in me as I trust in you." When he said that, he could feel the tension in her body leave. She exhaled and was for the moment, at ease.

He grabbed his Gucci backpack from the floor and Chasidy followed him to the side patio door right off the gourmet kitchen. After they made it to the sliding door, he turned to her and she looked deep into his eyes when she spoke.

"Bromise, give me forty-five minutes. Not forty-seven or forty-eight. Bae, just forty-five minutes, and then you come in here and handle your biz," she said and kissed his lips. "And don't shoot me this time."

Bromise slipped out of the side door and watched from a safe distance.

Future drove up in his big body white-on-white BMW 760 Li. Bromise sat patiently until he exited his whip. When Future entered the bungalow, he set his wristwatch for forty-five minutes.

# CHAPTER 16
*My First Move is My Best Move*
*PHASE I*

From the window, Bromise watched as Chasidy took Future by the hand and led him into the master suite. Bromise unzipped his Gucci backpack and removed the items he brought along. First he slid into an insulated coverall suit, a ski mask equipped with a Voxal Voice Changer built right in, throwaway shoes, black leather gloves, a dreadlock wig, and his Beretta PX4 semi-auto. Everything he needed. His Nike wristwatch was now at two minutes and counting down. His adrenaline was pumping.

Bromise opened the patio door and stepped inside. He expected this to be short and sweet, hence the reason for the one story bungalow. The house lights were low. He made his way through the gourmet kitchen and noticed Future's burner on the counter. He couldn't help but smile and be proud at the same time, for he knew that it was Chasidy's doing. After getting shot during their last lick, she learned quickly how to take certain precautions that would turn an excellent set-up, into a *perfect* set-up. Rule one: Remove all weapons from the robbery victim to avoid any unscripted complications.

Bromise shoved the .357 Magnum into his waistband and headed for the master suite, his Beretta aimed and ready. *Man I love this shit!* He was beginning to feel the rush as he walked over garments

166

leading up to the bedroom's closed door. He placed his ear to it and heard music playing mildly from the Bose stereo inside. Quietly, he opened the door and immediately had Future's wide bare back in front of him. He sat on the edge of the bed, smoking Kush with his head elevated.

Bromise darted his eyes around the room for a sign of Chasidy before realizing she was on her knees in front of Future. He slowly entered with his burner aimed at Future's head, making short steps around the massive bed and continued in stealth. Future's eyes were apparently closed behind his dark shaded Louis frames. Chasidy was so caught up in giving head that she didn't even notice that Bromise had entered the room.

He retracted his arm and with medium force, hit Chasidy over the head with the burner. She immediately dropped to the floor. Future was in utter shock when his face met with the tip of the Beretta.

"What the hell is this, man? I don't want no trouble!" Future was scared shitless. He dropped his blunt in his lap.

Bromise squeezed off two slugs into the mattress, inches away from Future's testicles, and slapped the glasses off his face.

"Stop di bumbaclot cryin' bwoy, eh!" Bromise yelled into the Voxal voice box with a Jamaican accent. The voice scrambler distorted his voice perfectly. He felt like a character straight out of the movie, *Shottas*. He was on charge, and Future wet the bed and floor with his urine. He looked down at himself and back up again with the sad clown expression. He was humiliated.

"Look, mister, I think I can satisfy you," he said, pointing his trembling finger toward a corner window. "I have exactly 108 ounces of dope and $30k cash money right outside that window. You can have it all. My whip is parked right out front, and it's all in there. It can be all yours, Mister. Just let me go," he pleaded.

While he rambled, Bromise gave him a once-over and was pleased with what he saw. As luck would have it, along with his iced-out rings and watch, he had on his favorite, most expensive chain as well. It was a 36-inch platinum chain that had a one-carat diamond embedded within each link. But it was the medallion that set it off! Valued at $197k, it was a platinum fist displaying the middle finger with the words "Fuck Haters" at the bottom, sprinkled in yellow and white diamonds. Even a few rubies were thrown in for good measure. *I gotta have that!* Bromise thought.

"Suh yuh 'ave strong money, eh? Tek off your bling cargo an' put it here," Bromise demanded and tossed a cotton bag onto the bed near him.

"Yes, anything, sir. Just take it all. Please don't kill me for it," Future cried and complied.

"An your whore, too. Get up, whore, an bruk yourself!" Bromise barked, but Chasidy wasn't moving. He looked down at her to get a closer look. She was unconscious. *Fuck! I didn't even hit her that hard.*

"I said get up, yuh likkle bloodclot whore!" He gently kicked the sole of her bare foot. Still, she didn't budge. "Well, get har up!" he barked.

Future rushed to the floor and placed her head in his arms. "Wake up, wake up," he said sternly and shook her until her eyes opened.

168

"Tie har to di chair now!" Bromise ordered and tossed a rope on the floor. He kept the burner trained on him and pulled from his pocket a throwaway cell phone. He dialed Freeway's cell number. In advance, Bromise had placed Freeway's cell in the glove compartment of his Lexus LS 460, which was currently parked in the garage of his Blue Island foreclosure home. Jay managed to lift the cell from Freeway's gym bag hours prior, while he was busy doing cardio at Hoops Athletics. When Freeway's voicemail answered, he set the second part of phase one in motion.

"Di main target, Black Mamba isn't here." Bromise maintained his Jamaican lingo and watched as Future tied Chasidy to a chair. "But deh is er half eediat here, a stoosh mon. Im fava a dinna pig with a wanga gut I evva seen," he quipped. "An a dutty slut with a fat batty an she a browning. Should I kill dem both?" Bromise paused, as if he was heeding an order.

"Wah yuh a fuckboy now, eh!" he erupted with anger and raised the Beretta from Future's chest to his face. Chasidy's eyes widened, and Future's knees buckled. He inadvertently fell onto the bed, pissing himself again. "Duh yuh move! Hands up!" Future threw his hands above his head.

Bromise stepped outside the room and shut the door behind him to continue the phone conversation in *private*, although he was sure Future could hear every word.

"Fuck yuh mean renegotiate contract, deh bwoy! Ah nah mi fault target wers nah here! Freeway, dat wers nah di bumbaclot—" Bromise cut his words short and stormed back into the room when Future was on his way out the window attempting to escape. He ran over and yanked him vigorously by the back of his neck, and Future crashed against the hardwood floor.

"Yuh an Black Mamba should 'ave been ded long time ago an gaan to bloodfire! Yuh two bloodclots are fuckin' wid mi money now, eh!" Bromise fumed and grabbed him up from the floor, and drove him against the wall with his forearm pressing his throat.

"What's your beef with me, sir?" Future asked politely while gasping for air.

"Don't flatta yourself, mon. Mi assignment wers to murda main target. Yuh and di fatty batty tramp are just inna di wrang place at di wrang time," Bromise said.

Having communicated with Jamaican Bill and his Rasta team for years, Future understood exactly what Bromise was saying. Bromise looked over at Chasidy. She was awake but still groggy. He released the pressure from Future's neck and took a few steps backward.

"I'm about business, and in this biz I can use a man like you. If you lemme go I would give you Black Mamba's head on a platinum platter, and his position on my team," Future said with conviction, meaning every word.

Bromise became instantly livid! He was currently a mere stranger committing this act against him. Future, on the other hand, was more than willing to set Bromise out when he'd been nothing but loyal to him since before he could remember. He wanted to kill him right then and there, and say *to hell* with his mission. So he wrapped his leather-covered finger around the trigger, and Chasidy broke her silence.

# VENOM IN MY VEINZ

"Mister, no!" she screamed from the chair. "Please, you don't want to do this. Just take what you want and leave us. Please, sir," she cried. Chasidy was a very good actor, but Bromise could tell that this wasn't an act. She was blessed with a deep intuition that he'd come to know. She was inside his head. She was right. They'd come too far.

Bromise came back down to reality and placed his finger under the trigger-guard. He charged at Future and hit him across the face with his burner. Future fell to the floor. Then he straddled him and struck him two more times before jumping to his feet.

"Let's guh now!" he said through his teeth, ordering Future to get up. He stood and Bromise shoved him in his back toward the exit, walking closely behind him. Before they left the room, he shot a glance at Chasidy's disoriented face. She was still out of it from the blow to the head, but he didn't have time to show sympathy. He had to stay the course.

"Please, sir, don't kill him!" Chasidy screamed one last time before they left the bungalow.

After Future exposed the money and three bricks, Bromise forced him into the BMW's trunk and shut it closed. He walked around and got inside the cabin, pushed the start button, and was off into the night.

About two miles north of his Blue Island home, a clique of car thieves hung out. Which was a small, yet important detail of phase one. He made it to the neighborhood and parked the flashy vehicle in the middle of the car thieves' block, and exited, leaving all doors unlocked with the keys in the ignition.

He walked near the trunk of the car with his Gucci bag filled with money and jewels in one hand, and

Future's cell phone in his other. He put it to his ear and started talking loud enough so that Future could hear from his crammed position.

"Ole bwoy Freeway is pon fuckery, mon. Yuh get er hole of di big shot an fix it, negga. Or mi breddas an I will murda yuh an your family. Yu have mi Kentucky numba. I will be deh afta tomorrow."

Bromise took a few steps to lean inside the driver window and pushed the trunk's lock-release. He quickly replaced his cell phone with the girth of Future's .357, and raised the hood. Future poked his head out in time to catch three blows to the head and face before he was out cold. Then he shut the trunk and kept it moving on foot. Although, he knew it wouldn't be long before Future woke up, he was confident that his whip wouldn't be around long enough for someone to hear his desperate pleas for help.

From there, Bromise crept into an alleyway and peeled off his coverall suit and the rest of the stuff that he brought along, and threw it in the garbage bin. His gloves remained on as he replaced his shoes. He was just about to smash Future's cell phone into pieces when it rang. Without bothering to screen the call, he put the cell to his ear.

"Let's do this, Future," were the words he heard coming from the other end.

In utter shock, his head reared back. He couldn't believe it. Bromise slung the cell phone as far and as long as it would go before it smashed to the ground in pieces.

"What the fuck do my uncle Cigar have to do with Future after being MIA for all these years?" he uttered, and like a ghost, he blended with the night.

# CHAPTER 17
*Positioning Pawns*
*PHASE II*

*12:32 a.m.*

After Bromise parked Future's 760Li, he went unnoticed through gangways and side streets. Chasidy's well-being was at the forefront of his mind. Both his thoughts and legs seemed to be in a race, as he sprinted through the darkness. And before long, he was at the front door of his Blue Island home.

Once he made it to the second floor, he peeled off his clothes and hopped into the shower. There, he spent about thirty minutes going over phase II in his head. The hot water was so soothing he didn't want to get out, but he had a schedule to adhere to.

He dried off and slid into fresh clothes, and it wasn't long before he was inside the kitchen and at the door that led to the garage. He deactivated the alarm to his Lexus LS 460 and sat on the bamboo leather seat. The vehicle wasn't a part of his whip-game lineup. He'd purchased the vehicle from his grandpa's oldest friend. He'd never been seen driving it before. It was brand new, paper tags and factory everything. It had a limo tint on every window except the windshield. He opened the glove compartment. Freeway's cell phone was still there safe and sound. Then he called, Chasidy.

"Wudup baby, you good?" he asked through his iPhone.

"Yeah, Porsha made it to the bungalow soon after

y'all left. I'm with her now. I just got off the line with Ayana, too. Her sister's boyfriend just skipped out on her and their kids, and she's stressin' big time about it. But yes, I'm cool," she said in a low-spirited tone.

"Are you sure? 'Cause you sound like—"

"Yes, I'm sure, Bromise," she said with a bite. "Besides having a golf ball-sized knot on my head and a splitting headache, yeah I'm good."

"Look, I don't have time for this right now. Are you packed and ready?" he asked impatiently.

"Yes, I'm packed and ready. Come get me." She ended the call.

It was a little before two in the morning when Chasidy and Bromise pulled up in front of Ayana's half duplex. Ayana was a stripper from Atlanta that Bromise met through Chasidy. She brought her back with her after a visit to Club Blue Flame, and she'd been a featured dancer at Reflections ever since.

Ayana was as fine as ever too. Bromise hooked her up with his main man, Fats, when she first arrived to Chicago a couple of years back. The two hit it off instantly and had been together since. They'd just had a baby boy three months ago, and their relationship was strong.

Bromise genuinely liked Ayana's flava, but above all, he trusted her loyalty enough to proposition her with an integral part in his mission.

She came running to the Lexus shortly after Chasidy summoned her from the car's speaker phone. "Wussup up, girl!" she said energetic-like. She bent down into the passenger window and spotted Bromise on the driver side. "Wussup to you too, Black Mamba."

# VENOM IN MY VEINZ

"Wudup, Ayana."

"I need you to do me a $5,000 favor," Chasidy said, getting straight down to business.

"Wussup, boo-boo?" Ayana asked, all ears.

"I need you to drop something off for me, but you can't tell Fats, or anybody else for that matter. I'll give you $2,500 now to make sure that this safe gets to where it needs to go. And $2,500 when I'm sure you did it." Chasidy patted a small Sentry safe that sat on her lap.

"Boo-boo, now you know I don't mind doing whateva, wheneva for you, but you know I don't like lying to my man," Ayana said in a way that revealed how much she hated to say *no* to Chasidy.

Bromise admired that about her, and even more he admired her loyalty to Fats. She didn't say anything that he didn't expect her to say. Unbeknownst to the both of them, Ayana's answer was a mere test that she passed with flying colors. Now it was time for Bromise to step in and make her understand the seriousness of her possible refusal.

"Look," he said, "that's my main man you're talking about. You know that I would never do anything to cause him harm. Furthermore, I'd never stand for you deceiving him either, much less put you in a position where you'd have to. Plus, there's no lying involved. Only silence and secrecy. You're simply withholding some crucial info that will undoubtedly harm him more if you told him, or if you refused to participate at all. Trust me when I tell you, Ayana, what we're asking you to partake in, and the conditions involved, is for the betterment of us all.

"To be frank with you," he said with sternness,

"you've already heard too much to say no. So fuck paying you now and later. I'ma give you the full $5,000 now, but you must listen to me closely, Ayana. If I can't find you for whatever reason, I'll slump everyone that I think you may have talked to. That means if I get wind of you talking to a bum on the streets about this, I'm taking out homeless shelters to make sure I get the right ass. If I hear about you catering to any of the city's gossip lines, I'm tearing down the whole chat room.

"I hate to be harsh with my words, but you need to understand how serious this shit is. I would prefer to see you collect good and enjoy your profits, 'cause it's going to be more jobs and much more money where this came from. I'd rather know beyond any doubt that I can trust you to keep a secret, than to see you die' cause your loose lips sunk the ship. Make sense?" he asked.

She shifted her weight to her other leg and nodded.

"Can you handle this, Ayana?" Chasidy asked in a way that was meant to smooth over the concrete that Bromise just laid down.

Ayana squatted and looked up at Chasidy. "Well, I trust *you*, and I know that Fats trusts you with his life," she said, looking over at Bromise. "So if it's in his and our baby's best interest, then I guess it's all right. I'll take care of that for you, boo-boo." She took her finger and outlined the side of Chasidy's sad face. "Damn, mami, what happened to the side of your head?" She noticed the bruised and swollen knot near Chasidy's hairline.

"I ran into a door," she said, glancing at Bromise

176

with a frown. "Anyway, girl, how's the baby?"

"He's asleep right now, but—"

"Ayana . . ." Bromise said, inviting himself back into their conversation. He didn't interject because he didn't care to hear about her kid. That was his mans' baby too. But right now just wasn't the time. "You'll get a thousand dollars a week, every week, for as long as you don't recall tonight's conversation between us. That's $4,000 a month, $48,000 a year, just to catch amnesia when this car pulls away from the curb."

According to one of Brisco's valuable lessons, at times, the most effective way to coax a *yes* out of someone is to leave them with no room to say *no*. He'd say, *"It's simple, grandson. Sometimes the best and easiest way to get a yes is to make a person fear what saying no might mean for them and their loved ones, and at the same time give that person a good reason to look forward to the benefits of saying yes."*

Bromise locked onto Ayana's eyes. "This goes for us too, Ayana. When we pull away from this curb in the next minute or so, the three of us will come down with a sudden case of amnesia. I won't recall why I'm giving you a yearly salary, and you won't recall why you're getting it. All I need to know is that I can depend on you when I need to, and you can be sure that you can call on me for anything," he said.

Chasidy handed her the safe through the window.

Ayana smiled, leaned into the window, and kissed Chasidy on the cheek. And to Bromise's surprise, she ran around to his side and repeated the same kind gesture.

He counted out five bands and handed it to her. "Here," he uttered and passed her a single piece of paper. "There's a phone number written on it. Call it and tell Remo that Freeway told you to call. Tell him that Freeway said code 55-55 and to pick up a package out of the garbage dumpster at the Shell gas station on Van Buren Street. You don't have to say nothing else or do anything other than what I'm telling you right now. Don't say your name, nor meet him anywhere. Just call from the gas station's pay phone and drop the safe into the garbage dumpster, and walk away. This will be the easiest five bands you've ever made," he said.

"Okay, I understand," she said, wearing her innocent smile.

"I like you, Ayana," he said honestly. "The last thing I want to do is hurt you . . . but it's still on the list."

Chasidy gave him a slight nudge as if to say, *"Lay off some, bae. She gets the point."*

He took heed and said, "Do you know where the safe is at the club?"

"Un-uh," Ayana uttered with a confused expression.

"Reflections' downstairs office has a stripper pole built into the floor. The stage is really a cover for the safe. If you turn the pole, it will twist up and off the floor like a screw. Once you do that, you'll be able to see the combination knob where the pole was." Ayana listened attentively to Bromise. "The combination is 24-25-24. There's a little over thirty-three bands inside. After you handle this small job, I want you to go to Reflections, get the money, and take a trip to ATL. Go spend some time with your family for a while. When you get there call me, but don't tell anyone where you're going, besides Fats. Oh, and tell your sister to hold her head up. If dude was that bogus to leave her and her lil ones high and dry like that, then fuck him. He didn't deserve her anyway."

"Are you serious?" Ayana asked and covered her mouth with her hand. Bromise didn't bother to answer. Instead, Chasidy handed her a spare key to the club.

"Are you really serious, Black Mamba?" she asked again, shocked and equally touched.

"Stay focused on your task at hand, so you can get home to your fam'," was all he said and drove the Lexus away from the curb. Bromise wasn't just being nice to Ayana. He had million dollar goals to reach, and she was now a pawn that he just placed on the face of his chessboard.

Inside the Sentry safe that Chasidy handed her was a blue drop off bag that they used regularly amongst the Convolution members. It was used only when either of them needed to drop off packages to the other when it wasn't safe to meet face-to-face, or talk over the phone.

Code 55-55 was the code they would use when situations were sticky, and when either of them needed a package picked up immediately. Both the blue bag and the code were designed to coincide.

Leaving the safe inside of dumpsters was also routine. The only people that knew about the code and their drop off habits were the Convolution members and their trusted lieutenants. Remo was Freeway's lieutenant. Bromise wasn't only sure that Remo was aware of their code of ethics, but that he also knew how to handle the call once Ayana made it. Bromise was confident that Remo would bite the bait.

# RUMONT TEKAY

In a code 55-55 situation, the protocol was simple. Act immediately and expect that all phone lines are hot. Don't use them unless later authorized. The blue bag contained Future's three bricks of dope, thirty bands, his jewels, the chain that Chasidy was wearing, and a note, which were all locked inside of the Sentry safe. They used these small safes because they were lightweight, mobile, fire proof, and its security locks could be easily broken into. Which was essential, considering they opted to never send keys along. The note inside the blue drop off bag read:

*It's not safe to talk or meet face-to-face. Drop the product off to Black Mamba, and tell him you're going to Kentucky. The money is yours. Meet me at the church at 3 a.m. for further details.*

Over the years, Fats had become the trusted lieutenant of Bromise's squad. He viewed him as the brother he never had, and he was also Bromise's surrogate. Whenever Remo couldn't find him, he'd report straight to Fats. So there's no doubt that Remo would take the message and three bricks to Fats. Bromise was purposely laying low for that reason.

He currently had Freeway's cell phone in his lap while he and Chasidy sped up Ashland Avenue, better known as Little Italy on the west side of Chiraq. The inside of the Lexus was quiet. Bromise was in deep thought when he felt Chasidy's fleeting glance.

"What's on your mind, baby?" he asked, stealing a good look at the side of her face before he turned back to the road. Even with the swollen bruise she was beautiful.

"You know, that was a real nice thing you did back there," she said, pointing her thumb behind her.

# VENOM IN MY VEINZ

"Making it possible for Ayana to go see her sister and the rest of her family. It's been a whole year since she's seen them last, and they haven't even laid their eyes on her newborn yet. I know her mama gon' be thrilled! Aw, Ayana misses them so much, too," Chasidy said and massaged the back of his fro.

"Yeah, well, I didn't do it to be nice," he voiced, remaining detached from his feelings.

She sucked her teeth and said, "Bromise, being nice from time-to-time isn't a weakness, and it don't make you soft. It's okay to have a heart, do good deeds, and it's okay to smile on the inside sometimes too, bae." She planted her hand on his thigh, as he caressed the heated wood grain steering wheel into a sleek left turn.

"I'll smile inside when I've conquered my mission in full. That's when I'll be happy," he said honestly, and joined her hand with his, interlacing their fingers.

"Well, I know of something that'll make you smile," she said.

"And what's that?" He whipped the Lexus into the church's empty parking lot and backed up into a stall. He shut off the headlights and turned to face her. "I'm waiting . . ."

"Bromise . . ." She gripped his hand then hesitated.

"What's wrong, baby?" he asked softly and stared into her hazelicious brown eyes.

"I'm pregnant," Chasidy said in a gentle tone.

*What? What the hell you just say!* were his immediate thoughts. Bromise tried to maintain his regular face, but he no longer knew what that felt like. He wanted badly to speak, but for once he was at a loss for words. For once he—

"I'm fuckin' with you, daddy!" She laughed and clapped her hands, completely amused by her own joke. "You should've seen the look on your face. Out of all the bullshit you've been through, you let a baby scare your ass!" She burst into more laughter, looking at him through watery eyes from laughing so hard.

"That shit just tickles you, right!" He wanted to be upset, but he honestly didn't know how to react. Then out of nowhere a smile spread across his face. He had to admit, as cruel as it may have been, she got him.

"Hell yeah, it's funny!" She giggled and calmed down her moment of hysteria. "I told you I could make you smile." She pointed to his lips. "Now you know better than to doubt me."

"You ain't shit. You know that, right?" he said, half-joking.

"I just wanted to see you smile. You're always so serious about this street shit that you forget to enjoy life. You're too young for that," Chasidy said sincerely. "With you it's always biz, biz, biz, and grind, grind, grind. I don't know if you love the game more than you love yourself, or did you forget that you're a man who needs time to relax like everyone else? Seriously, Bromise, you need to take it easy some. We're moving too fast," she said, while massaging his fro.

"Now ain't that 'bout a bitch. I know you're not talking that shit right now," he stated with a shocked look on his face. "You're runnin' this script like the game don't mean everything to you."

"With time, things change though, Bromise."

"Whatever." He wasn't willing to buy into

whatever new shit she was trying to sell. "Did you talk to your friend about the phone records I need?"

"See what I mean, it's always business with you." Chasidy was clearly agitated that he'd just robbed her of her emotional *talk-time*.

"Are you going to sit there and go on with the gibberish, or answer my question?" he asked sternly.

He didn't disagree with her entirely. Sure, he was jaded, living life in the fastest lane. The stress was starting to show on his face, and the sleepless nights were taxing his body. But mashing forward was a learned behavior, and he intended to proceed in the wake of that.

"She said that she'd mail the phone records to the P.O. Box the minute she gets her hands on them," Chasidy answered submissively.

"Well, I need for her to check on this number right here." Bromise memorized the number that Future had been obviously using to contact his uncle Cigar. He reached for a pen and paper and jotted down the number. "Here. I want to know the name and address of the person that this number is registered to." He handed her the paper and watched as she secured it in her Valentino handbag.

"C'mere, I've got something for you to see," Bromise said, and they exited the Lexus and used his key to enter the empty church.

Chasidy had no clue that she was currently standing inside of the Convolution's meeting place, so she was a bit thrown off.

"What the fuck are you doing with church keys?" Chasidy wore a curious frown.

"You own it, so why wouldn't I have my own set

of keys?" he teased. She spun around on the balls of her feet, studying the spiritual artifacts.

"Umm, I own it? Can you please explain yourself?" She placed her hand on her hip.

Before he committed to the details, he looked at his watch to make sure he had the time to do so. It was 2:25 a.m., which meant they had twenty-five minutes before Remo showed up, as directed in the note.

"You know Reverend Staples, right?" he asked her.

"Are you talking about the preacher that made all of that noise about helping the community, and then turned around and got busted with two thousand pounds of dope and child pornography in his church van?" she asked.

"Yeah, that's him."

"Didn't he just get killed last week?" Chasidy placed her index finger on her chin.

"Yeah, he did."

"I heard he got shot right after Jamaican Bill posted his—" She cut herself short before saying the word *"bail,"* as it dawned on her. "Is this *his* church? Bromise, you can't be going around killin' preachers!" She was suddenly acting brand new again, like she didn't know what *they* did for a living.

"Listen," he said. "The pornography was his, but the dope belonged to Jamaican Bill. The Reverend was an international mule for him, and had been for years. Jamaican Bill got word through inside intel that the Rev was looking to cut a deal with the government. So he had to be silenced. For Jamaican Bill to involve his mob was to implicate himself, so he called on me for the favor. And not soon after, I met the Rev in his study. You know how I do," he said, thinking back. "Don't get it twisted, the Rev was no angel. He was caught two other times before with kid pornography, and with videos of him fucking kids in other cities, *before* he relocated here with a whole new identity," he explained. "Either way he was a dead man. Whether it happened on the streets or in the pen, he was a goner for sure. 'Cause them boys up state would've tore his ass apart, literally." Bromise chuckled. "Seriously though, he even thanked me for coming myself and getting it over with quickly. He only had one request, and that was to allow him five more minutes of breath, so that he could finish signing over the church to his wife before he passed.

"He and Sister Staples both knew my grandpa really well, so I grew up being around them. When she gained knowledge that the church was hers free and clear, ironically enough she called on me for a little help. You know, she's pretty damn old, without family. She didn't have the strength to run and maintain it. So she offered to sell the church to me under the condition that she'd be allowed to dust and clean the statues and pews every week until she joined her husband. So I took the deal and had her put it in your name."

"Bromise, the lady died just two days ago. Her funeral is tomorrow in her home state."

"I know . . ."

"Did you send that old lady to her grave, too?" Chasidy asked, expecting to hear the worst.

"What? No! Hell no!" He raised his palms chest level. "Damn, baby, how could you possibly think that I'd do something like that? I'm a killer, but I'm not a monster," he said, taking a few steps back.

"Wow." Chasidy spun around again, taking it all in. She reached her fingers between the buttons on his Polo button-up, and began to caress his chest. "I didn't know." She kissed his lips and asked, "So what do you plan to do with it?"

"Well, I was thinking about what you said in the whip on the way over. You know, about how it's good to do good deeds and whatnot," he said, feeling the calming effects of her touch.

"And?" she pressed.

"And I was thinking that we could expand this place and turn it into a rec center that the neighborhood kids could feel safe to play in, and call their own. You know, like a Boys & Girls Club. God knows this neighborhood could use it."

Bromise expected an instant response, but she didn't say a word. He rested his chin on the top of her head and sighed heavily. Then he heard snivels as she pulled away and looked up at him with the brightest sparkle in her eyes. He crossed his hands in front of him, resting them on the handle of Future's .357. She stood there, stacked like a pit bull in a ring, with her hip poking out. Her long sleeve flower print dress stopped well above the knees and fit her body to perfection.

She leaned into him and said, "I forget how sexy you can be when you show heart." Chasidy reached under his shirt, simultaneously kissing his Adam's apple, and pulled the burner from his pants. "Hold this for me," she whispered into his ear, and filled his leather clad palm with the burner. She nibbled on his lobe then on to his chest and stomach. Chasidy kissed him with every button that she undid.

With his focus partially disturbed, he ran his eyes across the empty church, and before he could object, she was on her knees unzipping his pants with her teeth. An avalanche of thoughts flooded his mind. At the core were the integral parts of phase two. The plan he designed was no doubt a thorough one. Each phase played a crucial part, and the execution of each was going to be as easy as he allowed it to be, or as complicated as he allowed it to get. He had to stay free of distractions. His mind wouldn't let him rest. A mind overwhelmed with schemes only burdened its owner, and his burdens were heavy.

Currently, Chasidy only made matters worse with her failed attempt to seduce him. He could feel her warm tongue slowly licking him to an erection, and each lick only made him more uneasy. Only recently had she begun to pull this shit right before jobs. If he didn't know any better, he'd swear she was trying to get him slumped, as her screams to spare Future's life replayed in the back of his mind. *Did she scream to spare Future's life because it was the right thing to do at that time, or was it because she was becoming soft in the streets? Or worst, soft for Future? Was it the stress from these Chiraq streets that had finally caught up with her, to the point where she lost focus on the task at hand? Or was everything just a fucking test with her?*

In the very beginning of their relationship as adults, she very bluntly told Bromise something that stuck with him: *"Bromise, I can't stand a weak man, or a man that's too blind to see that I'm using his dick to walk over him. I honestly do love you, but if your young ass can't learn how to keep me in line, I'll eventually walk all over you too. Just like I walk over every other nigga that comes in my path. I won't try to—it'll just happen naturally because it's in my nature. Your grandpa knew how to keep my ma in line, and you have to do the same. You have to stand on a cold bitch like me."*

Bromise realized long ago that Chasidy could be a complex girl, because her mind and emotions stayed at odds. He only treated her the way she wanted to be treated—the way she taught him.

He was now fully erect. She took the length of him into her mouth, as he pointed the barrel slightly above her head and squeezed the trigger.

The blast echoed throughout the church, causing it to sound off ten times louder than usual. She screamed and jumped to her feet, holding her ears. He grabbed the back of her thick, wavy hair and shoved the barrel into her gut. Her eyes grew with panic. "No, Bromise, anywhere but there!" she screeched and grabbed a hold of the barrel, and moved it from her stomach up to her chest.

He took it as a challenge. "Oh, that's where you want it? Straight through the heart!" He pulled more of her hair, and cocked the hammer back.

She looked up at him with unveiled excitement in her eyes. The eyes never lie. He knew since they were little that she wasn't playing with a full deck. Chasidy was a bit on the crazy side for real, but he maintained his stone-face.

"We're past the point of playing childish games with each other," he said through his teeth. "So stop testing me. This is my last time warning your ass!"

"Bae, listen," she said in a coaxing tone.

"Bae listen my ass!" he fumed and put the barrel in her mouth. "We can't talk at the same time, and it's very beneficial that you hear me right now." He continued smoothly, "We play this game together and we always win, right?"

She nodded *yes*, and a single tear streamed down her high cheekbone.

"Anytime that you decide to switch sides and play the game against me, feel free to do that . . . I guarantee you'll lose, but it's your choice to make. Just don't pretend to be an asset to my squad, when you're really a fuckin' liability. There's nothing else you can teach me. I understand you. And your manipulation tactics does nothing but piss me off. So it stops now. Do you understand?" he asked politely.

Again, she nodded *yes*.

He freed her mouth of the burner and stepped aside.

"Bae, I don't try to play games with you on purpose," she tried to explain. "I honestly care about you. I love you and you know that. It's just in me to try to control a nigga."

"Good game, but I'm not a lame, so save that shit. I don't need excuses from you, Chasidy. From now on you make sure that you reserve those mental games for weak-minded niggas like Future, and remember who you're fuckin' with when it comes to me before I forget who you are and seriously fuck you up. Now fix my pants," he said frigidly.

She zipped and fastened his pants and he looked at his wristwatch. It was exactly 2:55 a.m. "Shit, it's almost time!" He grabbed her by the hand and headed for the exit. Bromise locked the church door and had just enough time to go over the conversation that she must lead with Remo. Then they heard a vehicle pull up at the back of the church.

# CHAPTER 18
## *Black Widow*

T his is it," he said, looking her square in the eyes and handing her Future's .357.

"I got this fool, daddy," she said with a confident smile and readied herself for the surprise of Remo's life.

Bromise wanted to give her sufficient time to work her magic, so he waited a few minutes before creeping around back to do his part.

Chasidy had a thing for chocolate, sexy men, or just a fine man in general would do, or at least a man with some form of swag. It made her job that much more enjoyable. But this clown, Remo, reminded her of something out of the *Walking Dead* TV series. Her thing was, how are you going to be as black as charcoal already, and still have darker rings around your eyes? To her, Remo resembled a coked up raccoon. And to add insult to injury, his awkward ass had no game when it came to women.

She recalled the night that one of her fly girls from the club pulled his card after he was talking king-ding-a-ling macho shit. She grabbed what she could of his little dick in front of the other women, and he clammed up like she knew he would. She ended up cleaning his ass out for 100 bands during the 90-day period that she was on his tongue. Now he was *Chasidy's* victim to toy with.

When Chasidy made it to the end of the building,

she had Remo in her sights. He parked his Cadillac Escalade beside Bromise's Lexus. He sat high on twenty-six inch Lexani rims. She put her best Beyoncé strut in motion in her 5-inch red bottom pumps until she made it to his passenger door. He leaned over to open it, and she climbed in. Immediately, she noticed the black .45 ACP on his lap. Bromise warned her about Remo's quick trigger-finger.

"Whut in the hell is you doin' here?" he asked, suspiciously, and placed his hand atop his burner.

"Freeway sent me. He couldn't make it out here to tell you everything himself, so he sent me. Shit is hectic out here for real. Didn't you get the damn note?" she said, trying to sound convincing.

"Yeah, I got da note, but it didn't mention nuthin' 'bout you," he responded seriously and made a fist around the pistol grip.

"That was the whole point of the note saying *meet at the church for more details*. Well, duh, nigga, I'm the details," she said, looking him straight in the eyes. "Listen, do you want me to call Future? 'Cause I can—" she bluffed.

"No, don't do dat." He reacted quickly. "Dat won't be wise, lil lady. We have a protocol—"

"A protocol that assumes all phone lines are hot. I know this, man," she said convincingly, batting her eyes.

His facial expression was that of both bewilderment and curiosity. "So how long have you been fuckin' Future?" he asked and licked his burnt, chapped lips.

"I don't think that's none of your damn business," she shot back, and saw a glimpse of Bromise ducking behind a dumpster bin.

"Okay, fair enough," he said, looking at her thick thighs that she made readily available for his eyes to feast on. "When dat lil nigga Black Mamba finds out you fuckin' Future, he's goin' to murk y'all both. You got to know dat, right?" Remo asked rhetorically. "I had a feelin' Future was knockin' yo fine ass down. But why you tellin' me dis shit now?" he coaxed.

"That's what I've been trying to tell you, if you'll listen, hun. Future is in the process of cleaning house. And the first person on his list to rid is Bromise—I mean Black Mamba."

With his fist still around the grip he said, "Wait a minute. Now it don't surprise me one bit 'bout Future. He's as shiesty as dey come. But you say it so freely, like you don't give two shits 'bout Black Mamba gettin' whacked. Damn!" He shifted in his seat and gave her another once-over, constantly licking his chapped, burnt lips. "I never knew you for the cold-hearted type. On second thought though, your ma was one of da coldest 'hos to ever stroll Chiraq streets. I guess the apple don't fall far from da tree, as dey say."

She bit her tongue and said, "Yeah well, I guess it don't. Listen, he sent Freeway and Fontane to hit Black Mamba out of town. Since it was short notice, Freeway asked me to drop off the Sentry safe in the dumpster and to meet you here at exactly three a.m." She tried to set him at ease, but he wouldn't take his hand off the fucking burner. Her time was running out, and she had to think of something fast. "Oh, and Future told me to welcome you to the Convolution." *Oops! Why in the fuck did I just say that?*

Remo squinted and withdrew into his seat. The

front of his burner raised a tad. "I thought lieutenants couldn't sit at the Convolution's round table, lil lady, since you know so much," he said and became even more suspicious.

*Fuck! What to do! What to do!* And without thinking, she leaned in and kissed his disgusting lips. "Hun, don't over think it," she whispered and kissed him again, longer than before. "Haven't you heard of *movin' on up* like the Jeffersons? It's called a promotion, and yes, even niggas on your level can get them if you work *hard* enough." Chasidy ran her hand across the baby bulge that his erect penis made in his pants. "Once Black Mamba meets his maker, you'll roll up into his position. Congratulations, hun, you'll be rubbing elbows with the men you used to run errands for."

He grabbed the back of her neck roughly, and kissed her. But this time he threw his tongue in. She tried her best not to puke. And just like that he was seduced.

According to Chasidy, pussy has always been the downfall of man since the beginning of time. She knew women and she knew men. Her philosophy was, "*Eve didn't tempt Adam with a fucking apple. Every woman knows that it's going to take more than a piece of fruit to make a man weak. It doesn't matter how dumb or stupid he is—it'll take more than an apple and a pretty smile to influence him to give up heaven, immortality, and cross God, all at the same damn time. Even if she is the only woman on earth. What happened was Eve tempted Adam with a hot, juicy, wet piece of kiwi pussy, and he couldn't say no to it because she made him believe that he had to have it.*"

# VENOM IN MY VEINZ

Remo caressed one of her full, perky titties with his free hand, while his tongue played spit tennis with hers. It was only a matter of time before he removed his hand from his weapon and went for her other tit. It was too enticing not to. And Chasidy knew it.

Desire makes a man weak. It's the same urge that a man possesses to get what he wants, that makes him overlook the fact that he might lose his life trying to get it. In most cases, men are so steadfast in their pursuit, that they don't even care about what happens in the process of reaching their end-game. From money to pussy, a man will put everything on the line trying to get it. Even his soul.

He was so desperately focused on his desire to get his small dick inside her kiwi that he was willing to disregard his intuition. The same gut feeling that saved his life more than once in the past. *But fuck a gut when trying to nut.*

The best part of cumming only lasted a few seconds. So the thought of getting a few seconds of pleasure was all it took for him to let his guard down— to forget what's going on around him, to forget how uneasy he was just a minute ago, or how none of the shit she was saying was making sense to him. It didn't matter. Because right now, all he cared about was his end-game. While Chasidy had something else in mind.

*I got that kiwi—that good-good pussy. And a universal bank she is. Now it's time to turn up!* Chasidy thought.

Bromise knew something was wrong the minute he saw Chasidy kissing Remo. From his position, he could tell she wasn't feeling him at all. He wasn't surprised, though. Remo didn't weigh enough in the game to capture Chasidy's attention. He was thirty-six years of age, and still doing flunky work for Freeway. Chasidy was no gold-digger, but she damn sure wasn't about to fuck with no almost broke nigga.

Bromise peeked around the dumpster that he was hiding behind, and then made his way to the back of his Lexus. He was close enough to look into Chasidy's face, as Remo kissed on the side of her neck. She noticed him, and over Remo's shoulder she mouthed the words, "*He has on a vest.*"

Remo never liked Bromise, and the feeling was mutual. But he was far from a dummy, and far from a pushover as well. The reason Bromise implemented these precautions was because he knew better than to underestimate any man out in these Chiraq streets. Moreover, Remo had a homicide record that was actively mounting up to his. Hitting him was much more complex than it appeared. He filled his palm with the Beretta PX4. It's time to get active!

The lustful steam inside the Escalade gradually fogged the windows until she could no longer see out of them. "It's hot, hun. How 'bout you crack your window?" she suggested. And without looking, he reached behind him and pressed the button on the door, cracking the window barely. *Ugh! His breath is killing me,* she thought.

"You gotta condom?" she asked.

"I sure do!" he said excitedly, and sat back in his seat and placed his .45 under his thigh. He unloosened his pants and pushed them down to his knees, and started to fumble with the condom package. He was geeked!

She parted her thighs and exposed her camel toe

through her crotchless panty. Remo became more excited and ripped through the package, dropping the condom on his floor mat. He quickly bent down to get it.

"Now you know if Bromise found out that you and me was fucking, he'd murk us both, right?" she said and slowly reached into her handbag. "Isn't that the comment you made about me and Future's fate?"

"Oh, don't get it twisted. It wasn't just a comment, it was da truth," he said as he rose back up with the condom. "But I ain't Future. And I don't give no fuck about Black Mamba. Muthafuck' him is whut I say!"

"Ay!" a voice came from outside.

In haste, Remo turned to his left and saw Bromise. He reached for his burner in vain as Chasidy let off two rounds into the back of his head. The blasts were deafening. Bromise dove to the ground as the bullets that exited Remo's head, zipped past him.

"Now that's my girl, right there!" Bromise said and hopped to his feet. He brushed himself off while Chasidy hit the button to the power tailgate and exited.

They met around at the Escalade's rear.

"That was a nice shot, beautiful," he said and stroked her face, smearing specks of blood across her skin.

"I learned from the best," she said and they kissed.

Bromise pulled Remo's body from the interior and carried him to the back of the Escalade. He dropped Remo's dead weight on the edge of the tailgate and pushed it the rest of the way until the body was completely inside. He shut the tailgate, and they both got busy with their individual assignments.

Chasidy climbed in the driver seat of Remo's

Escalade and watched as Bromise started the Lexus. She let the window down and said, "Get some sleep, bae. You look like shit."

"When you get your ass to your mama's home safely, then maybe I could," he responded honestly.

"I know . . . I would say don't worry 'cause I got this, but I know you won't listen." She put the gear into drive. "But I got this!"

"Now don't get cute. Get that truck to Rockford right away. Drop it off and get to your ma's. Are we clear?"

"Yes, daddy. Crystal!"

"Here, take this." Bromise tossed a black object from his window, and she caught it with her lap. "It's for the .357 and easier access. Be safe."

Chasidy looked at it. It was a thigh-holster. "Thanks, bae." She pulled off with him trailing her. He followed for about two miles before pulling alongside the Escalade. He mouthed the words *I love you* before he turned and disappeared along LaSalle Street. She merged onto the Dan Ryan Expressway with what felt like a one hundred pound weight around her neck. She was very apprehensive of what lay ahead, but her unyielding loyalty to Bromise gave her no choice but to meet it head-on. She gripped the wheel with both hands and headed for her destination.

# CHAPTER 19
*Past Investment Pays Off*

*Blue Island . . . (6:32 a.m.)*

No sooner than Bromise shut his eyes, an unexpected ring tone pulled him from his doze. It was a middle-aged Latin woman named Gossip, calling to share the latest buzz on the streets. He anticipated the word to get out, but he didn't fathom that the news of Future's robbery would spread as quickly as wildfire. But it had. His day hadn't even started, and his iPhone was already blowing up.

He met Gossip back when he was just a pup, and she wasn't the average clucker. Gossip was like the lines in the sidewalk: she was one with the streets and all the nickel and dime hustlers respected her. She had a pair of twin sons his age that were also about that life, reppin' the menacing Humboldt Park area. They were feared in the streets and had oppositions quivering in their shoes. After a six-month gang war resulted in hundreds killed, their bodies were found without limbs. Their joint funeral was the ninth one that week that Bromise attended. That was a year ago.

For five plus years, Gossip had been a loyal correspondent of Bromise. She'd been around since the beginning, and till this day she was still neck deep in her hustle, her habit, and her debt to him. Their arrangement was simple. He fed her habit, and in return she would keep her ear to the streets and run small errands for him.

As rumor would have it, Future had already announced a $50,000 reward for the recovery of his trademark neckpiece. And an equal amount for any valid tips that led to the culprit's capture.

"Did you hear me clearly, Black Mamba?" Gossip asked eagerly.

"Yeah, yeah, I'm listening," he said groggily and rubbed the sleep from his eyes.

"You have to wake all the way up and hear what I'm saying. Despierta ya, papi!" When Gossip got excited, she'd repeat whatever she said in English again in Spanish. Bromise picked up on some of the Latin language just from listening to her over the years.

"Okay, I'm up now. Talk to me." He sat up on his bed and placed the iPhone on speaker.

"I know Future is your friend, but don't fall for whatever b.s. he has goin' on. He's not tellin' the truth. Miente a traves de los dientes. I swear to it!" she said sincerely.

"Okay, I hear you," he said. "Now, I need for this shit to start making sense. What is he lying through his teeth about, exactly?"

"Papi, rewind your thoughts back to the last errand I ran for you."

"Okay, I'm there," he said, following her lead. He could tell she was as high as the Willis Tower. Her fast conversation and speech impediment pretty much gave that away.

"Are you there? Okay, papi, listen." Gossip took a deep breath in an effort to put her *geek mode* in check.

# VENOM IN MY VEINZ

"After I waited on Western Ave, out south for hours in da blizzard cold, I gave up on runnin' into Future. I know you gave me strict orders to remain in that area, but I tried to call your cell, papi, but couldn't get through. So I decided to leave," she said. "After drivin' for some time, I came by two men standing at the back of a white-on-white bimmer. One of the el burro I recognized as the fuckin' car thief you beat to a pulp for stealing the Dodge Challenger you gave to me years back. Obtuvo lo que merecia! Anyway, the car looked a lot like Future's, so I circled the block, parked, and put on my homeless gear like you taught me. As I approached unnoticed, papi, I saw the two men just laughing on and on. The closer I got, I realized they was communicating with someone inside of the bimmer's trunk. So of course I stalled my stroll, papi, just to be nosey-rosy. And you will not believe who was in the trunk the whole time?"

"Who?" he asked as if he didn't know.

"When those hoods opened the trunk, papi, Future came out hysterical, asshole naked, beat up and bleeding from his face and head. Te prometo que te estoy diciendo la verdad. I swear to you," she reported. "Then it dawned on me, maybe the only reason he didn't show up was because somebody got to him first and derailed his train, papi. So I rushed to my car and headed back to Western Ave, thinkin' just maybe he'll show like you said he would." She paused.

"So did he show up?" he asked impatiently.

"Yes, he pulled directly up to the address you gave me."

"Did he buy your story?" Bromise needed to know.

"Not only did he buy it, papi. He paid me forty bucks for being so helpful." She chuckled.

Bromise took a deep sigh of relief and put the iPhone close to his lips. "Okay, cool. Now keep all, and I mean *all* of what you just told me to yourself. I'll call if I need you." He ended the call and tossed the cell phone aside. Bromise ran his hands through his fro and reflected on what was taking place.

In truth, he knew Gossip well enough to know that she could keep a secret. On the flip side though, he wasn't naïve to how she earned her street name. But if he based his judgment solely on their history, then the odds of her repeating her report to anyone else were slim to none. But sometimes you just never know. The streets of Chiraq were unpredictable like that.

Bromise had no doubt that once Future had found himself free of his *crammed* situation, the first thing he'd do is check up on the bogus drop-off address that he texted to his phone. He would do this with two outcomes in mind:

1. Solve the mystery in hood record time.

2. To eliminate Bromise's possible involvement and make room for other potential leads.

And from the sounds of it, number 2 peaked. But after further thought, he needed more clarity to be certain. So he got Gossip back on the line to get a full detailed report of *what* and *how* her encounter went with Future. She was coming down from her high, which allowed for a calmer conversation. He needed to know everything, word for word, facial expressions, the whole nine. He remained quiet as he envisioned the scene from Gossip's perspective.

"No problema, papi. It was 5:30 a.m., and I know

that because that's the time I take my medication. I had just got back to Western Ave not even two minutes before the white-on-white bimmer showed up. At that point I was already sittin' on the stoop next door to the address you gave me.

"Ay you, c'mere!" Future yelled from the bimmer after he spotted Gossip. Without question, she got up and began to walk his way when he abruptly said, "Stop right there! Don't come too close to this whip." His voice shook her. She figured he didn't want her to come into view of his naked body. So she did as she was told and stopped in her tracks. "Have you seen anybody come and go from that house right there?" He calmly pointed to the house.

Gossip looked at the house then back at him, "I'm not so sure, papi . . . how much is it worth to ya?"

"Look here, you clucker-ass bitch. Take dis and you better tell me sumthin'!" Future balled up a twenty dollar bill and threw it at her feet.

She picked it up, unballed it, and examined it before she answered him.

"Well, as a matter of fact, I saw a guy step in and out of there all last night and up to the wee hours of this morning before he left, papi. He even sat a while on that front porch right over there." She pointed to the same house.

"How did he look?" Future questioned.

"I'm sorry, but I don't look at men like that. I'm gay, papi."

"Just describe the muthafucka, will ya!" He threw another balled up twenty at her feet. Again, she picked it up, unballed it, and examined it.

"Well, he was about yay tall, super dark-skinned

with bright white teeth. Oh, and he may've had a naturally curly afro. I kinda saw it when he got inside a car and took off his skully."

"What was he driving?" was his next question.

"One of those new foreign cars. An Audi—that's the name of it. It was a pearl black Audi sedan."

"Do you know the man in the Audi?" he asked, narrowing his eyes in her direction.

"No, not at all, papi," Gossip lied.

He stared her down further and asked, "Do you know who I am?"

"I'm sorry, papi" she replied, looking dumbfounded. "Not at all."

"Good. This conversation never happened, and you never seen me a day in ya fuckin' life. You got that!"

"Sure," she said, and he peeled off.

Gossip wasn't the slightest bit aware of what Bromise was up to. Aside from Chasidy, no one knew. Gossip was merely another pawn that he positioned on his chessboard. But he'd be lying if he said that her current position didn't leave him a bit uneasy. After what she had witnessed, along with the limited information he provided, it didn't take much thought to figure just maybe Bromise had something to do with Future being forced into the trunk of his own car.

For her sake, maybe she wouldn't give it much thought. And if she did, maybe she'd realize how critical it would be never to mention one word of it, especially not to Bromise.

Seeing too much of anything in Chiraq streets could be hazardous to anyone's health. He never meant for her to see Future in such a compromised state.

# VENOM IN MY VEINZ

Especially not during a time when she was *running an errand* that was in total alignment with what she saw.

Although, Gossip's well-played position provided him an alibi for now, he wouldn't think twice about sacrificing a pawn. Maybe Gossip was too close for comfort.

# CHAPTER 20
*OH! NO!*

*Rockford, Illinois . . . (6:44 a.m.)*

After being lead in circles by the Escalade's GPS system that took her an hour off course, Chasidy drove up a dirt road in search of Sims Industrial Junkyard. According to Bromise, the outfit had car crusher compactors on site. These colossal machines would crunch a vehicle from several directions until it resembled a large cube. This was ideal because it killed two birds with one stone: get rid of the SUV and Remo's corpse, therefore closing Phase II. Then she would head to her mother's house in Wisconsin and lay low.

Chasidy was able to get this set up through a dancer at her club. The girl entertained a john that happened to work the yard during the graveyard shift. After stopping at a small motel outside of town to rid Remo's blood from her body, Chasidy called the john, confirming that she was on her way. But that was over an hour ago, before both the GPS and her cell phone lost connection with the satellite and phone towers. She could only pray that he was still there, awaiting her arrival.

"Maybe this is it," she said and drove along a dirt road that had a barbwire, ten-foot fence that nearly came out to the road's edge. The sky radiated little light. The obscure partition woven between the diamond-shaped holes of the fence made it impossible to see what was behind it.

She had been driving alongside the fence for blocks now with no end in sight. *Bong!* The annoying sound alert for low gas startled her for a third time. Her eyes darted to the lit dashboard. The gas hand sat on E. "Shit! I'm going to run out of gas." She was becoming discouraged. Then out of nowhere her eyes widened from the moving object in her rearview mirror. It was the cops. *SHIT!* She nearly jumped out of her seat.

"Okay, be cool, be cool, Chasidy," she mumbled with both hands on the steering wheel. "You got this," she continued to self-talk while the cop car rode her bumper. The car seemed to be behind her for an eternity. Then suddenly the cop whipped around and drove alongside her, staring into her face. She kept her eyes straight ahead and paid extra attention to her breathing rhythm. *You're okay. You're just fine. Just think positive.* Chasidy maintained the posted twenty-five miles per hour speed limit. The cop wouldn't let up. She turned to him.

"Hi," she mouthed and waved. The cop waved back and sped away. She watched the vehicle's taillights until it disappeared into the early morning fog.

"Whew!" she let out a sigh and nipped the sweat from her brow when she noticed a small sign coming up ahead. It read: Sims Industrial.

"Yes, this is it!" Chasidy pulled into the driveway in front of the gate's entrance. She looked around in search of the john. "There he goes," she said with relief after spotting a burly white man approaching from the opposite side of the entrance. He was definitely dressed for winter with a Snow Mantra Parka winter coat with the fur hood around his face, snow boots, and thick insulated gloves.

He pulled back on the tall, heavy gate, allowing it to sway inward, and with his free hand he guided Chasidy in. The high beams caught his eyes, and he quickly shielded them with his forearm.

"Sorry," she said remorsefully as she drove into the yard.

It was clear from the outside that the junkyard was big, but it couldn't compare with her current view of the inside. The space appeared limitless in size as vast piles of smashed cars stacked some thirty feet, seemed to go for acres. Chasidy watched the john through the side-view mirror. He pushed the gate back into place and threw a chain around it before padlocking it. That didn't sit well with her. She rose in her seat as the man approached, appearing bigger with each step until he walked past the driver door and was now in front.

"Come, follow me," he yelled and proceeded to walk forward.

"I know he didn't mean get out," Chasidy thought out loud and decided to stay put. Instead she raised her foot off the brake, allowing the Escalade to cruise on its own. She assumed that she was doing what was expected as he continued to walk while she maintained a steady pace behind him.

Chasidy constantly checked her surroundings the further she drove through the narrow aisles of debris. The deeper she got, the more it became a maze as he directed her through turns and roundabouts, making it impossible to recall the route. Her thumbs rapidly tapped against the steering wheel. She was getting restless.

"Right here!" he yelled unexpectedly and threw his hand into the air, his palm facing outward. Chasidy stomped on the brake, causing the Escalade to rock. "I'll take it from here, darling," he said with a snaggletooth grin and pulled on the driver door.

Chasidy recognized his features through the small opening that his hood provided. He was a weekly client of her club that would cash the girls out with a smile. He was always respectful and never gave any of her girls problems. She was starting to have second thoughts about killing him.

She stepped out of the Escalade and traded places with him. Dressed incognito, she hid behind a trench coat, heels, a scarf over a red-haired wig, and Jimmy Choo sunglasses. He drove the SUV about twenty feet ahead into the compactor. She approached as he was exiting. She wanted to get an up-close look at the process.

"You like to see the show too, huh?" he asked, leaning toward the controls five feet away from her.

"Sure," she said, keeping it short.

"Did you happen to see the patrolman when you were coming in?" he asked, placing his glove on a lever.

"Yes," she answered. "I think I did, actually."

"Yeah, they patrol this area regularly," he said, "circling the compound." And with a blink of an eye he had a knife to her neck.

"Don't you say a word, Miss Fancy Skirt." A white cloud of vapor hovered above her shoulder as he spoke. "You gon' do what I say, how I say it!" He clawed at her face with his filthy gloves, and then threw her against a junk car with much force.

"Aghhh!" Chasidy shrieked in pain.

"You think I dunno who you are, do ya? You the fancy skirt that think she's too good to give out a lap dance or two," he said, undoing his pants. "Assume the position, you whore!" he roared and sent Chasidy to the ground from a solid backhand across the face, breaking her Jimmy Choos. He kicked her thigh with his steel toe boot, causing her to roll over in agony. Then he reached down for the flap of her trench coat. She struggled to crawl. "Where do ya think you're goin', skirt!" He grabbed her ankle and yanked back violently, running her stomach and chest over sharp rocks. She removed the .357 from her thigh-holster and turned in time to give him a facial. The sound from the blast echoed off the junk cars.

"That's because I own the joint, you red neck, sick, sorry excuse of a man," she rambled, squeezing the trigger consecutively until the loud bangs became nothing more than just a "click." Lying there, she stared at what was left of the john's face and head. There wasn't much.

She began to hear barking dogs in the distance. Quickly, she rose to her feet and limped over to the control panel. She had no idea which button or lever did what, so she just started pushing them all until the Escalade was nothing more than just a cube of twisted metal. She turned to the narrow aisles of debris and began to make a run for it.

"Aghh!" Chasidy fell to the ground. Police sirens echoed. Her injured leg would support neither her weight nor her determination. The sirens were getting closer, and the dogs were closing in. She couldn't just

# VENOM IN MY VEINZ

lie there and give up. *C'mon, Chasidy, you can do this!* With all the strength she could muster, she pushed herself up from the ground and only got so far.

# CHAPTER 21
*Skeletons*

*8:37 a.m.*

For the past two hours, Bromise tossed and turned, failing to patch things up with sleep. His mind felt like a stick of chewed up bubble gum, and on each side was an unsettling thought that pulled in opposite directions, spreading the gum thinner. Phase 1 was behind him. It was the closing of Phase II that contributed to the marching band that currently played inside his head. *Chasidy should've made the trip to Wisconsin by now. So what the fuck is up?* he pondered, trying not to think the worst. But it was kind of hard not to, since she hadn't answered or returned any of his texts or calls. *That's not like her.*

Gossip was partially to blame for poking at his intuition, and impelling his severely active mind. And then there was his uncle, Cigar. *What in the fuck does he have brewing with Future?* He feared him dead for the longest time, and his deceased mother suspected his involvement in Brisco's murder since the beginning.

Fats also crossed his mind. He needed to touch base with him and get an overall update on his business throughout *The Web*. "That's got to be her," Bromise thought out loud before realizing that iPhone #2 was buzzing, and not his personal one. He hesitated. *Future?*

212

# VENOM IN MY VEINZ

"Hello," he answered, and just like that, his mental question was answered. It was Future. The call was one-sided and brief. It was a summons to meet the Convolution at his eastside estate at 2:00 p.m. And after careful consideration on Bromise's end, two o'clock couldn't come quick enough. Not only was he going to show up, he was going to act the part and turn up if need be.

\* \* \*

*1:11 p.m.*

Bromise wanted to be sure to dress the part also. To be himself inside and out at all times was essential. He stood in the full-length mirror and glanced at his Audemars Piguet diamond watch after wrapping it around his left wrist. He raised his chin and gave himself one last look at his attire for the day. Besides the karats in his ear, he had on a pair of black Robin's studded jeans with a crisp button-up. An Audemars chain with a Jesus piece and a fresh pair of J's. He was gucci.

He checked the safety on both his .45 ACP's, then pushed them inside his double-shoulder strap. *So fresh and so clean.* It felt good to get into some fresh gear. On his way out the door, he grabbed his black and white Coyote fur coat off the hanger and threw on a matching Ralph Lauren skully. Once he made it to the garage, he hit the remote start to his white on white 3500HD Denali pickup truck. He called her Sadie. The engine sounded like a monster inside his two-car garage. She was a beauty indeed. And with the double wheels stabilizing her rear, she handled like a gem in the snow. Bromise walked past his Lexus 460 and climbed inside Sadie as "Addresses" by TI filled the

213

cabin.

Upon making it to Future's property at 1:57 p.m., he expected to see at least two, maybe three whips, parked in his driveway. But to his utter surprise, the only vehicle he saw was Fontane's Grand Cherokee SRT8. *Didn't he say the Convolution would be here? Then where's Freeway and Kill-Kill?* He pulled up to the Cherokee's back bumper and hopped out. He ran his hand over the hood. It was still warm. Then he proceeded to the front entrance of the stately residence, and Future was there to greet him at the door. The swelling around his face was clearly visible. He didn't say a word. Instead, he led Bromise through a hallway and into his secluded office. Fontane was already inside standing at the wet bar, pouring double shots of peach Ciroc into two glasses.

"Salutations, Black Mamba," Fontane greeted. He was draped in his usual business suit.

"Salutations as well," Bromise reciprocated the gesture and they shook-up.

"You already know," Fontane said and handed him the glass of Ciroc.

"Thank you." Bromise nodded.

Suddenly, the heavy door slammed shut, and "*decapitations*" was the first word that rolled off Future's tongue. They both looked up with hands on burners as Future walked around the dark oak and sat behind his prestigious hardwood Pergola desk. Fontane and Bromise assumed their respective seats opposite him. Future placed a small cloth bag on his desk and slid it across the two-toned wood finish. It halted just before the desk's edge.

"I need a job done, and I needed it done

yesterday," Future stated. "Inside that bag is a single address with two names. I want their heads off, literally. No questions asked. For your troubles there's also sixty bands inside. Thirty bands a piece."

Bromise was certain the two heads he wanted were the car thieves that freed him from his trunk. With Rudeboy dead, Future stood to inherit Jamaican Bill's reign. If the news of him getting robbed, kidnapped, and stripped, made it up the pipeline, he'd appear weak. And that simply was not an option, especially not during his campaign run for King of Chiraq. It's similar to how politicians would stretch to the extreme to protect their good name from the mud-slinging, except in the streets they lobbied much different. If Jamaican Bill caught wind of it, there's no way he'd bless Future with the position as his Successor. As far as Future was concerned, there were four loose ends that had to be tied ASAP in order to prevent that from happening, and two of their names were in the bag. Future desperately wanted (t)his problem resolved expeditiously, and that was the reason for Fontane and Bromise being there.

Bromise was undoubtedly the most lethal member, and Fontane's body count was respected in the streets. In the past, they'd only team up for major jobs that called for it. Small isolated incidents were usually executed single-handedly by one of the members, or their trusty lieutenants. Depending on the job, they were all capable. These factors made Fontane a bit inquisitive.

"So what is this about, exactly?" Fontane asked.

"Does it matter?" Future yelped. "I'm givin' you a job, and I'm payin' you for it in advance. Fuck you mean?"

"That's what I mean . . . that's the part that's not making sense to me," Fontane said. "Since when do you pay us for a job in advance? And you still haven't said shit about your fuckin' face. Yo' shit jacked, homie," Fontane said truthfully.

"I got into a car accident, period," Future replied quickly with a straight face.

"And since when do we do jobs collectively on a whim? I mean, I haven't seen or heard no intel, and no history on these fools, or a reason why I'm choppin' off a nigga's head," Fontane said and turned to Bromise. "Am I missin' sumthin'?"

Bromise shrugged and remained silent, while Fontane kept it going.

He had every right to question Future's motives. Bromise acknowledged to himself that he would've done the same had he been in his position. But Bromise's perspective was quite different. Fontane believed that Future was either overreacting about something trivial, or withholding crucial intel. Either way, Fontane wasn't feeling the vibe. And considering he knew firsthand about Future's shady tactics, it was understandable why he'd be so hesitant to agree on a blind mission.

On the other hand, Bromise was amazed at how cocksure Future came off. How firm he appeared in his position while barking orders at them. As if he wasn't crying like a bitch and pissing himself, just hours ago.

Listening to Fontane talk reassured Bromise of the type of man he was. When Future first brought him on board, Fontane was another one who had a chip on his shoulder like most of the old heads that looked down upon him and his peers. But over time they overcame their differences. Although Fontane always followed orders, he knew that Fontane hated Future's characteristics as a man, as much as he did. Call it a hunch, but Bromise was sure he wanted out of the Convolution altogether. But he was too spoiled by his lifestyle to do anything about it. At forty-six years old, his prime was behind him and so was his ambition as a contract killer.

"And what about Kill-Kill?" Fontane asked. "Why ain't that nigga gettin' dirty?"

"Do you even hear yourself right now?" Future leaned forward. "The man just came from under a double-life bid, after spending three years behind the walls . . . what the fuck do you mean why isn't he gettin' dirty?"

Silence took over as it dawned on Fontane just how dumb he sounded. "Okay, right, of course. He's fresh out . . . needs to get acclimated to the streets . . . he's laying low. I get it."

"Shut the fuck up!" Future struck his desk with his hand. "The muthafuckin' question should be, why in the fuck are you questioning me? Since when we do dat!" Future bellowed with rage and hit the surface of his desk again, except this time with a closed fist.

It took every muscle in Bromise's body to refrain from bursting out into laughter at Future's act.

"I don't mean to question you, boss." Fontane clammed up. "I was just asking for more information is all." He downed his two shots of Ciroc in one swallow.

"Well, that's all the info you need, nigga. Now run wit' it or run from it," Future warned. Bromise's thoughts went straight to his burner, knowing that he may have to slump Fontane right then if he respond the wrong way. He watched intentively.

"You know I'm down for whutever, man," Fontane assured him.

Bromise turned his glass up and ingested the peach Ciroc before breaking his silence.

"Well, it doesn't seem like there's shit else to talk about here." He placed his empty glass on a coaster and reached inside the cloth bag, pulling out his portion of the cash, and an index card with a single address and two names written on it. He quickly memorized them and handed the card to Fontane. He shoved the bands in his inside pocket and rose from his chair, as Future studied his every move. Then Fontane followed suit.

Bromise reached over the desk and shook up with Future. Fontane then did the same, and Bromise casually headed for the door. When he opened it, Angel appeared on the other side. Bromise held his composure.

"Whut? Whut can I do for ya?" Future asked, clearly annoyed.

"Nothing baby, I was just checking in on you to see if you want me for anything," she said and glanced around, taking an extra long look at Bromise. "I didn't realize you had company. Can I get you guys anything?"

"They were just leaving," Future spoke up.

"Damn, nigga, if you gon' stare that hard at least speak." She blasted Fontane.

Clearly caught off guard, he looked over at Future, who was squinting at him from under his swollen eye. "Oh, my bad. Didn't mean no harm." Fontane turned to her. "Hello, Angel. You look quite lovely today. I'm out." He threw up the deuces and walked past, exiting the office. Bromise made a motion to follow him.

"Ay, Black Mamba, slow up." Future walked up and fluttered his fingers as if to shoo Angel away. She must've gotten the clue, because Bromise caught a glimpse of her ass as she strutted down the hall. Future rested his hand on Bromise's shoulder and got close to his ear.

"You look exhausted, my nig. I'm talkin' dog-tired, like you haven't slept in days. Is there anything you would like to tell me?" he asked, breathing heavy like the walk from his desk was the distance of a marathon.

"What's to tell?" Bromise looked at him square.

"Like, how's bidness?"

"What do you think?" he shot back. "You said it yourself, I look dog-tired. Well, that's 'cause I've been puttin' in work, ya dig." He chuckled and they shook-up. "Bidness is real good. No need to worry about that."

"Oh, and about last night—" Future paused, his eyes narrowed. "It wasn't my intent to put you on hold like that, but some serious biz came up, and I had no choice but to tend to it. That's my word, B."

"Don't even lean on it, big homie."

"Wait!" Future tugged on Bromise's shoulder, gradually applying his weight. "There was one thing about last night that struck me as kind of strange, though."

"And what was that?" he asked, ready to make a move for his .45's.

"Your order. You only ordered three bricks and

that's way below your average. So are you sure bidness is good?"

"I'm more than sure. I'm positive. You know how I get down . . . hands on," he said, truthfully.

"Okay, well just as long as you keep up with your monthly quota, who am I to tell you how to run your bidness, right?" Future laughed mildly and patted his shoulder. "Just a heads up. I have a $50,000 reward out for my Jacob's piece. It was stolen out of my 760 last night," he said and sighed heavily. "I got a feelin' it was one of dem Rasta cats."

"Well, the only Rasta cats I know with balls that big is Jamaican Bill's organization," Bromise said, planting the seed.

Future left Bromise's side and reclaimed his sitting position behind his throne of a desk, and simply said, "I know."

"Well, if you want me to—" he started, before Future purposely cut him off.

"What I'm sayin' is the street chat line has its way of puttin' ninety on ten, ya know. Blowing shit out of proportion. So as my nig and my most loyal subordinate, I ask that you eradicate any exaggerated rumors and the source it's coming from."

"I gotcha'," Bromise said to comfort his bruised ego.

"And don't let Fontane pass that body on to you." Future leaned back in his chair and waited for it to set in, and when it dawned on Bromise, he finished with, "I know about everything that happens in Chiraq. Don't shit get past me. You remember that."

Bromise nodded and left Future with his thoughts. He pulled out his iPhone as he made his way through the lit hallway. Still no missed calls or texts from Chasidy. *What the fuck is going on with her?* He pulled her name from contacts and tapped *call* just as he exited the main entrance of the estate, shutting the door behind him.

"Well, long time no see, handsome," Angel said sarcastically. He turned to see her standing in the doorway, looking as fine as the last night he saw her. "I'm sorry. Are you on your phone?" She shut the door behind her.

He ended the call just as Chasidy's voice mail picked up, and shoved the phone into his pocket. *Now her shit is going straight to voice mail?* he thought.

"No apologies necessary. I can make the call later." Bromise looked Angel up and down.

"I just wanted you to tell Chasidy thanks for keeping her word," she said.

"O . . . kay," he said. "I'll let her know that. You take care." He turned and took the concrete stairs down to the pavement. He climbed into Sadie when a text came through from Fontane, saying to meet him at Grant Park. Home of President Barack Obama's victory speech.

The location was on his way, so he didn't give it a second thought. He tried Chasidy to no avail. Bromise also called both Porsha and Ayana, and neither had heard anything. And somehow he misplaced Brooke's number.

He arrived at Grant Park and passed by the Buckingham Fountain before he spotted Fontane's STR8 parked in a nearby parking lot. Bromise drove through and came to a stop beside him. He climbed in, blowing hot air into his hands.

"Man, it's cold out there," Fontane said and pulled the door closed.

"What's on your mind?" Bromise asked, cutting through the chase.

"I don't care what he says. Somethin' happened and Future isn't talkin'," Fontane said. "You heard, right?"

"Heard what?"

"Word is he got jacked and kidnapped last night, and I bet this job he gave us has a lot to do with it."

"Truthfully, I'd be careful who I repeat that to. Plus, I wouldn't give no fuck either way. And neither should you. It's a job. We gettin' paid for it. Simple. Now, is this what you got me down here for?"

"Would you wanna handle this body for me?" Fontane pulled out the cloth bag that he picked up from Future's desk.

"I got it, Fontane. Go home to your wife and kids. But if Future finds out about this, I don't think he'll be cool with it," Bromise said, reflecting on what Future said last.

"Man, fuck him. He don't know shit." He tossed the cloth bag in Bromise's lap.

"What's this?"

"That's thirty bands, my portion of the take like we always do. You do the job, you get the pay."

Bromise tossed it back to him and said, "Keep it. I'm doing pretty good these days, so I'm paying it forward. Now get the fuck out of my truck and go home before your wife crack that whip on your ass," he joked.

Fontane was pleased to say the least. They shook-up and parted ways.

# VENOM IN MY VEINZ

After he left Fontane, he brought Sadie to a slow pace up Michigan Avenue, admiring the tall buildings like a tourist would do. He spent so much time in the hood doing hood shit that he often forgot just how beautiful downtown Chicago really was. But for a good reason. Although Chicago is the birthplace of the skyscraper, looks are deceiving, because downtown didn't look shit like his neighborhood.

He took his knee to the steering wheel and used both hands to put a flame to his Irene Kush. The strain was heavy, and he was a loyal client to the hustlers who served it. He wrapped his lips around the tip of his neatly pearled Garcia Vega and inhaled cautiously, as the rugged terrain snow tires chopped through the slushy streets. Rich Homie Quan played in the background. He now had the Randolph Street Bridge in his sights. Suddenly, visions of Angel came to mind and his dick copped a tent.

All the while, Kill-Kill had been trailing him ever since he'd left Future's estate.

# CHAPTER 22
*The Closer . . . I've Got Your Back*

*Madison, Wisconsin . . . (2:32 p.m.)*

Chasidy sat in a wooden chair close to a window with her arms around her knees. One hundred and fifty miles away from Chiraq. The scenery reminded her of a postcard she once received from her mother when she was little. The bare trees and ground below were covered in new snow while huge flakes continued to fall from the sky.

The daylight was cheery and optimistic, but her disposition, not so much. Her heart was heavy, and her mind was confused. "I'm not happy," she said to herself and a tear tickled her cheek. She was so emotional that the muscles in her face involuntarily contorted, provoking her to sob and cry out loud. "Ouch!" She winced after her arm bumped the fresh bruise that covered her thigh. Since her arrival to her mother's, it had been a constant reminder of how she closed Phase II, and came so close to death. And thank God for Porsha being right on time as usual. If it wasn't for her smashing through the junkyard's fence and getting Chasidy out of there in a nick of time, there's no telling what the outcome would have been. She was pissed for having left her Hermes handbag, along with her iPhone, inside of Remo's twisted Escalade. Outside of that, she counted her blessings.

Then Bromise barged into her mind as he always did. She knew he'd be proud of how she improvised and closed Phase II, but she really didn't care about that right now. She was so mad at him! Tired of the senseless killings, the *jobs*, the whoring, the dealing, all of it. Chasidy wanted out! But she felt paralyzed without Bromise's approval. Yet, she wanted more. She was tired, lonely, and unhappy.

"Here you go, honey," her mother Brooke said, after she walked into her guest bedroom. "While I was out, I stopped by Verizon and replaced your iPhone." She handed it to her.

"Thank you, Mom," she said, low-spirited as she stared at her new iPhone. She wanted to call Bromise.

"You know, there were a couple of habits you would display when something heavy was on your mind." Brooke sat on the bed. "It was that cute little thang right there." She pointed to the Cabbage Patch doll that Chasidy now held in her lap. "And when you became a teenager it became her." She hinted toward her Mac laptop, which was streaming one of Mary J. Blige's older songs. "What's troubling you, dear?" she asked, very concerned.

"It's nothing you should be worried about. I'll be fine," Chasidy responded and looked away in an effort to hide her already roused emotions.

Brooke glanced at the bruise on her face and then her thigh. "Well, it looks like more than nothing to be worried about to me. But if you want to continue to be secretive about it—"

"What is it with you, mother?" Chasidy bellowed. "Since I got here you've been going on with these suggestive remarks. I said I'm fine, so just leave it at that. Since when do you care anyway?" She frowned to hold in the tears.

"Now what is that supposed to mean, Chasidy?" Brooke asked, kneeling in front of her. Chasidy looked away and out the window. "Are you going to at least talk to me, or are you going to continue with this immaturity?"

"Immaturity?" Chasidy's blood began to boil, and she stood to her feet.

Brooke locked her knees and stood face to face before her daughter. For the both of them, it was like looking in a mirror.

"Well, isn't that fuckin' ironic," Chasidy said. "So, you leaving me in Chiraq to fend for myself was mature?" she scoffed. "You didn't even come to see me before you left me. You didn't have the caring decency of a mother to at least say goodbye to her daughter—*me*—your baby girl." She pointed her thumbs to herself. "So don't you dare scorn me about immaturity!"

"Are you still hung up on that—" Brooke said, then decided to take another approach. "Sweetie, you were sixteen, and it's not like I just up and left you by your lonesome. I left you in the care of your older sister, who was twenty at that time. You two were inseparable back then."

"But Mom, you didn't even tell Porsha you were leaving. You just up and left without saying a word to either of us."

"Now that's not entirely true. I left you both an in-depth letter," Brooke said, trying to justify her actions.

"Letter? What kind of source of comfort is a letter going to bring to a couple of kids that have just been abandoned by their mother! The only depth that piece of paper had was when I buried it underneath a ton of

226

garbage!" she cried.

"You wouldn't have left Chicago even if I would have asked you to. You loved your friends and life down there."

"Not more than I loved my mother. Besides, that should've been my choice. Or were you afraid that I might've surprised you and decided that I wanted my ma more than anything?"

"You were in the middle of your senior year at Whitney Young. There was no way that I was going to pull you out of school, anyhow. You were doing so well in your studies, and on the verge of graduating."

"A graduation that you received an invitation for, but didn't care to come to," Chasidy said. "Don't matter though, because I dropped out that year anyway."

Brooke hung her head at the news. "Look, what more do you want me to do or say?" Brooke asked sincerely.

"Ma, it's been seven years . . . seven whole years since I saw you last. I want you to admit that what you did was wrong, and I want you to apologize for it. But I want you to mean it," she replied.

"Look, I didn't expect that I'd be gone from you girls that long. All I was trying to do was find a better life for us."

"A better life for *us*. Are you fuckin' serious right now! You can't be! 'Cause the only thing you were trying to find was another trick to turn for that raunchy-ass pimp you were sniffing behind, like the whore you are!" Chasidy exclaimed harshly, and before she could guard her grill, Brooke whaled her across the jaw line with an open hand.

Chasidy reached for her face in shock and looked at her mother. "I'm pregnant . . ."

"What!" Brooke gently wrapped her arms around her daughter. "Did you just say what I think you said?" Then she fought to remove the hair that was sticking to Chasidy's tear-soaked face, and looked into her eyes. She knew her baby girl was scared. "Come here, honey," Brooke took Chasidy around the shoulders again and hugged her compassionately. "I'm so sorry for hitting you. I am so sorry for everything." She squeezed tighter.

Chasidy didn't reciprocate. Instead, she stood with her arms to her sides and shut her eyes. *Not only do I not know this woman, I don't trust her. Did I make a mistake coming here?*

*** 

Bromise had just entered the Englewood District on Chiraq's south side, heading for the address that he memorized from the index card at Future's crib. On the way, he stopped at a hardware store and bought an ax.

In his opinion, Future was rattled for sure. He tried to disguise his fear, but the Don Corleon reenactment bit that he performed at his estate was a dead giveaway. He called them *tell-tale* signs. Right now, Future was hiding out in the safe comforts of his stately residence nursing his wounds, while he utilized his resources to uncover the identity of the dreadlocked bandit.

Bromise chose to wear a dread-wig during the lick for a reason. If there was a crew in all of Chiraq that would have a problem with Future taking the reigns post-Jamaican Bill's retirement, it would be the Rastas. They had all, including Future, had their run-ins with them. And several of their members voiced their objections in the past to Future's rise.

It was evident that he was taking the necessary measures to keep the Convolution out of the loop and still achieve his objective.

Bromise bent the Eighty-third Street corner looking for his targets at one of their low-key shops. He observed two guys under the hood of a Maserati Quattroporte. *That's them.*

"These fools stay taking exclusive whips," he thought out loud and circled the block to check out the neighborhood. The one good thing about Chicago's winters was that it kept people inside. It was like a ghost town in broad daylight. *I'm going to have fun with this.* He parked Sadie about a half block down and slid out of his fur and tossed it in the backseat. Bromise pulled his skully and replaced it with a black baseball cap and pushed his arms into the sleeves of his black Carhartt winter coat. His leather gloves were snug, and the clips to the .45s were filled with hollow points. He was ready.

He set the burners back safely inside their holsters and climbed out of Sadie. He cut through the alley and pulled out one of the 45s. He positioned the burner behind his back and walked up to the garage like he belonged there. As he got closer, he recognized the high-yellow dude with the freckles. Gossip was right.

"What it do, Chris and Mike?" Bromise greeted them by the names that were on the index card. They came from under the hood and screwed their faces. "I got six bands for a clean whip. How y'all inventory lookin'?" he asked.

"Who da fuck is you? And how da fuck you know

us!" the taller of the two asked and slammed the hood shut.

Bromise would've dropped them both right then, but he didn't want to have to go out there for a second time because he slumped the wrong two men. He needed to confirm their names at least.

"Listen, man, I didn't come all this way for trouble," Bromise said. "I just got my taxes, and Curtis said y'all had whips for sale. There it is, cash money," he said, tossing a bundle of bills on the hood of the Maserati. The freckled-face dude's eyes lit up at the cash.

"It's all good. We know Curtis. We just had to make sure you wasn't dem jakes," he said. "My name is Chris and this here is Mike." He extended his hand. "You look familiar . . . what you say yo' name is?" Freckle-face narrowed his eyes.

"I'm the death dealer," Bromise sneered and swung the burner from around his back. It was like the Fourth of July inside of the garage and he had the Roman candle. When the smoke cleared, they both lay in a pool of their own blood, dead.

Bromise scanned the garage floor and spotted a thick block of wood. He propped it under freckle-face's neck and reached into his coat, pulling out the axe. He raised it over his head and came down with a heavy blow, severing his head from his body in one chop. He repeated the same act with his partner.

Then he proceeded to put the heads inside of a garbage bag. He grab his cash off the hood when he heard something. He turned to an armed man charging through the door from outside, shooting uncontrollably in his direction. Bromise reached for his burner, but it was too late. A series of blasts deafened him as he dove to the floor and guarded his head. To his bewilderment, the armed stranger fell to the ground next to him. He was lifeless.

"Get up, papi!"

Bromise jumped to his feet and threw his back against the drywall. Both 45's filled his palms. "What the fuck are you doing here?" he yelled in Gossip's face.

"Well," she said with a tremor. "After what I saw, I figured Future would order the car thieves to be hit. And I figured that it'd likely be you who'd be doin' da poppin', papi. So I came on my own to watch your back," she said shyly.

Bromise peeked outside the garage door to see if there was any more unexpected company waiting in the wings to slump him.

"Well, did you stop to think that if Future finds out that you've witnessed what these two dead muthafuckas did, that he just may order your ass dead too?" He raised the garbage bag from the ground and swung it over his shoulder. "You shouldn't have come here," he said somberly and snatched her burner from her hand and shoved it in his pocket.

"My bad," she offered, looking remorseful.

"Damn it, Gossip! You see way too much shit than what you're supposed to see. You're not going to be satisfied until you make me do something I really don't want to do." He turned and ran his hands through his fro.

"I'm really sorry, papi. Realmente me disculpo! What ya want me to do?"

"Just get the fuck out of here before I change my

fuckin' mind! NOW!" he snarled.

\*\*\*

"You still haven't talked to Remo at all?" Future asked.

"Nah, not today," Freeway responded, making sure to keep up with the street signs as he passed them. Future had given him a direct order to go out to Bromise and Chasidy's home in Lincoln Square. "Okay, I'm pullin' up now, boss," he said through his Bluetooth.

"Good. I just received a text from Black Mamba, so he's not there. But if you run into Chasidy, be sure to snatch dat bitch up and bring her to me!" he yelled through the earpiece.

After Freeway got inside using a skeleton key, he defused their alarm and searched high and low. There was no sign of Chasidy. Before he left, he wired the entire house for sound with state of the art listening bugs that could pick up even the tiniest of sounds.

Meanwhile, Future was inside his home office laughing at the picture messages he just received from Bromise. It was multiple still shots of the side and front angles of the car thieves' decapitated heads. He was pleased.

\*\*\*

After their little spat, Chasidy and Brooke started anew. The two of them sat on a couple of stools at her kitchen counter, sipping on cranberry juice and conversing.

"Brisco Balducci was so good to you, your sister, and I," Brooke said. "He made it so that we ate well and remained safe while doing it. After he was killed, a big part of me died with him. Though I was with him

**232**

for twenty-three years, I played second fiddle to his wife of fifty years. All of his assets went to her, as it should have. I was merely the other woman that no one knew about, so who was I to demand or even expect a crumb? Needless to say, his untimely death broke me down physically, emotionally, and financially. After twenty plus years of living the glamorous life, I had to resort to doing what I did best just to put food on the table. That was prostitution. So much had changed since I was last out there, so I made the vital mistake of subscribing to a pimp that you talk understandably bad about. He called himself Milwaukee . . . that's what led me to Wisconsin, and away from you two. I honestly had dreams of making it better for us, you know, like how it was before Brisco died. But with the murky influences of Milwaukee, both the city and the pimp, things went from looking almost like sugar, to being actual shit. Excuse my language, but I'm telling you, baby girl, I'd never wish what I went through on my worst enemy. Not even the bastard that took me through it. But by the grace of God," she said and raised her hands slightly above her head. "I was able to persevere through the trauma and retire from that lifestyle. And God made it so that I could purchase this house just a year ago."

"Wow mom!" Chasidy looked around the modest, two bedroom home. "That's so awesome. Good for you!" Then she looked at her mom. Her smile suddenly dropped and her grip around the glass tightened. "Mama, how did Mr. Brisco really die?" she asked with riveting curiosity. "I mean, I know that a US Marshal shot him, but was it a setup?"

"You've heard the story," she looked away and

sipped her juice.

"Yeah, but you know how the street chat lines can be. They're hardly ever accurate. Plus, they're reporting more than just one story, and they all can't be true."

"Yes, it has become somewhat of a folktale," Brooke agreed as her palms began to sweat, avoiding eye contact.

"But you were the last one with him. I remember seeing him in our living room, and the next thing I know he's lying dead in the street. From the time that he sat on our sofa, to the time that he was pronounced dead, couldn't have been no more than an hour tops. So you must know something, or more than what the chat lines were reporting, at least," she insisted.

"Yes, he was in our living room on the morning of his death, but I'm afraid that I know nothing more than what anyone else knows," Brooke maintained.

"Well, from what I hear it has to be between Jamaican Bill or his ex-son-in-law, Cigar."

"And that would be a shame. He treated Cigar like his own son. In Brisco's eyes, he *was* his son," Brooke said. "What does Bromise think?" she asked, finally raising her face.

"He finds it hard to believe." Chasidy sucked her teeth.

"What about you? What do you think?"

"I know that the love of cash is the root to all evil. And at the end of the day, niggas will sell their souls for it," she said, believing every word.

"And again, I know nothing more than you." She swiftly changed gears. "Now, how about you and I talk about the subject that you're obviously avoiding?" She pointed to Chasidy's flat stomach. She wasn't even showing yet. "So how far along are you?"

"Seven weeks." She took a sip from her glass.

"Wow! So is it—"

"Yes, of course it's his." Chasidy knew exactly whose name she was leaning toward. "Who else would it be!"

"Excuse me," Brooke said sarcastically. "Just checking . . . Well?"

"Well what?" she asked playfully.

"Well, have you told him yet?"

"No."

"And may I ask why not?" Brooke asked politely.

"Because when I mentioned it to him—"

"Wait," she interjected. "I thought you said you didn't tell him yet?"

"What had happened was, I told him—but afterwards I told him that I was playing."

"What!" Brooke nearly fell off the stool in confusion. "Now why would you go and do something like that, sweetie?"

"I know it sounds messed up, but listen . . . When I broke the news to him you should've seen him. That boy looked as if he saw a ghost and was about to run for his life, and out of mine forever. So I panicked and told him that I was just fuckin' with him, and you should've seen the look of relief on his face when I said that."

"So what are you going to do now, Chasidy? You have to tell him  sooner or later," she said with a motherly stare. Chasidy avoided eye contact. "I know you're not contemplating an abortion. Are you?"

"Mama, that boy is too deep in the streets. Trust

me, he ain't ready for no baby. Shoo, I'm not even sure if I'm ready for that matter."

"Chasidy, listen to me, baby girl." She set her glass on the counter. "I was pressured to have an abortion with both you and your sister Porsha, but I refused and look at how beautiful the both of you have turned out. Baby, hardly anyone is ready to bring a child into this world. It's just something you do when God blesses you with the opportunity."

"I'on know, ma," she said, unsure. "I don't want to do this by myself."

"And I doubt very seriously that you would have to. You and your sister both have had your share of men that I didn't care for, and although Bromise is not perfect, I've always secretly cheered for you two," she said. "You two have been around each other since you were kids. He knows you as intimately as you know him, and I don't mean that in a sexual way. What I'm speaking of transcends lust and sex." She sat back on her stool, and Chasidy's iPhone received a text.

"Oh, this is my friend, Ayana," she announced and read the message: "*Hey gurl! Just letting you know that Lil Fats and I just touched down in the 'A' and couldn't be happier about this trip. Thanks again for everything, friend ☺.*"

"Is she a good friend of yours?" Brooke asked

"Yes, she is," Chasidy said and looked on with a smile.

"I guess what I'm trying to get across to you is," Brooke continued, "Bromise is the heir to certain qualities that came from a giant of a man that I truly loved. So I'm positive that he has a heart of both steel and gold. The steel is only to protect him like body armor while he's on the battlefield, but the gold is for the love he has for his mother, his grandfather, and you. What he didn't learn from his beloved grandfather, he learned from you. And I'm sure that having his baby would only enhance the gold in his heart, to the point where he'd realize that gold is much stronger than steel, and much more precious. He would leave the streets by the wayside.

"I hear you, ma but—"

"But what?"

"I hear how you talk about the way Brisco treated you, how he made you feel secure in y'all's future in spite of how it turned out." Chasidy looked down at her hands. "With Bromise, I just don't know. . ."

"What is it, baby?"

Chasidy raised her face. "I don't think he even expects to live long enough to see his twenty-first birthday."

Brooke sighed heavily. "I believe strongly that your baby will teach you two how to become better people. How to evolve from a burden that you're so convinced you cannot let go of, only because you think that you cannot do anything better with your life," she preached.

"You don't understand, ma. When Bromise is committed to something, he has tunnel vision. The end is all he sees. And he's not going to let up until he wins or dies trying."

"Are you speaking about something in particular?" Brooke asked.

Chasidy cleared her throat and shifted in her seat. "No, not at all," she lied, "I'm just speaking about his commitment to the streets in general."

# RUMONT TEKAY

"Listen." Brooke touched Chasidy's knee.

"I knew from the start that both you and Porsha were genetically pre-disposed to being just like me, just as Bromise is to Brisco. But I'm here to tell you, baby girl, that it doesn't have to be that way. I'm admitting it to you now that Brisco and I were both terribly wrong for molding you two into what you are today. Bromise, a killing machine, and you, a conniving temptress that preys on the weaknesses of men. Brisco and I made a selfish mistake in that respect, and I know that Bromise is a very dangerous man because of it." She paused to take a sip from her glass. "However, I also know that Brisco instilled in him the importance of protecting you. You two were designed for each other. Now, the only wall that y'all need to overcome is gaining true understanding that the streets don't have to continue to be your life's map. We all make mistakes, have struggles, and even regret things in our past. But you are not your mistakes, you are not your struggles, and you are here today with the power to shape your future, baby girl."

Chasidy rose from her stool and limped over to the refrigerator. Brooke got up and made her way around the oppsite side of the island, meeting her daughter.

"Otherwise, the streets are going to swallow you both. You see"—she took Chasidy by the hands—"the both of you can rise above and beyond the self-destructive paths that we led y'all on. You two can create your own fate, and I strongly believe that little miracle that's growing inside of you will help the both of you make that transition. Understand that your heart may be on the left side of your chest, but its always right. So listen to it. And make Bromise listen to you, because he will."

"I hear you and everything, but I just don't know, Mama," she said and her cell chimed again. She screened the call and stared at the name. It was Bromise. She let it go to voicemail.

"Well, you can't keep avoiding him," Brooke said, knowing exactly who it was.

"I know. I just need some time to think is all." Her cell chimed again. It was a text from Porsha. "Ma, Porsha is outside," Chasidy said and turned on the balls of her feet.

"Well, tell her to bring her butt inside."

"She's about to take me to one of the malls that this itty-bitty town has to offer." She chuckled. "Plus, I need to buy a purse." Chasidy kissed her and limped to the guestroom to get some last minute things. She opened the dresser and reached for the .357. She hesitated. *I don't have nothing to be afraid of in this small town,* she thought and left the guestroom without it. She limped to the front door and Brooke met her there.

"You really need to let me take you to the hospital and get that leg looked at," she said.

"Nah, it'll be fine," Chasidy said. "It's just a little sore. I hope you really meant it when you said that your home is my home, 'cause I may need to stay for a while. You know, just until some things blow over in Chiraq."

"Baby." Brooke looked into her eyes. "You can stay for as long as you need to. Maybe you and Bromise should think about moving here. It's the perfect place to raise a family, and you can really thrive here. Your sister has decided to make the move."

"Really?" Chasidy was surprised. "She didn't mention that to me."

"Yes. Well, she put in an offer on a home just a few blocks from here," Brooke said with a proud smile. "She's ready to change her life, and you should too. Just think about it."

"Okay, I will . . . and Mama . . ."

"Go on, sweetie."

"I'm sorry for calling you a whore earlier."

"I've been called much worse in my lifetime, so don't stress yourself over it, baby girl," she said.

Chasidy hugged Brooke and said, "I love you soooo much, Mama. And I want you to know that I don't blame you for anything."

"I love you, too," she said. "And thank you." Brooke placed a kiss on Chasidy's cheek, and her daughter walked out of the door, misty-eyed.

Porsha was sitting patiently in her rental car with the engine running. Chasidy met her at the curb and got inside. "Whew, it gets just as cold here as it does in the Chi," she said, referring to the brisk wind.

"If not colder," Porsha said. "Girl, this is Wisconsin." She chuckled. "Did Mama talk your ear off?"

Chasidy smiled. "She has gotten pretty deep, huh?"

"Girl, yes!" Porsha said. "That woman goes to church every Sunday, and sometimes on Monday."

Chasidy glanced around the interior of the new rental car that Porsha was forced to get and immediately felt guilty. "Foremost, I wanna say thank you again for saving my ass in Rockford."

"Oh, it ain't nothin', girl. Don't worry about it," she said and waved her hand.

Chasidy caught it and held on to it. "No, it is something. I mean really. If it wasn't for you coming to get my ass, I don't know how the fuck I would've gotten out of there. Plus, you had to drive your Range through the fence and shit."

"That's what full coverage insurance is for," Porsha said and smiled.

"Yes, and make sure you give me the bill for your deductible. I got you," Chasidy said and rubbed the top her hand as her eyes watered. "You always come through for me, sis, and I don't say thank you enough. I love you, sissy."

"Aw," Porsha uttered. "You're going to make me cry." She fanned her face and they hugged.

"I really do appreciate you, Porsha," Chasidy whispered into her ear.

"I appreciate you too, little sister," Porsha said as a tear fell. "Now where's my lip gloss?" she asked as she released Chasidy. "I can't go anywhere without my gloss. My lips have to stay poppin'." She chuckled and buried her face in her purse.

"Mom told me that you just put in an offer for a home not too far from here."

"Yes, I did. I was offered a job out here, so I figured why not," she said, still rummaging through her purse. "It's time for a change, sis. Chicago is not the place to be any more."

"Wow . . . I hear you there." Chasidy noticed a Mercedes Benz SUV parked just across the street.

"Here it is, girl," Porsha announced happily and spread the gloss across her full lips. "West Towne

**241**

Mall, here we come—"

Chasidy smiled and turned to Porsha, who was looking past her with the most terrified look in her eyes. Out of her peripheral, Chasidy saw the silencer over her shoulder.

"Nooo!" Chasidy screamed, but it was too late! The Rasta behind it closed his eyes and squeezed off multiple shots.

Chasidy ducked as shattered glass burst inside the vehicle. The door swung open and two Rastas snatched her by the hair and coat. "Let me go!" she screamed.

They ignored her pleas and ripped her out of her seat. She reached out for Porsha, whose body was slumped over and bleeding profusely.

# CHAPTER 23

*It's a Small World*

*Hartsfield Airport . . . (5:35 p.m.)*
*Atlanta, Georgia*

Ayana's flight had landed on time. *ATL turnup!* She was so happy to be back in her hometown. She hadn't been here since before she got pregnant. Speaking of Lil Fats, he was bright-eyed and bushy tailed right beside her. He was looking up from his car seat with a smile as big as Georgia.

"Aren't you so happy to be here, huh booboboo," she said, playfully. They were at the baggage carousel eagerly awaiting their luggage, as the merry-go-round of bags amused him.

"Heeeeyyy chica!" Ayana turned to her sister, Roni's voice. She had her arms opened wide. "Look at you," she said, admiring Ayana's Islay Halter maxi dress and suede wedges. "I love the dress and those shoes are mean, sis!"

"Hey, love! Girl, I couldn't *wait* to leave that snowy-ass city, so I could rock these shoes. I see the little sexy number you rockin', too!" Ayana gave her a once-over and they hugged and bounced around in excitement.

"And this must be my handsome nephew?" Roni said and picked Lil Fats up from his seat.

Ayana spotted their luggage. Three suitcases total. She pulled them from the carousel while Roni showered Lil Fats with a riot of kisses. An iMessage lit up the face of her cell. It was a text from Fats, asking had she landed safely yet. She texted him back that all was well and Lil Fats and her would give him a call once they got settled at Roni's.

Once they made it outside, Roni took them to her Toyota RAV4. They secured Lil Fats in the backseat and loaded the luggage and laughed about everything in between. They were so giddy and excited just to be around each other. They both got inside the SUV, and Ayana reached back to check on Lil Fats.

"Sis, that boy is so handsome," she said for the umpteenth time.

"Lookin' just like his conceited ass daddy," Ayana half-joked. "Ain't that right, mama's baby?" She playfully pinched his chin and he laughed uncontrollably. He loved when she did that.

"His daddy a'ight," Roni jested, and Ayana turned to look at her.

"Bitch, you betta check yo' mouth about my man. You know he fine." She giggled.

And on cue, Roni started singing Nivea's song. "Don't mess with my man, or I'ma be the one to bring it to ya." They both laughed.

"Speaking of men," Ayana said and turned in her seat. "Continue telling me about this man you met at the airport while waiting for us. Mmm hmm." She pressed her lips together.

"He flew in from Miami. Girl, all I can say is Choco-late," she emphasized in a playful, seductive manner. "That dark-complexioned man was a man for real, honey. Almond-shaped eyes and girrrrrl, his teeth were perfect. Not none of that gold-cap shit." They laughed again and continued to chat it up until suddenly they found themselves trapped in a traffic jam. Now bumper-to-bumper, Roni was forced to bring her RAV4 to a complete stop.

"Ain't that sumthin'?" Ayana asked out of the blue.

"What's that, sis?"

"Who mama would name their child after a Swisher Sweet? But then again he probably named himself that."

"What are you talkin' about?" Roni asked with interest.

"Look right there on the license plate." She pointed out a red Porsche Panamera with matching rims. It was on the left, next lane over and just ahead of them.

Roni squinted in the Panamera's direction and read the license plate aloud. "Cigar?" she uttered and reached for her purse.

"Yeah, sis, that's what it says," Ayana said sarcastically. "And those are Miami plates too. Whoever that is must own a damn *cigar* company 'cause that whip is badass." She noticed the puzzled look on Roni's face. "'Sup, sis?"

"That's him!" Roni said. "That's the guy I was telling you about. The guy I met at the airport." She handed Ayana his business card, and she read it aloud.

"Cigar Buchanon. Owner of Cigar's Auto-Design & Parts." She reverted her attention to the Panamera, and compared the name on the card to that on the license plate. "Yep, certainly is spelled the same. And you said he looked like brand new money, right? Well?"

"Well what?"

"Well, that's gotta be him!"

"And your point?"

"My point is pull up some and talk to him. Or at least pull up and see if it's really him," Ayana insisted.

"I dunno, sis," she whined and inched forward.

"You got this. Don't be so shy."

"Ayana, to be truthful, I'm not studdin' that man. I didn't have no intention on callin' him anyway. You know I'm engaged."

"Sistah, stop playin'! That broke down fiancé of yours has done very little if anything at all for you and your kids, except bring pain and heartache for years to come," she said, speaking her mind. "And you haven't even seen or heard from that nigga in weeks. You betta see what's to this Cigar character. He just may be what the doctor has ordered for you, and the way you were tellin' that story of how y'all two met, you'd think that it came straight outta a romance novel. Talkin' 'bout you wasn't gon' call him. Sistah, puh-leese," Ayana said and sucked her teeth.

"If I described anythang that was remotely close to being romantic, it was only innocent flirting. That's it! And I don't see what's so romantic about that. Like I said, I'm not studdin' him."

"That dead-beat baby daddy of yours is the bum you shouldn't be studdin'," she said matter-of-factly. "Now c'mon, it won't hurt none to see if that's the same nigga you was talkin' to in the airport," she coaxed.

"Okay, Ayana, damn!" Roni submitted to her wishes and pulled ahead as much as the car in front would allow. The Porsche was at a standstill. Slowly,

Roni drove alongside of it while Ayana boldly looked.

"Shit, his windows are too damn dark," Ayana said, displeased.

"I told you it wasn't no use! Now you got this ignorant bastard behind me blowing his horn like he crazy. Don't he see that we all in gridlock. Fool!" She blew her horn in return. "He ain't goin' nowhere fast. None of us are!" she sneered and flipped the disgruntled driver the bird.

"Wait, look!" Ayana nudged Roni.

The tinted window began to decline.

"Is that him?" she asked nonchalantly, trying not to make a big fuss.

Roni didn't answer. She couldn't. Instead she sat there spellbound by a set of white teeth that contrasted perfectly against the most flawless chocolate skin she'd ever seen on a man.

Ayana also was checking him out from her seat. *Damn! I see what she meant.*

"Sis." Ayana nudged her. "Let the window down. The man is trying to say something." Roni let the window down slightly.

"Now what could be more pleasant than seeing you twice in one day? I'll tell you. Nothin'," he said with a chuckle. He was reclined in the passenger seat, puffing on a Zino Platinum Cigar. "And you must be, Ayana?" He looked past his focal point and planted his eyes on Ayana. "Hi, my name is Cigar, and this is Boston," he said, referring to his driver.

*How in the hell does this stranger know my name?*

"Your sister told me a little about you back at the airport," he said, answering her mental question.

"Oh, I guess I forgot to disclose that minor detail,"

Roni said, breaking her silence and still smiling.

"Hi," Ayana said and waved. "Nice meeting you two."

"Y'all could pass as twins too, ooh wee," he said and looked over at Boston. "Wouldn't you agree, B?" he asked him, and his friend nodded in agreement. "As beautiful as you are, and you're that beautiful." Cigar looked into Roni's eyes. "The beautiful one that I'm checkin' for hasn't even given me her status yet. Shall I take that as a sign, beautiful?" he asked, exposing his bright white smile again.

Ayana couldn't believe how stuck in a trance Roni was. She woke her up with another nudge.

"Um, it's kinda complicated," Roni said.

"Too complicated to talk about it?" he asked, not willing to give up.

"Maybe," she responded. "I have your business card. So we'll see."

Traffic ahead started to ease and horns blared behind them.

"Fair enough," Cigar said and puffed again. "Y'all enjoy the rest of the evening, and I will look forward to your call." And just like that he was behind tint again.

After they drove ahead and out of sight, Roni became herself again. "Whoo wee! I gotta admit, that dude is Blair Underwood fine. *So sophisticated* like Rick Ross say!" She smiled and took notice of Ayana's sudden silence.

"Yeah, that much is true. His smooth black skin, perfect white teeth, and charming attributes, I'd say that he's definitely something worth looking into. It's something about him though," Ayana said, rubbing her chin. "I can't quite put my finger on it, but I either

248

# VENOM IN MY VEINZ

know him in some way, or he reminds me of
somebody . . ."

# CHAPTER 24
## *The Web*

**B**romise parked Sadie in front of a UPS store, bumping "Go Get It" by TI. He went inside, retrieved his mail, and was back on the road. He placed the manila envelope in his middle console with the intent of getting to it later. It was time to have a talk with his lieutenant, Fats, and decipher precisely where he stood within this quandary. Up until this point, he hadn't exactly clued him in to his secret scheme that was fully underway. And for good reason: need to know basis. When there's no need to know, then there's no basis to tell.

It wasn't at all that Bromise didn't trust him—it was a matter of him thinking security at all times. Brisco once said: *"To think security is to be snapped up and on point during each tick-tock of every minute of every hour. Devote your closest attention to detail. Dot your I's and cross your T's. And don't reveal anything until it's time."*

With that in mind, Bromise headed for *The Web*. The Web was a carefully designed fortress that consisted of a multiple street setup that Fats spent the past five years organizing at Bromise's direction. It was an ingenious setup that would impress a skilled engineer. And it was in the heart of K-Town.

There were three borders often referred to as *Gun Lines* that outset The Web's core. The first one starting at Keating Avenue, then Kilpatrick Avenue, and on to Kingsdale Avenue. Hidden surveillance cameras were strategically positioned on each of these blocks, and all of them routed back to a fortified basement that sat at the core.

As Bromise stopped at a stop sign on Keating Avenue, he threw up his palm in a greeting gesture before going again. He knew exactly where the cameras were positioned, and he was sure that Fats was back at the fortified basement standing over the video monitors. Bromise drove casually, taking in his surroundings as he drove further into The Web. There were specific houses on each block that were utilized for particular tasks. Between each inconspicuous *lookout* house was a well-positioned *house-of-arms*, where two to three snipers were posted at all times. Kolmar Avenue was the street they referred to as the *strip-of-finance*. Off the corner were two trap houses side by side, and next to it was a designated safe house. The three houses had a secret underground tunnel that led from basement to basement.

Kilbourn Avenue was considered the core and home of the fortified basement. The brains of it all. It was his very first trap house. This spot was completely renovated and designed to focus on surveillance, video monitoring, police scanners, and other spy work. From that basement alone they were able to watch and listen to the happenings throughout the entire Web, due to hidden recording devices.

If ever the squad deemed it necessary to shut down The Web and secure the entire area, there would be no way of getting out of it. It was a web in that sense and what influenced Fats to give it the title. It was also a web in the sense that each intricate part had a reciprocal relation. Under Fats' supervision, runners moved product back and forth underground to the bagmen, the bagmen pushed the product to a hasty clientele, and the security men kept their eyes out for anything that wasn't routine. All that Bromise had to do was keep up with the demand by delivering product by the trunk load.

Outsiders were prohibited. Bromise's childhood squad was still with him, and they carried out the day-to-day activities throughout The Web. Jay, KO, Trent, BG, and Fats. They were all still one unit, and stronger than ever. Plus, other tried and true associates that he recruited along the way.

From the outside looking in, The Web didn't appear to be any different from the many other poverty-stricken ghettos throughout Chiraq. But no one, not even the residents, knew the half of it.

Bromise pulled Sadie into the alleyway and parked behind the fortified basement. He dialed Fats and summoned him outside. He showed up in a nick of time, trudged through the snow, and climbed into the truck.

"Wudup, Joe?" Fats said and they shook-up.

"Same shit," Bromise said. "Talk to me."

"Everythang on point, B," he said. "The cash, product, time sheets, err'thang."

"Cool, that's good to know." He looked at him.

"Wudup, Joe?" Fats felt awkward by his stare.

"I know you, and I haven't spoken in a while about anything outside of the operations of The Web," Bromise said, driving out of the alleyway. "So I wanted to spend some time with you today and learn what's on your mind." He looked out at the street.

Fats shifted in his seat. "If you're barkin' up that

tree, then I'm right beside you barkin' too. I'm down for whatever. You know dat." Fats drove his fist into his palm.

Bromise knew that no matter how discreet he'd been with his scheme, Fats was too close and intelligent not to have picked up on something. He was curious as to how much he knew and simply said, "Elaborate."

"Well, Future got licked. Then Remo called. I met up with him and he hands me three bricks to hold for you. Then he tells me a story about leaving for Kentucky and having no time to explain." Fats continued, "Freeway doesn't know shit about shit, 'cause he stopped by the block about an hour ago in his Hummer, asking have I seen Remo. And then for some odd reason, you can't be found all of a sudden." Fats looked at him with telling eyes. "C'mon now, B, I've been soaking up game from you for over five years now. You know I know wusup."

"Do you really think so?" Bromise kept his eyes on the road. "Well, enlighten me. 'Cause at this point I need rooks, not pawns," he said solemnly.

Fats shifted in his seat again. "Keepin' it all the way gutter with you." He sighed. "I'm not sure if you're going to hit Jamaican Bill, but I'm pretty damn sure that you're setting the stage for Future to take a spill."

"Okay, let's entertain that thought," Bromise said as he clicked on his turn signal. "So what if I was? What would you think about me making such a dangerous, forbidden power move that could get us all slumped?" He sat in the turning lane and watched Fats closely for telltale signs.

"I would think that it's about fuckin' time somebody stood up to Future's shyster ass. He deserves to get knocked down to size!" He punched his palm again. "Check dis out, Joe. I never had shit. Not a mother, father, sister, or brother. Not a pot to piss in or a window to throw it out of. Not until I met you and joined your squad. Before then, I slaved at the trap house door for Goldie, and I did it for food scraps," he said. "No, I'm serious, Joe. Goldie would actually pay me in food. If I worked, then I ate. If I didn't work, then I went to sleep with my stomach touching my back. You feel me?"

Bromise caressed the wheel into a sharp turn.

"On the night you made your physical stance and demanded your position, initially I was scared to death. I ain't gon' lie. But I knew something good would come of it, 'cause it couldn't get no worse.

"After you had slumped Goldie that night, and John-John and I piled into the whip with Future, he told us flat out: 'One of you niggas is a dead man ridin' right now. The only man standing will be the one that Youngin calls for. Until then, shut da fuck up!'

"Later that night, Future had us locked up in some kinda dungeon or some shit. An all-concrete room that reminded me of a jail cell, except there was no cot or toilet. We were blindfolded the entire trip, so we had no clue where we were," he continued. "Then the next day, Freeway came down the cement steps and murked John-John, execution-style, right in front of me. Joe, I was so close to the nigga that specks of his blood went into my eyes and mouth. Then without saying a word, he just left. Days went by, and just when I thought I was going to die from the foul smell of John-John's corpse, you called for me, Joe," he said with a sincere smile.

"Man, I was too happy to get up outta there. But to keep it gutter, every day when I reported to work, I thought you was going to murk me for something, who knows." He slightly chuckled. "The fact is, I didn't know, so I kept my mind on the grind and hustled my ass off. In the beginning I thought there was a catch to you, till you positioned niggas under me and really gave me a shot to run shit. I knew then that you were giving me the game to last in this game. And the tools to keep the screws and bolts tightened. I guess what I'm saying is . . ." He paused. "My loyalty is to you and only you, so it's whatever, Joe. I trust you."

Bromise couldn't help but feel Fats' sentiments as he spoke them. He was pleased with what he heard. "So how's my main man, Lil Fats doing?" he asked, changing the subject.

"Oh man, Joe." Fats lit up. "He's gucci all the way around the board, and getting big too!" he said excitedly. "He and Ayana flew out to the A to visit her fam'. This is his first time meeting them. I miss them already, B."

"So you and Ayana," Bromise said. "Everything gucci with you two?"

"Couldn't be better, Joe." He smiled. "She's the love of my life. Like I said, err'thang I got I have it because of you."

"Nah, I can't take credit for that." Bromise massaged the steering wheel. "That's all you. You're the reason for everything you have, including Ayana and Lil Fats. You've worked hard for it, and you deserve it, Joe." They shook-up. "Ayana is a good woman too. She's loyal to you, and I'm happy for you both. I got love for y'all, Joe." Bromise tapped the left side of his chest.

A sudden silence came over them and their minds drifted. Thoughts of Ayana and Lil Fats penetrated Fats mental, while Bromise's went straight to Chasidy. He still hadn't heard anything, and he was starting to get even more worried.

"So, if you don't mind me asking," Fats said. "How's thangs going with you and that beauty vixen of yours, Chasidy?"

"We good," he said, looking straight ahead.

"Are y'all looking to have a kid of y'all own some day?"

Bromise glanced out his side window. "I guess I never thought about it. Plus, I doubt she'd even want a baby. You know how vain she can be about her perfect shape." He chuckled. "We too deep in these streets, anyhow. I'm not in no shape to help bring a child into this shitty world, right?"

Fats shrugged. "You'd be surprise how something as precious as bringing a shorty into this world can change any situation. It would change the way you think, your outlook on life, the way you rotate and demonstrate. I'm talking err'thang shifts and it shifts for the better, Joe."

"Yeah, you may be right." Bromise said it like he was giving the idea some thought. Then he quickly changed gears. "So when Freeway came by sniffing around earlier, what did you tell him?"

"The way I viewed it was if his own lieutenant ain't checkin' in with him, then what da fuck makes him think I will," Fats said with an angry look. "So I told him I haven't seen nor talked to Remo."

"My nigga. Now that's what I'm talking about . . . a thinker," he said and they shook-up.

"That reminds me," Fats said and pulled out his iPhone. "You know I get the security feeds straight to my cell, right?"

"Yeah, I recall you telling me about it before," Bromise confirmed, wondering where he was going with this.

"Well, I noticed something odd earlier when you drove up," he said, raising his iPhone as Bromise pulled Sadie over near a curb. "When you made it to the stop sign on Keating Ave, I noticed this whip right here." He pointed to the iPhone's screen. "I didn't think much of it until the same whip showed up on the same nine monitors thirty to forty-five seconds after yours did. Which can only mean one thang . . ."

"It was following me," Bromise said as he looked at the still image of a black Mercedes SUV.

"Exactly."

"Well, did you look further into it?" He rose up in his seat.

"No, I didn't have time to. You called and I came out as quick as I could," Fats explained.

"Okay, play the video back," he said, and brought his face closer to the screen. "Right there. Stop. Can you zoom in?"

"No doubt." Fats zoomed in on the driver side window of the Mercedes.

Bromise studied the image. "I know exactly who that is." He sat back in his seat.

"But how?" Fats questioned. "The windows are tinted."

"I know that silhouette from anywhere." Bromise said. "That's Kill-Kill. Apparently, he's been keeping me under his watch. For how long is what I wonder."

"So what you wanna do?" Fats was eager for action.

"Nothing," Bromise said plainly. "Let me handle Kill-Kill. What we're about to talk about next is what I want you to focus on. Cool?"

"Cool."

Bromise turned up the music and began to explain his role in the scheme, detail by crucial detail. Fats listened attentively and was more than ready to perform his part. Bromise didn't reveal his current worries about Chasidy, because he needed Fats sharp and focused. By the time their conversation came to an end, Bromise had crossed The Web's borders and pulled into the alleyway behind the fortified basement.

"Talk to the squad, fill them in on their roles, and I'll be in touch," Bromise said.

"Will do," Fats said and left the vehicle.

Bromise kept his foot on the brake pedal and watched as Fats walked away, trudging through the snow. Brisco entered his mind: *Grandson, never ask a man to do a job after you've told him about the benefits he'll receive for doing the job. Instead, ask him to do the job only after you've made him aware of the grim risk involved. It's much easier that way to discern whether he's doing it out of loyalty to you, or out of self-gain or greed. This tactic will also reveal his true colors in determining whether he's a true blue crony, or just another associate in the end.*

Bromise came out of his daze and noticed that Fats had disappeared into the fortified basement. His foot left the brake pedal, and Sadie cruised before turning out of the alleyway. Bromise made another sharp left onto Kilbourn Avenue, and what he saw next totally caught him off guard.

At once, men and women began to materialize in front of houses, between gangways, and out of parked cars. Some were visibly armed. The core of The Web resembled a gorilla war zone. Then Bromise spotted his entire childhood squad in the mix, and even Gossip, who stood in the same spot where the Bogus Boy clique trap house used to be. All of them were facing Bromise as he drove at a snail's pace.

"Yo!" Fats called out from the front porch of the fortified basement. He waved Bromise to stop and jogged over to him as he let the window down. "Unless our adversaries are as ready and as thirsty for blood as we are"—he paused and extended his arms out to his sides, gesturing to their strength in numbers—"It's going to be more of a slaughter than it will be a war." Fats wore a look in his eyes that Bromise had never seen. He even noticed a different tone to his voice.

"So just to be sure we're on the same page . . ." Bromise narrowed his eyes. "Although it's unlikely that we'll survive this, you're still willing to die trying?"

"Look at me, Joe." Fats met with his gaze. "You and I are reading the same book, chapter, page . . . hell, we're reading from the same line," he said and extended his right hand. "You can count on us, Joe. We'll follow you to the ends of the earth and back again."

Bromise didn't say a word. He took his hand and they simply shook-up. Fats walked away and stood tall on the curb. Then without warning, he turned to Bromise and saluted. Bromise looked around as several hands followed, before every warrior on the block was saluting. And they were all saluting in Bromise's direction. He smiled, for he knew, no matter what happened, his grandpa would be proud of that moment. He was ready for Phase III—the final stage.

He reached for his remote control and maxed the volume. Then he stepped outside of his truck, put his heels together, and stood at attention in the middle of the street. When the bass line dropped, and with one crisp motion, Bromise saluted his squad. "The Heat is On" by DMX, rocked the entire block.

***

Bromise pulled into his three-car garage in Lincoln Square, sure that Brooke's cell number had to be written somewhere inside. Before he vacated Sadie, he reached into the middle console and retrieved the manila envelope, then went inside. He set the envelope on the side table and started searching for any signs of where Brooke's number could be. He checked countertops, shelves, hard to reach places, cupboards, coverts, dresser drawers, Chasidy's vanity table and cases, jewelry boxes, closets, you name it and he probed through it. He even looked under beds and couches in each room. Nothing.

He flopped on the floor and sat his back against the wall. *I know her number is right under my nose,* he thought and ran his fingers through his fro. "But where!" he shouted in frustration. He wiped sweat from his brow and walked into the living room exhausted, picking up the manila envelope on the way. Bromise sat on their leather sectional and tore through the envelope. He removed the documents, and a smile touched his lips.

Thanks to Vanessa St. John, VP at AT&T, and an associate of Chasidy's, he currently held in his hands, phone records that date back to the unforgettable month that Brisco was killed. The full thirty-one days that led up to the worst day of Bromise's life was now in his possession. The documents consisted of all incoming and outgoing calls on both Brisco's cell and home phone.

"Wow!" he uttered as he filed through the many pages. The stack was pretty thick. "Grandpa was a very busy man that month. This is definitely going to take some serious man hours," he said and reached for his iPhone.

"Hey, Black Mamba," Ayana said excitedly. "That's funny. I was just about to call you—"

"Have you heard from Chasidy at all?" he asked, cutting her off.

"No, I haven't," she said, sensing the tension. "Is everything okay?"

"Yeah, I'm sure she's gucci. I should be hearing back from her soon," he said, minimizing his worry. "Didn't you say you wanted to tell me something or was about to call?"

Thrown off balance, she said, "Um, damn, that's funny. I've suddenly forgot."

"Okay. Well, if it was important it'll come back to you, and when it does just hit my line. In the meantime, if you hear from Chasidy before I do, tell her to get at me ASAP."

"Okay, will do," she said and ended the call.
*Ring!*

His iPhone chimed in his hand. "Chasidy!" he blurted.

"No, I'm sorry. This is Vanesssa . . . Vanessa St. Cloud. Is this Bromise I'm speaking to?"

"Yes, this is he."

"I'm sorry, did I catch you at a bad time?" she asked in a professional tone.

"Nah, you gucci—I mean, this is a good time. Wudup? I mean, how can I help you?"

"Okay good," she said. "I'm calling in regards to a phone number that Chasidy requested to be traced back to its owner. I would have mailed it to your P.O. Box, but she said that it was pretty urgent and to call you at this number."

"I'm grateful," he said. "So, did anything turn up?"

"Well, that's the thing. I traced the number back to a cell phone, which comes back in the name, Frank White. I'm almost certain it's an alias. Considering there's no paper trail, and the only Frank White that I know of was in the movie *King of New York,* and not residing in Atlanta, GA.

"Atlanta? How's that possible?" Bromise's brows furrowed.

"Well, yes. Although the phone is actually registered in the city of Chicago, which explains the 773 area code, however, out of 75,000 used minutes, 50,000 of them bounced off of our Atlanta towers. Our towers in Miami picked up the remaining minutes," she explained, and what she said next reminded Bromise of why her fees were so pricey. "I'm not sure if you're aware, but that number is no longer in service. And after a little digging, I was able to come up with the new seven-digit number that Mr. White so hastily switched over to. In fact, even before Chasidy had given me the number to trace, Mr. White had already switched to his new one. Would you like to have it?"

"Sure," he said quickly and jotted the number down. "Quick question?"

"Shoot," she encouraged.

"Have you by chance spoken to Chasidy?" he asked with his fingers crossed.

"Not since she called about the urgency of tracing Mr. White's number," she said truthfully.

"Do you think you could track down a number quick to a Brooke Berry? She lives in Madison Wisconsin."

"I know the area," Vanessa assured him. "Unfortunately, it's after business hours, and I'm currently at home. But I'll do this . . . I will get on top of it first thing in the morning."

"Okay, yes," he said, disappointed. "Well, thanks again for all of your help."

"Sure, anytime," she said, "And tell Chasidy hi for me."

Bromise stared at the new number that he'd written on a sheet a paper. *Mr. Frank White.* It was clear that Cigar must've sensed something shady the second Bromise answered Future's cell. That would be a good explanation as to why he changed numbers so abruptly. Cigar was his only uncle. One of his favorite people, next to his grandpa and mother. He looked up to him. He was the only blood family that he had left in this world, and he'd love to see him. But his mother was so adamant about her ill feelings toward him.

There had to be a reason he left and never came back, much less reach out to his only nephew. *Did he play a part in grandpa's murder? What does he have going on with Future?* Bromise's feelings were mixed. He propped his Air Force 1's on the ottoman and sighed deeply. "Atlanta, Georgia."

# CHAPTER 25

*The Heat is ON!*

Brooke sat still inside the hospital's waiting room with her hands between her shut thighs. Her head hung low as the priest sitting next to her read scriptures from the Bible.

"John 14:1-4, Let not your hearts be troubled. Believe in God; believe also in me. In my Father's house are many rooms. If it were not so, would I have told you that I go to prepare a place for you? And if I go and prepare a place, I will come again and will take you to myself, that where I am you may be also. And you know the way to where I am going."

"How could this be? How could this have happened!" Brooke sobbed.

The priest shut his Bible and placed his hand on her knee. "One of the most difficult things to deal with in life is the death of a loved one. Even for the Christian, death is a part of life. Unlike they that do not believe, the Christian has a blessed hope, that is the return of the Savior Jesus to catch up His church and bring them to eternal life with Him and God the Father in Heaven."

"But she was just a child," she cried. "She hadn't even lived yet. She was only twenty-five years old . . . she was just about to start anew. Why couldn't the Lord just take me instead!"

"Let it out, it's okay to cry." The priest comforted her, and she collapsed in his arms, as two Madison policemen approached.

"Excuse me, ma'am. My name is Officer Douglass and this is my partner, Officer Rhymes," he said with a pen and writing pad in his hands. "I know this may not be a good time to ask, but didn't you report that you had two daughters? And they were in fact together when this murder took place?"

"Chasidy! Oh Lord, help me Jesus!" She fell to the floor trembling and wailed a long mournful cry.

***

*Snap it up!* Bromise bolted from his doze like he'd escaped a nightmare. The phone documents fell to the floor. He glanced at his Audemar watch. "Shit!" He didn't mean to fall asleep in his Lincoln Square home. It wasn't exactly safe. The hairs on the back of his neck stood up. Something wasn't right. He filled his hand with a burner and went over to the front window and peeked beyond the drapes, and spotted the same black Mercedes SUV from earlier. It was parked inconspicuously further down the street.

"Kill-Kill," he uttered. "This nigga must really want to see me." Bromise sprinted to his master bedroom and walked over to his gun collection for ammunition. He removed the clips from his 45's and replaced the hollow-point rounds with fresh copper tip bullets that exploded upon impact. He pushed them in their holsters and sprinted back downstairs. He walked over to the phone records, rounded them up from the floor, and headed into the garage where his stealth gray Jaguar XK resided.

The second he drove his foreign whip onto the road, he caught a glimpse of the Mercedes out the side of his eye. It wasn't until he made it to the street's end before the Mercedes headlights shone and began to trail. "Yeah, c'mon if you think this is what you want," he said and bent the corner. Seven seconds later, so did the Mercedes.

Bromise continued to cruise at a steady pace while the Mercedes kept at a reasonable distance. He dialed both Chasidy and Porsha's cell number. Voice mail. "Shit!" he bellowed. "I'm convinced something's gotta be wrong." He kept a close eye on the rearview. He had no intentions of stomping on the gas and leaving the Mercedes in the dust, as the XK was most certainly capable. He had other plans.

Bromise pulled into Club Reflections' valet area of the parking lot. From the activity outside, the place appeared to be rocking as people stood in the cold behind the velvet rope. He reached for the burners and placed them both on his lap, waiting patiently for the Mercedes to show up. *Tick-tock.* He glanced at his Audemar. Ten minutes had passed. "Where are you, muthafucka?" He replaced the 45's in their holsters and rose out of his XK.

"Wudup, Black Mamba?" a deep-voiced bouncer greeted him as he walked up to the side entrance.

"Wudup, Big Tank?" he said and tossed him the keys. "Has Chasidy been here today?"

"Nope, not yet," said Big Tank.

Bromise went to go inside, when he heard his name called. He looked over his shoulder and spotted three ladies waving anxiously for his attention.

He exposed his famous smile. "They're coming in with me."

"Done," Big Tank said and pointed the women out. "You, you, and you," he said and Bromise watched as they stepped out of line, strutting their physical assets.

"Jeez!" Bromise uttered at the view and held the door open for the ladies. Then each of them gave him a hug and a peck on his cheek as they passed. He visually scanned the parking lot area one last time, and then followed them inside.

Chasidy came up with the club's name after the creative process of its interior ended with floor-to-ceiling mirrors attached to every square inch of the place. Tonight was Ladies' Night, and it appeared to be more women than men enjoying the provocative shows. There were seven stages with a naked dancer on each, and countless lap dancers were shaking their asses on the floor to T-Pain's "Booty Wurk." The place was packed. Bromise looked around in search of Diva, the club's sexy manager and caught a glimpse of her heading to the back.

"Hey," he called out to a female waitress. She walked up with the biggest smile. "Show these fine ladies to a VIP table and a bottle of Ciroc on me." He gestured to the ladies that walked in with him.

"No problem," she said and looked at the women. "Shall we?"

"Thank you, Black!" they said in unison.

"You're welcome," he said and then caught up with Diva in the back.

"Hey there, Black Mamba," she said. "Can I help you with something?"

"Yeah, have you seen or heard from Chasidy?"

"Not today I haven't. I tried calling, but her phone goes straight to her voice mail."

Bromise sighed deeply and looked off. "So how's everything here?"

"So far so good, except one of them guys over at the VIP section bought one of the bars. Him and his crew are drinking like fish and passing out liquor, but no one has paid up yet," she said with concern as Bromise looked in the direction that she was referring to. "I was just about to ask Big Tank to handle it when I bumped into you."

"Don't worry about it. I'll look into it," he said.

"Are you sure? Because Big Tank can—"

"Yup, I'm sure," he insisted.

"O . . . kay," she said with a sly smile and walked away.

Bromise watched until she left the corridor and then he turned to the VIP section. He watched attentively as Freeway's team (minus Remo) popped bottle after bottle. Their female waitress appeared to be under duress as they called her out of her name and ordered her around. He had seen enough and walked over.

"Whutcha' waitin' on, bitch," the man yelled. "Go get us some bottles!"

"Stop right there," Bromise said over the music to the stressed waitress who stopped in her tracks. Then he turned to the disrespectful man. "You sure have a rude way of addressing the staff here at Club Reflections."

The man quickly recognized who was in front of him. "Nah, Black Mamba, I ain't mean no harm." He was drunk. "I'm just talkin' shit. You know how we do."

"Not here you don't," Bromise sneered, pointing down to the empty bottles of Grey Goose, Remy Martin, Kettle One, and Hennessy. "This shit costs money." He looked over at the waitress. "How much is the bar tonight?"

"That particular one is $25,000" she answered.

"Okay," Bromise said, turning to the entire VIP group. "Who's planning to cover this tab?" He stared into the men's faces. "Well, don't all speak up at once." He opened the front of his fur coat. He wasn't interested in playing the silent game.

"Well, well, well," a familiar voice spoke behind him. He turned in time to see Freeway underhand toss a neatly rolled band of bills to the waitress. "Nice catch," he said.

"Thank you, sir," she said. Her voice was shaky.

"Twenty-five bands in full," Freeway said. "Make sure you count it." He smiled and walked up to Bromise. "Salutations, Black Mamba." He extended his hand.

"Salutations as well," he said and they shook-up.

"Please excuse my team. We don't won't no trouble. Not here of all places," he said with a chuckle and extended his arms to his side. "This is your wifey's establishment, so you know we respect it," he said and leaned in. "Speaking of your wifey, how's she doing?"

Bromise looked at him and wanted to slap the saucy smirk from his face. The eerie pitch in Freeway's tone made the hairs stand on the back of his neck. But he kept his cool. "Y'all have a nice evening," he said and turned to walk away.

Freeway raised his hand, pointing two fingers directly at Bromise's back, then blew the tips as though his hand were a gun. Bromise caught the image in the mirror and kept it moving.

As he turned the corner, he heard Freeway yell out, "We all one family, Black Mamba. Don't you forget that!"

Bromise took the stairs to Chasidy's office and used his key to get inside. He stopped short at her desk to look at her belongings in the manner she left them. She was so neat. Everything had its place was her motto, and Bromise appreciated that about her. He glanced at the framed photos. One was a close-up of them taken in Atlantic City, and the other one was of him, Chasidy, and Porsha when the three of them went on a cruise last summer. He put his hand over his mouth, shut his eyes, and sighed heavily. His mind was going a million miles an hour. He shook it off and sat behind Chasidy's desk, and pulled up the security feeds on her Apple Mac.

*"It's not what you say, but how you say it,"* were Brisco's words that played in Bromise's head. Chasidy was in trouble. He was sure of it. And Freeway's tone implied that he knew something too. He rewound the video ten minutes and watched from a different angle as Freeway raised his hand and pointed to his back. "So you wanna shoot me in my back? You coward," he said, then pulled up the live security feeds. "What the fuck—" he said, taking notice to four Rastas sitting in a booth, drinkless with big coats.

These Rastas were a part of Jamaican Bill's team, and they had never stepped foot inside Club Reflections till now. He watched as the men rejected the ladies over and over again. It was clear they weren't there for the entertainment. Bromise rose from the desk and left Chasidy's office. He took the stairs and was now back on the floor when another twerk song began. The Rastas now had a clear view of him as he intended. He wanted a reaction, a telltale sign as he watched them watch him. He casually walked to the other end of the club when he bumped into a scantily clad guest that could've passed for a dancer.

"Hey, sexy chocolate," she said, appearing from under the dim lights.

"Oh, wudup, Donnie?" Bromise said, clearly recognizing his old fling.

"Is that all I get, baby?" She grabbed a handful of his limp dick.

"Whoa! What the fuck are you doing?" He swiped her hand away from his groin.

"Don't act like you don't want *this*." She pointed to her curves.

"Donnie—" he said but stopped when he saw two of the Rastas checking around for his location. They were no longer being as discreet about their intentions. "C'mere," he said and grabbed her by the waist roughly, pulling her close, and threw his tongue down her throat. He caressed her ass and put his tongue to work. When the Rastas took notice and kept it moving, he released her. "It was good seeing you," he said, leaving her standing there, discombobulated.

Bromise walked around casually speaking to staff and shaking hands as he scanned the club nonchalantly for other Rastas. He went behind the bar and pretended to pour himself a drink. All along he had one eye on the Rastas, who were now on their feet, impatiently waiting for something.

"Black Mamba," Big Tank called out and walked over to the bar. "Here, Fontane dropped this off not too long ago and asked that I give it to you." He handed him a folded piece of paper. Bromise brought the note waist level and out of view of anyone on the opposite side of the bar. He unfolded its corners and read silently: *If you're still inside, then I suggest that you get out of there fast through the private exit. I'll be there with the whip waiting for you. Code 55-55.*

Bromise folded the note and slid it in his pocket. When he looked up, he noticed Big Tank still there, leaning against the bar with his back toward him.

"Big Tank, lemme holla at you," he said, and Big Tank turned.

"What can I do you for?" he asked in his extra-deep voice.

"I know you don't have a whip yet, just getting out of the pen and all . . ."

"That's right."

"Well, seeing as though you already have my keys," Bromise said, "how about you go and find you a lil dip and take her out on the town or some shit."

His eyes lit up. "Really?"

"Yeah, really."

"Are you talking about that foreign thang outside?" he asked, hoping so.

"That's the one, Joe," he said. "Go now. Don't worry about here. I'll make sure you're covered."

"I can leave now?" Big Tank wanted to be sure.

"Yeah, right now," Bromise said. "Before I change my fuckin' mind. Get outta here." He smiled, and the lighting changed as the DJ introduced the next featured dancer.

That was Big Tank's cue. "Thanks, bro," he said and mixed into the crowd.

Bromise followed suit but in an opposite direction of the club. He made it to the stairs unseen and took them by twos until he was back inside of Chasidy's office. Then suddenly, his iPhone #2 chimed. He prescreened the call. It was Future.

He took a deep breath and answered. "Salutations," he said.

"Salutations as well," Future responded. "I thought you should know that your monthly has just been dropped off to Fats, exactly five minutes ago."

"Cool, good lookin', big homie," Bromise said.

Then there was silence.

"Where are you right now, Black Mamba?"

Bromise ran his fingers through his fro. "I'm at Club Reflections," he said, knowing that Future already knew.

"You're not planning on leaving the city no time soon are you?"

"Nah, you know me. I'm hands on," Bromise said. "I got a quota to meet, right."

"That's what I wanna hear," Future said. "Ai'ight then, keep in touch."

The call ended.

"Shit!" he yelled out. "He knows." This was the second time today Future had called him on iPhone #2 in the five plus years he'd had the phone. When it came to doing business it had always been done via text encrypted through code, never actual conversations. "Fuck!" Bromise said and dialed up Fats. It went straight to voice mail. He tried again, and again it went to voice mail.

He stood behind Chasidy's desk and pulled up the live security feeds. He zoomed in on each Rasta until they filled all four corners of the Apple Mac screen. Then he peered out the window blinds. Bromise could see the valet area. It was busy. More cars were driving in as people loitered in the lot. He watched Big Tank drive away in his XK. He quickly darted his eyes to the Mac and stared at the screen and held his breath in anticipation. "C'mon, c'mon," he said repeatedly. And then it happened. "Yes!"

One of the Rastas became visibly alarmed after he reached into his pocket. He went to the others clearly yelling and showing something in his hand. "Stop moving," Bromise uttered as he attempted to zoom in on the device. "I knew it!" It was a standard transmitter to a tracking device attached to Bromise's XK. "Fuckin' amateurs," he said and watched the frantic Rastas bolt out of the club, pushing people down in the process and yelling out Jamaican curse words.

Bromise hightailed it out of the office and nearly cleared the stair casing in one leap. He slowed his pace when he made it to the corridor, passing staff as he neared the private exit. He put his hands inside his fur and wrapped his palms around his twin .45s. He pushed the door open, ready for whatever when the high beams from Fontane's whip caught his attention. He sprinted over and got inside when iPhone #1 chimed.

"Oh Bromise, thank God! This is Brooke," she said. "I've been searching for your number high and low."

Bromise became immediately alarmed.

"Is everything okay? Where's Chasidy?" he asked as Fontane sped out of the lot.

"No, Bromise, one of my babies is dead and the other is missing. They took my babies!" she wailed through the phone.

"Who is they? Who's dead and who did they take?" Bromise shouted through his cell and noticed they were driving through a dark alleyway, when out of nowhere a black van erratically cut them off. Fontane stomped on the brakes as bright headlights charged from the rear. Tires screeched loudly. Bromise dropped his cell and went for his burners.

"Don't make me do it, Black Mamba!"

Bromise turned to Fontane, who had a sawed off double-barrel shotgun aimed directly at his face. Bromise's hands were still in his fur.

"Are you serious right now?"

"Remove your hands very slowly."

"Are you really doing this?" Bromise asked, not complying.

"I don't want to do this, but I will," Fontane warned.

"Look around you. There's no way out of this."

Bromise scanned his surroundings and quickly realized what he meant. There were six Rastas in front with assault rifles drawn and Freeway and his team at the rear, also with burners aimed.

"Okay. Okay," Bromise said, removing his hands from around the 45s. He opened the door and rose with his hands in the air. The Rastas charged at him and relieved him of his weapons. Then they took turns whaling on him while Freeway held him up in a full nelson hold. And Fontane looked on. After they thought he'd had enough, he released him and Bromise crashed to the ground like five hundred pounds of steel.

Three of the Rastas picked him up and carried him to the back of the black van. He was barely conscious. Through his bloody eyes he was able to fixate on Fontane's face.

# VENOM IN MY VEINZ

"Really?" he said in a low tone and was thrown in the van. They slammed the doors. It was pitch black. He rolled over to his back and uttered, "Chasidy!" Bromise smelled her perfume before passing out cold.

***

# RUMONT TEKAY

## About The Author

By his eighteenth birthday, Rumont TeKay had a  thirty-five year prison sentence in front of him, with only bleak appeal hearings to look forward to. The gang life, fast money, fly whips, and cherry-picking women, was nothing more than just a painful memory.

Like many of his peers, Rumont took to the streets at the impressionable age of 10 years old. After his initiation, he quickly climbed the ranks within a notorious street organization out of Chicago aka Chiraq. At eighteen, he'd grown to become one of its largest distributors in the cocaine trade. Twelve years later, Rumont has been released from captivity with a different vision: Spread Venom through his Mighty Pen!

# VENOM IN MY VEINZ

## READING GROUP QUESTIONS

1. How did you *experience VENOM in My Veinz?* Were you immediately drawn into the story--or did it take you a while? Did the book intrigue, amuse, disturb, alienate, irritate, or frighten you?
2. Do you find the *characters convincing?* Are they believable? Compelling? Are they fully developed as complex, emotional human beings--or are they one-dimensional?
3. Which characters do you particularly *admire or dislike?* What are their primary characteristics?
4. What *motivates* Bromise's actions? What motivates Chasidy's actions? Do you think his and her actions are justified?
5. Do any characters *grow or change* during the course of this first installment? If so, in what way?
6. Who in this book would you most *like to meet?* What would you ask—or say?
7. If you could *insert yourself* as a character in the book, what role would you play? You might be a new character or take the place of an existing one. You choose.
8. Is the *plot well-developed*? Is it believable? Do you feel manipulated along the way, or do plot events unfold naturally, organically?
9. Is the story *plot or character driven*? In other words, do events unfold quickly? Or is more time spent developing characters' inner lives? Does it make a difference to your enjoyment?
10. Can you *pick out a passage* that strikes you as

# RUMONT TEKAY

particularly profound or interesting--or perhaps something that sums up the central dilemma of the book?

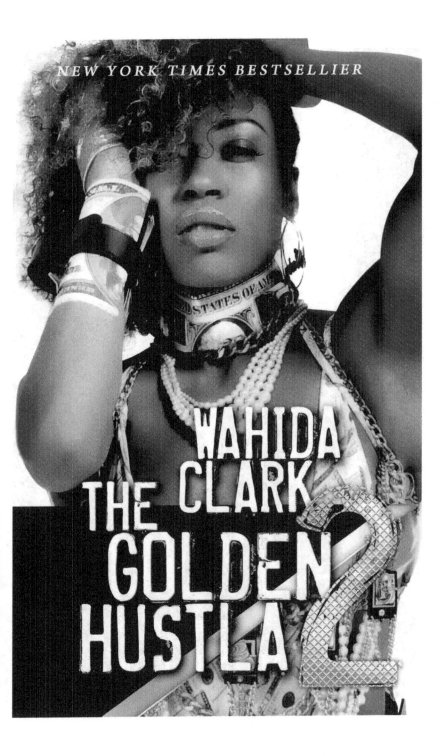

NEW YORK TIMES BESTSELLIER

WAHIDA
CLARK

THE
GOLDEN
HUSTLA 2

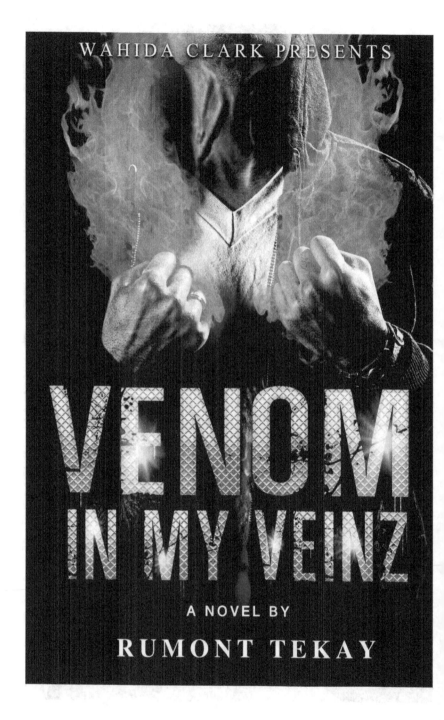

WAHIDA CLARK PRESENTS

# VENOM IN MY VEINZ

A NOVEL BY

## RUMONT TEKAY

WAHIDA CLARK PRESENTS

*Butterfly*

A NOVEL BY

Michael A. Robinson

CPSIA information can be obtained at www.ICGtesting.com
Printed in the USA
LVOW04s1442310814

401739LV00017B/591/P